Also by Karin Gillespie

A Dollar Short:
The Bottom Dollar Girls Go Hollywood

Bet Your Bottom Dollar:
A Bottom Dollar Girls Novel

Dollar Daze

THE BOTTOM DOLLAR GIRLS IN LOVE

KARIN GILLESPIE

**Doubleday Large Print
Home Library Edition**

Simon & Schuster

New York   London   Toronto   Sydney

This Large Print Edition, prepared especially for Double-day Large Print Home Library, contains the complete, unabridged text of the original Publisher's Edition.

SIMON & SCHUSTER
Rockefeller Center
1230 Avenue of the Americas
New York, NY 10020

SIMON & SCHUSTER and colophon are registered trademarks of Simon & Schuster, Inc.

Manufactured in the United States of America

ISBN-13: 978-0-7394-7279-8

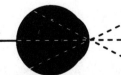

**This Large Print Book carries the
Seal of Approval of N.A.V.H.**

*To the most wonderful and supportive
parents in the entire world, my mother,
Magda Newland, and my father,
Edward Gillespie.*

*Also dedicated to all of the small towns
of the South, but especially
Milledgeville, Georgia.*

Dollar Daze

**If love is blind, why is
lingerie so popular?**
—Comment overheard under the hair dryer at the
Dazzling Do's

CHAPTER ONE

It was the night of the annual Sweetheart Dance in Cayboo Creek, South Carolina, and the cinder-block walls of the high school gymnasium were festooned with foil hearts and crepe-paper cupids. Frank Sinatra crooned "Fly Me to the Moon" on the oversized boom box while a crush of couples clung to each other on a makeshift dance floor beneath the basketball hoop.

Mavis Loomis, who was manning the punch bowl, clucked her tongue as she saw her friend Attalee Gaines seductively grinding her bony hips for the benefit of her white-haired date, Dooley Prichard.

"Someone needs to take a fire hose to those two," whispered Birdie Murdock, who was selling baked goods next to Mavis.

Mavis shook her head in dismay. "I'm surprised either of them have any spark left. Attalee's on the downhill slide of eighty, and Dooley can't be far behind."

"Oh, he's a far *younger* man," Birdie said with a snigger. "Attalee was bragging about it the other day, saying she'd snagged herself a seventy-eight-year-old stud."

"Leave it to Attalee," Mavis chuckled.

"All that wooing and cooing," Birdie said, waving a funeral home fan in front of her flushed face. "I'm glad my dating days are done."

Mavis knew she was expected to agree with her old friend. Both she and Birdie were widows and their respective husbands had been dead for over ten years. Since then, Mavis's love life had been as lively as a wet firecracker. She knew Birdie's hadn't been much perkier.

"Sometimes I think it'd be nice to have a beau," Mavis said as she swayed to the music. "Seems everyone's part of a couple these days. Look at Reeky and Jerry."

Birdie glanced at Reeky Flynn and Jerry Sweeny in the far corner of the dance floor. The couple was fused together like Siamese twins. Reeky, the owner of the Book Nook in town, had always deflected the advances of Jerry until her cat died a couple of months ago. As a surprise, Jerry, who was a taxidermist, had Moonbeam freeze-dried and mounted, creating a lasting memento of Reeky's fallen feline. Now Moonbeam had a prominent place on top of her piano, and Jerry was spending most evenings beside Reeky on her love seat.

"Reeky's a young woman in her thirties." Birdie refilled her cup with strawberry punch. "It's a bit late for us, my dear."

"I think we're still pretty darn fetching for a couple of mature women," Mavis said, smiling at her friend.

Birdie's best feature was her head of silver hair, shiny as a new dime and styled into sleek waves around her face. At the age of sixty-two, she still sported a girlish figure, save for a slight swell of tummy that could be discerned underneath her red wool dress.

Mavis was shorter than Birdie, with close-cropped hair, the salt-and-pepper color of a schnauzer's. Her best points were soft brown eyes (the color of malted milk balls, her late husband Arnold use to say) and shapely calves.

"Fetching or not," Birdie said, "I have no interest in—"

Gracie Tobias, who'd been taking tickets at the front door, darted across the slick gymnasium floor to the refreshment table.

"Did you notice Attalee's vulgar behavior on the dance floor?" she said. "I think it's time for a faster song."

Mrs. Tobias, who wore a boxy black jacket with slim skirt and pearls, knelt next to the boom box. In moments, "Fly Me to the Moon" was replaced by "Double Shot of My Baby's Love."

"There." Mrs. Tobias brushed her hands together. "Much better. How are things going at the punch bowl?"

"Not spiked yet . . . unfortunately," Mavis said.

Mrs. Tobias laughed and helped herself to a cup of punch. "I know what you mean. I could use a bit of a toddy myself."

Mavis tapped her foot in time to the music and looked longingly at the throngs of dancing couples. "I'd settle for a turn around the floor."

"Maybe later," Birdie said with a yawn. "I'm bloated from all the punch I've been drinking. "

"I didn't mean with *you*," Mavis said with a sigh. "Nothing personal, but I'm tired of dancing with my girlfriends at these functions. For once, I'd like to be in the arms of a man."

"All evening long she's been in a state," Birdie said to Mrs. Tobias. "Going on about moons and Junes as if she were at the junior-senior prom again."

Mrs. Tobias dabbed at her mouth with a napkin. "Heavenly day! I'm grateful to be done with romance. All that groping and heavy breathing that comes with courting. In my book, there's nothing more *common*. Besides, I'm sixty-three, not sweet sixteen, and much too old for such shenanigans."

"Last month's *Good Housekeeping* claimed that sixty is the new forty," Mavis said. "Plenty of women have romances at an older age."

"Oh really?" Birdie asked. "Name some."

"Well, there's . . . Joan Collins," Mavis said.

"Didn't she marry a young Swedish gold digger?" Birdie said.

"Yes, but *then* she divorced him and re-married and is supposedly happy as a lark with her current husband," Mavis said. "And what about Barbra Streisand and Jim Brolin? Theirs was a late-life romance."

"Celebrities don't count," Birdie snapped. "It's a cinch to attract a man when you have millions of dollars and can scamper off to a plastic surgeon at the first sign of a wrinkle or a bulge. Try snagging a man when all you have to offer is creaky knees and your AARP discount card. Give me an example of *one* ordinary older woman who is having a romance."

"Attalee," Mavis said.

"Oh, well, Attalee." Birdie pursed her lips into a smirk. "She's hardly ordinary."

"That's for certain," Mrs. Tobias said with a titter.

Birdie glanced at her watch. "I hope this dance wraps up soon. I'd like to catch an episode of *Murder, She Wrote.*"

"I heard that was in syndication," Mrs. Tobias said. "What channel does it come on?"

Mavis made a face. "I'm tired of sitting at home and watching old-lady television shows. I don't know about you gals, but I'm going to go and find a fellow to dance with."

She surrendered her punch ladle to Birdie and flounced away from the refreshment table into the semi-darkness of the gymnasium.

"Good luck, Mavis," Mrs. Tobias called after her. Turning to Birdie, she said, "She's not herself. Maybe I should take her to my garden club meetings. Plunging a trowel into the soil is a wonderful diversion."

"She *is* behaving peculiarly," Birdie said. She stared at the clutch of dancers on the floor.

"About what Mavis was saying . . . Do you ever think about?"

"Never," Mrs. Tobias said with a resolute lift of her chin. "I was married to my late husband Harrison for thirty satisfying years, and that's all I'll ever need."

"I know what you mean," Birdie said. "My Max was the love of my life."

"Besides," Mrs. Tobias said, casting her eyes around the gymnasium, "it's not as if there are any suitable men to be found around here."

That's precisely what Mavis discovered as she wandered through the knots of partygoers at the dance. Instead of encountering an eligible man to partner with, she found legions of lone women like herself. DeEtta Jefferson sat in the shadows wearing a red satin party dress, chewing Cracker Jack and looking mournfully in the direction of the dance floor. A posse of women from the Ladies' League at the Rock of Ages Baptist Church were passing out buttons that said "Down with Dancing," but Prudee Phipps, the president, betrayed herself by unconsciously tapping her foot to the beat.

Jewel Turner, who was two-stepping on the fringes of the dance floor, grabbed Mavis's arm and said over the din, "Why don't Baptists make love standing up?"

"Why?" Mavis asked.

"'Cause it might lead to dancing," Jewel said. She jerked her head in the direction of the members of the Ladies' League. "Those gals need to learn to put a little 'fun' in their fundamental."

Mavis chuckled and pressed on, disturbed that someone as pretty and young as Jewel was forced to dance stag. Jewel, who was the owner of the Chat 'N' Chew diner, had a pile of wavy, red-gold hair that reached to her shoulders and a waist as cinched as a bud vase.

Mavis simply had to find someone to dance with. It didn't matter who. After making such a big fuss in front of Birdie and Mrs. Tobias, she'd be too humiliated to return to the punch bowl a failure. All she needed was one single man willing to do the Carolina Shag. Squinting through the gloom of the gymnasium, Mavis didn't see any suitable candidates. Then, just behind her, she heard a familiar hacking cough.

The song "Be Young, Be Foolish and Be Happy" cued up and the dance floor grew packed with moving bodies.

"What do you say, Mrs. Tobias?" Birdie extended her hand. "Shall we trip the light fantastic?"

"Well, I—"

"Come on." Birdie snapped her fingers to the beat. "It's fun."

"One dance," Mrs. Tobias said. "And you'll have to lead. I've never shagged before."

The two women joined the twisting masses. Attalee, who was being flung around by a surprisingly limber Dooley, noticed her two friends and let out a hoot.

"Shake yer groove thing, y'all!" she hollered over the music.

Birdie and Mrs. Tobias launched into a stiff shag as Birdie mouthed the words to the music. Then, directly under the floating spangles of the mirrored disco ball, Mavis and her dance partner appeared.

"Good godfathers," Birdie breathed. "Can you believe it?"

"Not in a million years." Mrs. Tobias was struck motionless.

Mavis threw herself into an enthusiastic shag with Roy Malone. Roy, who was trailing an oxygen tank, had to stop every few seconds to cough up some phlegm.

"Bless her heart," Mrs. Tobias murmured. "She really *was* desperate."

Just as Roy was about to dip Mavis, he lost his grip on her waist, and she fell flat on her bottom.

"Roy!" Mavis shouted over the music, struggling to get up. "Are you okay?"

Roy, who was clawing at his chest, turned purple as a plum and crumpled to the floor.

"Medic!" Mavis screamed. "Please, somebody! Help!"

A half hour later, Mavis was slumped on a folding chair in the middle of the gymnasium while Birdie and Mrs. Tobias hovered over her like a pair of brooding hens. They were the only three people remaining. After Roy's collapse, the Sweetheart Dance had lost most of its zing.

"Now, Mavis, it's not that bad." Birdie patted her shoulder.

A mottled-faced Mavis looked up at her friend. "Yes it is. I could have killed Roy. And all because of my silly vanity."

"Nonsense," Mrs. Tobias said. "You heard what the paramedics said. Roy's going to be fine." She cleared her throat. "Well, as fine as a man with an advanced case of emphysema can be. He just has to avoid aerobic exercise from now on."

"Ladies." A shiny-faced custodian poked his head into the gymnasium. "I gotta be locking up soon."

"We were just leaving." Mavis rose from her chair.

Birdie pinched the sleeve of Mavis's navy-blue mackinaw coat. "I should come home with you."

"No," Mavis said. "I think I'll stop by the store first. I've got work to do." Mavis was the proprietor of the Bottom Dollar Emporium, a general store on Main Street.

"I could help you," Birdie said, tying a muffler around her neck.

"I'm fine, really." Mavis managed a faint smile.

The women emerged from the school into a night as dark and velvety as the inside of a jewel box. Mavis waved good-bye to Birdie and Mrs. Tobias and sprinted to her white Chevy Lumina. A smattering of frost had formed on her windshield, so she had to crank the engine and wait while the defroster cleared the glass. Her late husband Arnold used to keep a scraper in the glove compartment for such occasions, but Mavis had misplaced it several years back.

Frosted car windows, leaky pipes, loose floorboards. She'd coped with them all and more since heart disease had claimed Arnold two weeks shy of his fifty-third birthday. Over the years, she'd gotten handy with a wrench and Philips screwdriver, wondering sometimes if Arnold was looking down from heaven at her in astonishment. As a young bride, she'd been all thumbs when it came to tools.

Once the ice cleared from her window, Mavis backed her car out of the school parking lot. Goodness knows what had come over her in the last few weeks. For more than ten years she'd been relatively content to be on her own. There'd been the odd moment when she'd waxed nostalgic for male companionship (watching a broadcast of *The Way We Were* on TNT, hearing Brenda Lee sing "Sweet Nothings" on the oldies radio station), but for the most part, she'd been fine.

Lately, though, she'd been visited by an array of confusing emotions. Several nights in a row she'd woken in the middle of the night with such an aching emptiness that she'd grabbed handfuls of her flannel nightdress and gently rocked back and forth against her headboard, soothing herself to sleep. That lonely ache, instead of lifting with the first faint light of dawn, stayed with her all day, like a persistent twinge in the joints.

Why now all of a sudden? Mavis suspected it had something to do with Attalee and Dooley's recent romance. Attalee had worked for years with Mavis at the Bottom Dollar Emporium and although she could be wacky and rough as a cob, she was still Mavis's dearest friend. Ever since Attalee had started dating Dooley, she had little time for Mavis. No more weeknights watching reality television together on Mavis's living room sofa. (Attalee knew the comings and goings of the cast members better than her own grandchildren's.) No shared suppers or evening strolls.

To be fair, Attalee often invited her along on outings with Dooley, but Mavis would just as soon stay home. The two of them were constantly kissing—sounding like the suction cups of a rubber mat being pried from the tub—and Mavis felt like a fifth wheel.

As a result, she'd been left to her own devices in the evenings, and every day her loneliness grew stronger. She yearned for a man's company, but the eligible men in Cayboo Creek were as picked over as a garage sale at noontime. She'd even considered posting her picture on a dating site on the Internet. But every time she sat down in front of the computer, she imagined her dear departed mama spinning in her grave at the thought of her daughter rendezvousing with strange men in dingy coffee shops. Besides, Mavis would die of shame if anyone in town found out. She could hear the gossip now: "Did you see Mavis Loomis's picture on the World Wide Web? Poor, desperate thing. She's auctioning herself off like a used lawn mower."

What a pickle I'm in, she thought as she parked in front of the Bottom Dollar Emporium. Here she was stuck with this continual longing, with no notion of how to satisfy it.

As she climbed out of her car and stood on the curb in front of her store, she squeezed her eyes shut and mouthed a silent prayer. She hadn't often asked God for a leg up. The last time she'd called on Him was when her business had been threatened by a large chain store. At the eleventh hour, He'd come to her aid like the cavalry charging over the hill on white horses.

Maybe this time, you won't wait until the last minute. Mavis immediately bit her lip at her ungracious thought.

She completed her prayer and turned the key in the lock. It was in His hands now.

I use to have a handle on life, but it broke.

—Sign in the break room of the
Bottom Dollar Emporium

CHAPTER TWO

In a stucco bungalow situated on the banks of Cayboo Creek, Elizabeth Hollingsworth stood over a seafood soufflé and glanced at the clock on the oven. Her husband was now officially thirty minutes late for supper, and her soufflé was sinking faster than a leaky rowboat. Occasionally Timothy lost track of time, lingering with the fellows who hung out at his bait shop, but, since it was Valentine's Day, she thought he'd make a special effort to be punctual.

Certainly she'd knocked herself out for the holiday. Never mind the seafood soufflé (which cost her a burnt thumb, a half-dozen eggs, and some frayed nerves), she'd also laid out a beautiful table with Grandmother Tobias's china and silver and a bouquet of pink tea roses as a centerpiece.

Setting the mood for romance, Elizabeth had put Glenda, their ten-month-old daughter, down for the night and slid a Nat King Cole CD in the stereo. Then she misted her wrists and earlobes with Jovan Musk and draped herself seductively over a love seat, where she'd been for the last half hour until she'd gotten up to check on the soufflé.

Where was he? She eyed the champagne bottle on the counter and was about to pop the cork and toss back a glass or two when she heard her husband's key turn in the latch.

"Honey, I'm sorry I'm late." Timothy sauntered inside, removing his baseball cap from a tangle of dark curls. In greeting, their dog, Maybelline, flung her portly body against her master's legs. Timothy knelt down to scratch the dog's shiny black head, saying, "I tried to call but all I got was the answering machine."

"The answering machine," she said sharply. "That's impossible, I've been here the whole—" Abruptly she remembered turning off the ringer of the phone just before Glenda's afternoon nap. Had she remembered to turn it back on? Obviously not.

"I was late because I had to drive across the river to pick up *someone's* Valentine's present," he said with an impish grin. "They accidentally shipped it to the post office in Augusta instead of here in Cayboo Creek."

"Oh, Timothy!" She flung her arms around his neck. "I thought you'd forgotten what day it was."

"How could I forget my best girl on Valentine's Day?" he said, hugging her close to him. Then, over her shoulder, he spotted the champagne cooling in the ice bucket.

"Time for a toast, I'd say." Timothy popped the cork and poured champagne into two glasses, handing her one. He regarded her with dark eyes that glowed indigo in the soft light of the kitchen lamp.

"I remember the first time we ever drank champagne together," he said, lifting his glass. "It was our wedding night. You took a sip and said, 'It's like tasting stars.' I fell in love with you all over again." He fixed his gaze upon her face. "To Elizabeth, a wonderful wife and mother."

Her crystal glass made a satisfying "ting" as it touched her husband's. Timothy was such a doting spouse; she should have guessed he'd have a good excuse for being late for Valentine's Day dinner. Elizabeth was the one with the problem. Lately she'd been uncharacteristically sensitive, apt to tear up at the most minor of slights.

"I smell something delicious," Timothy said, his nostrils twitching. "Do you want your gift before dinner or after?"

"Before," Elizabeth said. She'd never been particularly patient when it came to presents. Even at the age of twenty-seven, she still got up with the roosters on Christmas morning.

"Wait a minute." She picked up a red gift bag from the kitchen counter and handed it to him. "Your gift first."

Timothy eagerly tore away the tissue paper from the bag and let out a low whistle when he saw the box inside.

"A Pro Caster XL. Best darn reel on the market. I've had my eye on this thing for months." He planted a kiss on her cheek. "Thank you, Elizabeth."

He weighed the aluminum reel in his hand, marveling over it for several moments until she was forced to noisily clear her throat.

"Oops. I almost forgot your present. It's in the truck." He ambled out the kitchen door into the garage.

Elizabeth had made some strong hints about a white-gold heart pendant she'd seen in the Zales flier in last Sunday's paper, but Timothy had been buried deep in the sports section at the time and might have missed her comments. She heard him grunting in the garage and when she peeked out the door, he was grappling with something big and unwieldy.

"Do you need some help, honey?" she cried out. Maybe it was that rattan armchair she'd admired on the Pier One Web site. Not the most romantic gift in the universe, but it would go well with the couch in the den.

"Nope, sweetie. I've got it." After a moment or so, he strutted into the kitchen proudly pushing a baby buggy.

"A stroller?" Elizabeth tried to disguise the disappointment in her voice.

"A stroller," Timothy said with a snort. "That's like calling a Rolex a watch. *This,*" he said, flinging his arm out in an exaggerated fashion, "is the Amphibian."

"The *what*?"

"It's the Jaguar of strollers. The women in your Mommy Time group will be pea-green with envy when they see this. It's got the suspension of a Porsche. You could roll over a pothole, and Glenda wouldn't even blink. There's also mosquito netting and a sun cover that adjusts to three positions." He pushed his foot down near the wheel. "Not to mention a parking brake. And see these big wheels? They're for off-road handling."

Elizabeth folded her arms in front of her chest. "Hmmph. I suppose they'll come in handy when I take Glenda four-wheeling over rough terrain."

Timothy's face fell, and she instantly regretted her unkind remark.

"You don't like it," he said softly. "When I ordered it, the saleswoman claimed that every mother dreams of owning an Amphibian."

"Every mother, yes," she said, stroking his hand. "But on Valentine's Day, I want to feel more like a wife than a mother."

"I'm a big dolt." He knocked his temple

with his knuckles. "A stroller *isn't* a very romantic gift, is it? What was I thinking? I should have gotten you flowers or jewelry."

Elizabeth planted a kiss on his forehead. "I was just a little surprised. I'm sure once I try it out I'll wonder how I ever lived without the Salamander."

"Amphibian," Timothy said, quickly recovering his jovial mood. "It folds down completely to fit into the trunk. I got it in aubergine, but if you don't like that color, we can swap it for sand, marine, khaki, or plaid."

Elizabeth tuned Timothy out as he continued to marvel over the many features of the stroller. For weeks she'd been trying to hide her misery from her husband, but it was getting more difficult to pretend she was the same happy-go-lucky woman that he'd married.

Logically, she should be one of the most grateful people on the planet. She had a doting husband, an adorable baby daughter, and a gaggle of girlfriends who'd give her the bras off their backs if asked.

Still, for the last couple of months, she'd been slogging around in the doldrums. Sometimes she didn't get out of her nightgown until eleven A.M. and too many of her days were spent suspended on the couch, watching the Lifetime Channel or thumbing through old fashion magazines. When Timothy got home and asked her about her day, she'd invent little white lies.

"Glenda and I took a long, bracing walk along the creek bank," she'd say with false cheer, or "We went to story hour at the library," when in fact the farthest she'd ventured from the couch was to check out the Dorito supply in the pantry. She'd packed on eight pounds over the last couple of months, but Timothy either didn't notice her new girth or didn't care. He was so tickled to be a daddy that he assumed everything was wonderful in their little cottage by the creek.

Elizabeth wished she'd listened more carefully to the advice of her mother-in-law, Daisy Hollingsworth.

"I'd have gone stark raving mad if I'd stayed home with Timothy," Daisy had said when Elizabeth turned in her resignation at Hollingsworth Paper Cups to be a full-time mother. "Not everyone is suited for that sort of thing, and you're such an ambitious young lady."

True, she'd loved her marketing career, but she'd been eager to trade it in for what she considered to be the most important job in the world. Timothy was especially adamant about her decision to stay home with their baby. As a child he rarely saw his own mother and had been raised by a series of nannies. "My nannies were all very nice women, Elizabeth," he'd said with a sad little droop to his mouth. "But I always longed for my mother."

When their daughter Glenda was born, the wisdom of Elizabeth's decision to quit her job seemed confirmed. As soon as she gazed into the tiny, pink face of her brand-new infant, she was entranced.

But then came the sleepless nights, cracked nipples, and whining bouts of colic. Everyone told her things would get better after three months, and an addled-brained Elizabeth counted the days off on her calendar like a prisoner. But even after Glenda made her transition from red-faced she-devil to a placid, saucer-eyed Gerber baby, Elizabeth still faced a host of adjustment problems. She coped by trying to throw herself into motherhood, reading parent magazines cover to cover and memorizing the steps of the Ferber method of getting babies to sleep through the night (or "Ferberizing," as it was called by parents in the know). She even learned to make her own baby food. But then, several weeks ago, when she was preparing a dish of Tiny Tot Turkey, she started crying into the bowl of puréed fowl.

What are you doing with your life? The question echoed so loudly in her head it nearly made her ears ring. Quickly, all the advantages of being an SAHM (stay-at-home mom) swam up in her mind: She'd be the primary role model for her daughter. Her child wouldn't be raised by strangers. She'd never miss an important milestone due to a staff meeting or a business trip.

She'd stared straight ahead as if in a trance, wooden spoon slipping from her hand. It wasn't enough. Much as she loved her daughter, much as she wanted to be a great mother, she wasn't cut out to stay home every day with a small child. She'd been fooling herself.

Elizabeth couldn't share her misery with Timothy. He wanted to believe she was the perfect little mommy leading the perfect little life, but it was all a big, fat lie. *If you only knew,* she thought helplessly as Timothy concluded his animated spiel on the Amphibian.

"We'd better eat before everything gets

cold." Elizabeth set her soufflé dish on a silver trivet on the dining room table.

Timothy sat down and served both of them from the chafing dish.

"It may not look beautiful, but it tastes fantastic," he said through enthusiastic bites of egg fluff.

"Glad you like it." Elizabeth moved her food around her plate with her fork, but didn't really eat much of anything.

Timothy continued to chew with satisfaction, washing his supper down with great gulps of iced tea. Then it came: the dreaded question.

"So, what were my two favorite girls up to all day?"

Fortunately, she'd been much more productive than usual. She'd forced herself off the couch to shop for and prepare the Valentine meal.

"The usual. Shopping, cooking. Busy, busy, busy."

"Can you believe Glenda is almost a year old? It seems like we brought her home from the hospital yesterday." Timothy reached across the table to squeeze her hand. "Maybe it's time we started working on a little boy."

Elizabeth dropped her yeast roll. "What do you mean?"

"What do you think I mean?" He lowered his eyelids with a knowing glance. "After all, we both agreed we wanted to have a bevy of babies."

Bevy? The tiny bit of supper she'd ingested churned in her stomach. *How many babies were in a bevy?*

"We might as well get rolling, seeing how thoroughly you've embraced motherhood." He wiped his mouth with his napkin. "By the way, the O'Quinn place is up for sale. I stopped by today. It has six bedrooms, perfect for a large family. We should take a look."

So a bevy meant five, unless, of course, Timothy planned to stack their children in their rooms like cordwood. Elizabeth imagined rows and rows of bunk beds spilling over with kids.

"Excuse me," she said with a tight smile. "I need to visit the powder room."

"I'll clear the dinner dishes while you're gone."

Nodding, she tried not to run to the bathroom. As soon as she opened the door, a piteous cry welled up in her throat. She turned on the tap full blast to muffle the sound of her sorrow. How could she possibly have a bevy of babies when she was miserable with just one?

"She Looks Good Through the Bottom of My Shot Glass"
—Selection D-9 on the jukebox
at the Chat 'N' Chew

CHAPTER THREE

Mavis tottered on a stepladder, planning to take down the chubby cutout of a cupid that hung in the window of the Bottom Dollar Emporium. After the evening's fiasco at the Sweetheart Dance, she didn't want to look at the decoration. Certainly none of the arrows in the cupid's quiver had been meant for her.

When she reached for the cupid, she jostled a glass jar filled with candy conversation hearts on a nearby shelf. Pastel sweets rained from the container onto the oak floor. As she stepped off the ladder to clean up the spill, she heard the purr of a motor and the jingle of the bell above the door. She guessed her visitor was Birdie, dropping by to check on her. As she crawled on her knees to reach for an errant "Sweet Talk" heart, Mavis saw the leather toe of a cowboy boot in the entryway.

"What are you doing here?" she gasped, backing away. A strange man towered over her.

"Aren't you open?" he asked. "The lights are on, and the front door was open."

"No." Mavis struggled to get up from the floor. "We closed hours ago."

"Allow me, ma'am." He extended his arm to assist her. Warily, she put her hand in his, noticing how delicate and childlike it looked on the bed of his meaty, oversized palm.

He helped her to her feet, and as she rose, she took in legs thick as dock pilings, a neatly trimmed Vandyke beard, and green eyes bright as the feathers on a parrot.

"Is there something I can help you with?" she asked.

"No," he said with a smile. "If you're closed, I'll just come back tomorrow."

"It's okay. I don't mind." She smoothed her hair with the back of her hand.

"That's mighty kind of you." His eyes swept around the room. "You don't see many general stores like this anymore. Is that an old-fashioned soda fountain in the back?"

"Yes, but I'm afraid I can't make any sodas. Attalee . . . I mean, my soda jerk isn't here tonight."

"Actually I didn't come in for a drink. I was looking for something a mite more practical." He surveyed the wooden signs hanging over each aisle.

"Dry goods, housewares, apothecary." As he read the signs under his breath, Mavis noticed something vaguely familiar about his face. He took a step in her direction and she backed into a display of wind chimes, which embroidered the night with a cacophony of clangs, rings, and dongs.

"Clothing!" he said triumphantly. "I figured a general store like this would carry a little bit of everything. Do you happen to have a pair of overalls? Extra large?"

Mavis tried to recover her voice, which seemed to have sunk to the pit of her stomach.

"Let me check what I have in stock," she

said in a near whisper, knocking over a display of sock monkeys with her hip. The stranger leaned down to pick up the wayward toys and righted them on their shelf while Mavis trotted down the aisle, the wooden floor squeaking against her Rockport walking shoes.

She arrived at the clothing aisle and sorted through a stack of men's overalls, peering at the tags sewn into the fabric.

"Extra large." She shook out a pair of the heavy denim overalls and handed them to the stranger. He took the garment and held it up to his chest. The legs just skimmed his ankles and were clearly too short.

"What do you think?" He patted the overalls down on his chest and grinned.

"You're a very brawny man." Her voice betrayed a breathiness she hadn't intended.

"What the hey," he said, folding the dungarees. "They'll have to do until I can find me a big-and-tall store in these parts."

In an effort to disguise her self-consciousness, Mavis became all bustling efficiency. She strode to the cash register, rang up the purchase, and slid his credit card through the machine. Her heart nearly stopped when she glanced at the raised name on the card: Brewster Clark. Instantly a vision of a tall, muscular boy wearing a letterman's jacket materialized in her mind.

"Brewster Clark?" Mavis said softly, staring at the card. "Cayboo Creek High School Class of 1959. Quarterback for the Flying Squirrels?"

"That's me all right, and you're . . ." He tapped the side of his head. "Don't tell me. Let me guess."

"Mavis Flump. Actually, Mavis Loomis now. I'm sure you wouldn't remember me."

"Mavis Flump? Were you a cheerleader?" His face was pensive.

"No. I was marching band, actually. I played the bassoon. And I was treasurer for the geography club," Mavis said in a soft voice.

"Oh," Brewster said, as if he now understood her rank in the adolescent hierarchy of high school. She'd been one of the invisible girls who faded into the gray landscape of the hallway lockers. A little plump, a tad shy, and definitely not the sort who would turn the head of an Adonis like Brewster Clark.

"You use to date Prissy Stevens, the homecoming queen," Mavis offered. "I always imagined that the two of you got married."

"No. Prissy went away to college, and I joined the Navy. We kept in touch through her junior year, and then she married a rich real-estate developer from New York." He stroked his beard. "The name Loomis sounds familiar to me. Did you marry some-one from high school?"

"Arnold Loomis. A lot of kids knew him be-cause he was the Flying Squirrel mascot."

"Why sure," Brewster said with a grin. "Old Acorn Arnie. I remember him. A slight fellow. Had wires coming out of his mouth."

"Headgear." Mavis nodded. "He had a pro-nounced underbite."

"How the heck *is* Arnie? Does he still stuff his cheeks and make that crazy squeaking sound?"

She bowed her head. "Actually, Arnold passed on about ten years ago. He had a heart attack."

"Gee, I'm sorry," Brewster said with a pained look. "I lost my wife Nettie two years ago." He glanced up at her underneath dark lashes as luxuriant as a film star's. "So you're a widow and I'm a widower. I'll be dogged."

Mavis blushed and slid his overalls into a

brown paper shopping bag. "What brings you back to Cayboo Creek?"

"My great-aunt passed on about six months ago, leaving me an old house on Chickasaw Drive. The property's all grown up, so I need to clear it up some and decide what to do with it."

"So you won't be with us long?"

"Maybe. Maybe not. I'm retired now with not much family to speak of, so there's a possibility I could stay on here in Cayboo Creek. Get away from the cold winters up north. I was living in Chicago."

"Brrr." Mavis handed him his purchase.

He started out the door and then glanced back at her. "Hope to see you around town, Mavis."

A girlish giggle escaped her lips.

"You too, Brewster."

"Call me Brew," he said with a wink.

As she scurried to the window to watch Brew drive off in a little red sports car, she remembered her entreaty to the heavens not ten minutes earlier.

Heavens to Betsy! That was quicker than Domino's pizza.

She swept up the rest of the candy hearts

on the floor, turned out the lights, and locked up for the night. As she headed to her car, she noticed that the cloud mass overhead had broken up, allowing one faint star to prick through the murkiness. *God sure does work in mysterious ways,* she thought. *And sometimes he even delivers.*

**Kids in the backseat cause accidents.
Accidents in the backseat cause kids.**
—Bumper sticker on Katie Costello's minivan

CHAPTER FOUR

Elizabeth sat in the small meeting room of the Cayboo Creek Library, listening to Katie Costello, president of the Mommy Time group, talk about pacifiers.

"To binky or not to binky, that is the question," said Katie, a serious-looking young woman with long chestnut hair and oblong eyeglass frames. "I wouldn't be so presumptuous as to answer that query myself, so I've brought in a guest speaker. Please give a big Mommy Time welcome to Dr. Flythe, a pediatric dentist from Augusta."

The group of mothers clapped while a balding man garbed in a white coat strode to the podium.

"I have just one word to say to you fine ladies." He surveyed his audience with watery blue eyes. "*Overbites*. Those are the consequences you'll face unless you choose orthodontic pacifiers for your children."

Elizabeth ignored the droning dentist and studied the young, earnest faces of the members of the Mommy Time group. Lydia Caruthers was doodling smiley faces on a pink Post-it note; Gail Anderson was eagerly taking notes, as if preparing for a final exam; and Connie Dye was sniffing her baby's diaper. If distress churned behind those Madonna-like masks, Elizabeth couldn't detect it. Instead, the club members' expressions were placid, as if motherhood was a favorite sweater they'd slipped into with ease.

Glenda squirmed on Elizabeth's lap. Other babies were getting restless as well. Trevor Lyons was slapping his mommy's cheek and saying "Doh" over and over, while the Barton twins across the table were winding up for a major fuss festival. The room in the library was too small and confining for the Mommy Time group, leaving no space for active babies to crawl or careen across the carpet.

"Thank you, Dr. Flythe, for that useful information," Katie said, leading the group in polite applause. Just before he left, the dentist passed out child-sized toothbrushes embossed with the name of his practice. Once he was gone, Katie consulted her notes and said, "Now it's time for our treasurer's report. Elizabeth?"

Elizabeth stood and began passing out materials with one hand while holding Glenda with her free arm. "Thanks, Katie. I've prepared a portfolio for everyone, complete with diagrams. Now, if you'll look at page one, you'll see graphs projecting our future earnings over the next five years."

It took Elizabeth several minutes to give her talk, utilizing the overhead projector as well as her laptop for an elaborate PowerPoint presentation. When she finished, she took her seat and smiled expectantly at Katie.

Katie shot her an odd look, saying, "Thank you, Elizabeth. That certainly was a thorough report."

"It sure as heck was considering there's only forty-five dollars in the pot," said Dottie Brubacker, a large, brassy blond who'd recently joined the group. "Could we get to the chow now?"

Embarrassment blazed in Elizabeth's cheeks. She realized the group didn't have a lot of funds, but that was no excuse to be slipshod about their management. She'd toiled over that treasurer's report and had looked forward to her presentation for days. Now she just felt foolish.

"Who's on this week's cookie committee?" Katie asked. Before anyone could respond, someone knocked on the door.

"Come in," Katie called out and the elderly librarian, Miss Goodbee, tiptoed into the room. "I'm sorry to interrupt," she said. "But some members of the genealogy club want to know if they can come in and set up early. They have a slide presentation today."

Katie glanced at her watch. "We're scheduled to have the room for fifteen more minutes."

Not waiting for an answer, Prudee Phipps and Mello Vickery pushed past the librarian, carrying a film projector and screen.

"Gangway, ladies," Prudee said with a

merry wave of her hand. "Never mind us. We'll be quiet as church mice. Mello, hand me that extension cord, please."

Mello, her eyes as dark and glittering as the glass orbs of her fox pelt, glared at the mothers. "So this is the Mommy Time group?" she said. "I'll thank you to clean up after your offspring. Last week a member of our club nearly slipped on a soggy piece of zwieback."

Prudee was at the white board, writing "Getting to the roots of your family tree" with a squeaky blue marker.

Katie pushed her glasses higher on the bridge of her nose and sighed. "I guess we'll save the cookies for next time. Meeting adjourned."

The women rose from their seats, retrieving coats, children, and plastic baggies of Cheerios. The only person to take Elizabeth's report was the two-year-old Lyons child, who was gnawing on the corner of a folder. Once the mothers had filed out of the room, Elizabeth started picking up the abandoned reports and shoving them into her briefcase. Katie, who'd presumably been lecturing the librarian about the genealogy club's infringement on the group's time, came back into the meeting room to pick up her diaper bag.

"You know how scatterbrained moms are," Katie said as she helped Elizabeth gather the rest of the reports.

"I know." Elizabeth tried to swallow back tears. "I just—"

"Hey, there." Katie clamped a hand on her shoulder. "It's okay. I know what you're going through. I'll walk you to your car."

Outside, the drizzling sky was the color of dove feathers. Oak leaves, which had long since fallen and littered the parking lot, were slick and muddy under the women's feet.

"You're the first in the group to know this, but I'm going back to work." Katie tugged her red slouch hat down on her forehead.

"What?" Elizabeth stopped in her tracks.

"I can't stand it anymore," Katie said, rubbing her son's back with a gloved hand. "I can't bear twenty-four hours of binkies, blankies, and Blue's Clues. Staying at home isn't for everyone."

"What'd your husband say?"

"Jack's okay with it. He misses some of the extras my income used to buy. I'm enrolling Kiefer in Wee World next week. The teachers seem nice, and the place looks cheerful. You can do it too, Elizabeth. It's okay to want to go back to work. It doesn't mean you're a bad mother."

Elizabeth shook her head and continued toward her car, hugging Glenda close to her chest. "My husband would pop his cork. He thinks mothers should stay home with their children. We talked about it at length before Glenda was even born."

"That was then." Katie quickened her pace to keep up with Elizabeth. "Maybe he's gotten more flexible about it. I remember meeting your husband at the Mommy Time family picnic, and he seemed like a really nice fellow."

As they neared the parking lot, Katie fished her car keys from her pocketbook. "It couldn't hurt to discuss it with him. Surely he doesn't want you to be unhappy."

"Is my misery that obvious?" Elizabeth asked, her eyes stinging in the winter wind.

"I suspected. But I wasn't sure until after you gave that treasury report. Then, I said to myself, 'There's a girl who's desperate to get out of the nursery and back into the boardroom.'"

"I don't know. I keep going round and round, and—"

"If you do decide to stay home with Glenda, maybe you can be the new Mommy Time president. That is, if we can find another place to meet."

"What's wrong with the library?"

"Mello Vickery is what's wrong. The librarian just told me she wants us out for good. Mello claims the conference room smells like poo-poo diapers after we leave. Unfortunately, she donates a ton of money to the library every year, so she has a say in the matter."

"Oh for heavens sakes," Elizabeth said just as Katie's son let out a cranky cry.

"I better go," Katie said. She paused for a moment and reached out to squeeze Elizabeth's hand. "Cheer up, Elizabeth. It's all right to want to go back to work, really it is." Then she turned and plodded to her car.

Elizabeth strapped her daughter into the backseat of the Ford Expedition that Timothy had bought just before Glenda's birth. (It had eleven cup holders, more evidence of his plans to keep her pregnant for the next decade.)

She fastened her seat belt and sat frozen with her hands on the steering wheel. Maybe Katie was right. Surely Timothy wouldn't want her to continue to stay home with Glenda if it made her unhappy, no matter what they'd agreed on before. After all, she'd worked since she was sixteen, first managing the Bottom Dollar Emporium for ten years and then signing on with the marketing department at Hollingsworth Paper Cups.

She'd gotten only a taste of her dream job at the cup factory when she discovered she was pregnant. She and Timothy hadn't intended to have babies so quickly (a leak in her diaphragm led to Glenda's conception), but when they'd discovered a child was on the way, they'd been overjoyed. Who could have predicted that she would miss her career so much?

Elizabeth put her SUV into reverse. She'd made up her mind. As soon as possible, she'd have a talk with Timothy. She couldn't go on like this much longer.

Jesus is coming. Look busy.
—Sign outside the Rock of Ages Baptist Church

CHAPTER FIVE

"Say spaghetti," Birdie said as she prepared to take a photograph of Mavis, who was posing beside the old-fashioned cash register at the Bottom Dollar Emporium.

"Spaghetti," Mavis said through tight lips.

"I'm so out of practice." Birdie closed one eye to peer through the lens of her camera as she snapped the picture. "I wish Chiffon was still working at the newspaper. I miss her."

Birdie was publisher and reporter for the

Cayboo Creek Crier. Her former photographer, Chiffon Butrell, had gone into business for herself, leaving Birdie to take all her own photographs again.

She made another small adjustment to the camera lens. "This time say *gesundheit.*"

"*Gesundheit,*" Mavis repeated, her hand touching her mouth. "I wonder if this lipstick color is too racy. It's a darker shade than I usually favor."

"It'll read fine in black and white," Birdie said as the flash went off. "So Mavis, how does it feel to be nominated by the chamber of commerce as Business Person of the Year?"

Before Mavis could answer, the bell above the door jingled and Elizabeth wandered in, carrying her daughter and a ceramic dish garden flourishing with sprigs of dracaena, ivy, and palm. Her hair looked uncombed and there was a strained carrot stain on her beige sweater.

"Hey, Mavis, I heard your good news and I—" She eyed her friend's appearance. "You look gorgeous."

"Thank you," Mavis said with a modest smile. She was dressed to be photographed, wearing a navy pleated skirt with matching jacket and a silk blouse underneath. A paisley scarf, tied around her neck in a jaunty knot, completed the picture.

Elizabeth set her gift on the checkout counter. "This is for you. Congratulations on your nomination for Business Person of the Year. I just know you'll win."

"How sweet, Elizabeth." Mavis leaned over the checkout counter to admire the plants. "You should share in this honor. After all, you're the one who turned this business around." Two years ago, Elizabeth had devised a new marketing strategy for the Bottom Dollar Emporium when a competing national chain store opened nearby.

"The only thing I'm turning around these days is Glenda when she crawls into mischief." Elizabeth laughed, but there was a false note to her merriment. Mavis raised an eyebrow at Birdie.

"Shoot, I gotta go." Elizabeth glanced at her watch and hurried to the exit. "Glenda has an appointment with the pediatrician. Congratulations, Mavis."

"I didn't even get to cuddle my godchild," Mavis said with a pout. "Thanks again for the plant," she called as Elizabeth slipped out the door.

"She's not herself," Mavis said, turning to Birdie.

"She's a mother now," Birdie said.

Mavis bit her lip. "That's not it. I've never seen her look so unkempt. And her eyes—the sparkle's missing. Something's troubling her."

"Make way!" Attalee Gaines burst through the front door, her gray sausage curls bobbing on her shoulders. "Hedonism II, here I come."

"What do you have?" Birdie said, looking at the card that Attalee held high in the air.

"It's my ticket to tropical titillation," Attalee said with a gummy smile. "It's called Caribbean Cash."

"Not another lottery ticket," Mavis said.

"What's Hedonism II?" Birdie asked, peering over Attalee's shoulder.

"An all-inclusive resort in Jamaica. They have pj parties, wet T-shirt contests, and drinks with little umbrellas stuck in 'em. It's for singles, eighteen and over. If I win I'll take Dooley."

"Well, you certainly qualify for the age part," Birdie said. "Several times over."

Attalee scratched at the ticket and squinted at it through her glasses. "Durn. I won only two bucks. Not even enough for a piña colada."

"Do you know what the odds are of winning the Lotto?" Mavis said with a shake of her finger. "You're just flushing money down the toilet."

Attalee ignored Mavis and dropped into a chair beside Birdie. "I had my heart set on Hedonism. Looking forward to doing a little oil wrestling."

"Speaking of hedonism." Birdie craned her neck to examine a red spot on Attalee's upper shoulder. "What is *that* thing, pray tell?"

"It's a love nibble," Attalee said. "Dooley came over last night and things got steamy."

"Attalee," Birdie said in a prim voice. "I hope you're not compromising your virtue."

"Too late for that," Attalee said. "My virtue got compromised more than half a century ago in the backseat of a 1938 Nash. But I wouldn't fret about things going too far 'twixt me and Dooley. Every time I invite him over, my roommate Myrtle sashays into the parlor wearing a skimpy little nightdress. *Claims* she's looking for her liver pills, but I believe she's trying to horn in on my man. If I was out of the picture that chippy would be all over Dooley like dew on Dixie."

"Why don't you just go over to *Dooley's* place, then?" Birdie asked.

Attalee frowned. "He lives in a boarding-house, and his landlord don't allow female guests. That's why I was hoping to win that trip to Jamaica, so Dooley and me could have us some sparking time."

The front door flung open, and Mrs. Tobias strode in.

"To the future Business Person of the Year," she said. "I'm so proud of you, Mavis."

"Word travels around fast," Mavis said.

"By the way, did I just miss my great-grandchild and her mother?" Mrs. Tobias said. "I thought I saw Elizabeth's car pull out of the parking lot just before I pulled in—" Her eyes alighted on Attalee's shoulder. "Goodness, gracious, Attalee. Your shoulder is inflamed. Were you bitten by a spider?"

"It's a hickey," Attalee proudly said.

Birdie rolled her eyes. "You really should put a Band-Aid over that thing, Attalee. It's attracting far too much attention."

"I believe you're jealous," Attalee said, rubbing the spot with her finger.

"Jealous?" Birdie sputtered. "As I told Mavis at the Sweetheart Dance, I'm glad to be done with courtship once and for all."

"Horse feathers!" Attalee tugged her white soda-jerk jacket from the hook on the wall and slipped into it. "A woman never loses her yen for a good man. That's like saying you've lost your taste for a hot meal."

"I disagree," Mrs. Tobias said. "I'm quite content to be single."

"Here, here." Birdie clapped her hands together.

"I'm with Attalee," Mavis said. "It's nice to have a man about."

"Particularly if he's a red-hot French-kisser," Attalee said.

"After that embarrassing incident at the dance, I thought you'd be soured on men, Mavis," Birdie said. "Besides, there aren't any eligible males our age around here."

"There is now." Mavis smiled. "Brewster Clark from high school stopped by the store recently. He's in town to fix up some property his aunt left him."

"Brewster Clark," Birdie breathed. "Big, strapping quarterback with more dimples than a golf ball? That Brewster Clark?"

"One and the same," Mavis said with shining eyes.

"He never gave me the time of day," Birdie said with a frown. "And I was no slouch in high school, what with being editor of the *Flying Squirrel Times* and captain of the javelin team. Instead, he preferred frivolous girls. Cheerleaders and prom queens. Tore through them like notebook paper, finally settling on that blond minx, Prissy Stevens." Her eyes gleamed with curiosity. "What does he look like now? Paunchy, bald, or both?"

"Nearly the same as he did in high school, only with more crinkles around his eyes," Mavis said. "Best of all, he's single. He was widowed a while back."

"Poor, dear Prissy," Birdie tsked. "She *was* always frail."

"Not Prissy," Mavis said. "She married a big shot in New York City. Brewster's late wife was named Nettie."

"And where's this house that he's fixing up?" Birdie asked.

"On the corner of Chickasaw Drive," Mavis said. "It's the place covered up in wisteria."

Birdie pushed a stray silver thread of hair behind her ear. "I still say men are more of a nuisance than a comfort. Even Max, God love him, was a trial at times. The TV clicker was like an extension of his hand. I'd be happily watching a movie on the tube and in a blink, we'd be flung into the middle of a duck-hunting show."

"Arnold wore scratchy wool socks to bed, even in the summer," Mavis said, with a faint smile.

"Harrison used to listen to his Vivaldi records at such a deafening volume it made my china rattle in the cabinet," Mrs. Tobias said. "Men are simply a different species entirely."

"I should be going." Birdie picked up her camera case. "The morning's flown out the window, and my in-box is piled with papers."

"I'm game for another cup of mud," Mavis said as she waved good-bye to Birdie. "Join me, Mrs. Tobias?"

"I prefer tea," Mrs. Tobias said. "But I'll get it."

"No, you sit." Mavis gestured to her regular chair in the break area. "You like lemon, don't you?"

Attalee didn't join them. She had her nose pressed up against the front window of the store.

"I smell a bird," she said in a suspicious voice.

"You mean a rat," Mrs. Tobias said.

"I mean a *bird*," Attalee said, jerking her

thumb in the direction of the window. "A *love*bird about to warble her mating song."

"What are you jabbering about, Attalee?" Mavis said as she split open a box of teabags.

"Birdie claimed she had a desk piled high with papers," Attalee said with narrowed eyes. "So how come instead of taking a left on Main to the *Crier* she took a right in the direction of Chickasaw Drive? Right into the arms of that Brewster fellow y'all were talking about."

"That's silly, Attalee," Mavis said. "You heard Birdie. She has no interest in men anymore."

Attalee shook her head. "I don't give a hoot what she said to you. She buzzed out of here like a queen bee hunting down her drone. I'm telling you, Mavis, if you're interested in that Brewster fellow, you better get cracking, 'cause our girl Birdie is hot on his trail."

**At the feast of ego,
everyone leaves hungry.**
—Sign outside the *Wagon Wheel Restaurant*

CHAPTER SIX

When Birdie left the Bottom Dollar Emporium, the gray dampness of morning had been swapped for a clear blue sky, shimmering with the pale pastels of a fragile rainbow. Her eyes followed the hoop of color, which disappeared behind a huddle of pine trees on the corner of Chickasaw Drive. It certainly wouldn't hurt for her to take a short detour to find out *who* might be at the end of the rainbow.

As publisher of the *Crier,* it was part of her

job description to call on new people in town. The newspaper had a section called "Welcome, Neighbor" that featured stories about Cayboo Creek newcomers. Therefore, she had a perfectly legitimate reason to call on Brewster Clark.

Although she'd tried to conceal it from Mavis, she was intensely curious about her former classmate. When Birdie was a sophomore in high school, she'd been crazy about two boys: Frankie Avalon and Brewster Clark.

But even the velvet-voice Frankie crooning "Venus" on *American Bandstand* couldn't compare with the real-life thrill of having Brewster Clark as her lab partner for biology. He was the only boy in class who managed to look sexy in safety glasses.

Clipping over to Chickasaw Drive in her navy-blue pumps, she felt a brief pang of guilt. After all, Mavis had made it clear she was interested in Brewster herself. Was she being disloyal to her longtime friend by popping in on him?

No, Birdie convinced herself as she traveled down the boxwood-lined sidewalk. Her visit to Brewster was completely innocent, born out of inquisitiveness and journalistic duty. One look at her former classmate and whatever spell he'd cast over her in high school would most certainly be broken. It'd happened with Frankie Avalon. Birdie had seen the former teen idol hawking Twilight Tan Exfoliating Cleanser on the Home Shopping Network, and now she could never think of him in the same way.

She reached Chickasaw Drive and spied a red convertible sports car parked in front of the corner house. Tidying her hair with her hand, she took measured steps as she pushed past the ragged overgrowth of tea olives and clematis surrounding the two-story house. The structure was an elderly Greek revival with columns weathered to the color of unpolished silver. With its ornate cornices and gabled roof, it had clearly been a showplace in another era. But now the eaves sagged, the shutters hung crooked, and the façade was freckled with mildew.

"Anyone home?" Birdie sung out as she climbed the steps leading to the porch, threading her way through pieces of peeling wicker furniture. Just as she was about to knock on the heavy walnut door, it creaked open and Birdie found herself staring into a pair of dazzling emerald eyes.

"Avon calling?" said the man, in a puckish voice. He grinned, and Birdie was treated to a blinding, white smile.

"Brewster Clark. As I live and breathe. You've not changed a smidgen since high school."

Brewster bowed at the waist. "Thank you, m'lady, for the kind words, but I *have* changed. My eyesight has weakened over the years, so forgive me if I can't place you."

Birdie chuckled to herself. What a diplomatic way of saying he didn't know her from a knot in a log! Unlike Brewster, she'd changed a great deal since she walked the hallowed halls of Cayboo Creek High School. Her blond hair had turned silver, and her once reedy frame had swelled over the years.

"Mealworms," Birdie said as a prompt. "We studied their life cycle together. I was your lab partner in Mr. Phelp's class."

"Who could forget Formaldehyde Phelp?" Brewster clapped the side of his face and squinted at her. "You're not that little snip of a girl who used to dress like a peppermint stick?"

She'd forgotten all about her red-and-white striped dress with the flared skirt. It was identical to a dress that Suzy Parker had modeled on the cover of *Harper's Bazaar.* In high school, she'd worn it at least once a week.

"Yes." She extended a hand. "Birdie Purdy. That's me. Rather, Birdie Murdock now."

"Birdie," he mused, eyeing her up and down. "Is that a nickname?"

She blushed. She'd acquired the nickname Birdie because she'd been such a scrawny teenager. Her real name was Bernadette.

"You look different now. Much curvier." He chuckled. "Sorry. I didn't mean to get too personal."

"No, not at all," Birdie said coyly. "We shared a dissection kit, after all."

"I like bumping into folks from high school. Brings back great memories." He puffed up his chest as he spoke. Brewster was still a big man and looked rock-solid under his plaid work shirt and blue jeans. "I'm glad you decided to pay me a visit. What can I do for you on this fine day?"

She felt uncharacteristically flustered. "There was nothing in particular. I just . . . I'm the publisher of the *Crier,* and I interview new people when they come into town."

"I'd love to be interviewed by you," he said with a grin. "Specially since you're a big-time newspaper publisher."

She consulted her wristwatch. In fifteen minutes she was expected at a school board meeting. "How's tomorrow around this same time, Brewster? It won't take long."

"Suits me fine. And look here, why don't you call me Brew?" He smiled at her. "I'm looking forward to it, Birdie."

"Likewise," she said, backing down the crumbling concrete steps of the porch. She was so flummoxed she tripped over a plaster pot and nearly fell, but Brewster lunged forward and caught her elbow just before she hit the ground.

**They're not hot flashes,
they're power surges.**
—Bumper sticker on the back of Attalee Gaines's
Buick Skylark

CHAPTER SEVEN

Attalee parked her Buick Skylark in front of a large storefront on the Aiken-Augusta Highway. The aging vehicle continued to stammer and lurch long after she removed the key from the ignition.

"Is it supposed to do that?" Gracie Tobias grasped the armrest until the car finally wheezed to a stop.

"It's temperamental, all right." Attalee kicked open the door with the heel of her shoe.

"I should say so," Mrs. Tobias said, folding up her white kid gloves and tucking them into her clutch bag. "We should have taken my Caddie."

"Other folks driving makes me nervous." Attalee slid from her car seat and pointed to the flapping banner on a pole that read "Last Chance Flea Market." "Here it is: shopping paradise."

Mrs. Tobias surveyed the decaying building, which had formerly been a Kmart. "I've never been to a flea market before. Are you sure we can find a nice present for Mavis here?"

All of Mavis's friends had chipped in money to buy her a special gift, which they would present to her at the banquet for Business Person of the Year. Mrs. Tobias and Attalee had volunteered to choose and purchase something appropriate.

"You betcha." Attalee hitched her battered vinyl pocketbook on her shoulder. "The flea market has one-of-a-kind items. Couple of weeks ago, I bought my daughter one of them moving waterfall pictures. You won't find something that classy at the Wal-Mart. I'd get Mavis one too, but she's got a tendency towards seasickness. And my boyfriend Dooley works here. He's got a booth inside, and I told him we'd meet him for lunch."

"Lunch?" Mrs. Tobias asked. "There's a restaurant inside?"

"Course there is. With rib-sticking country eats," Attalee said. "I recommend the chicken-feet casserole. It's so good it'll put your granny in a branch."

"Oh my." Mrs. Tobias's stomach flip-flopped. "I still think we would've been able to find a more suitable gift at Rich's in the Augusta Mall."

"Bor-ing! We need a present with piz-zazz," Attalee said as they crossed the park-ing lot. "Maybe a lava lamp or one of them singing fish."

"Well, you *have* known Mavis longer than I," Mrs. Tobias said. "I suppose you're more familiar with her tastes."

The women pushed open the glass door and were greeted by a medley of food aro-mas. The scent of piping-hot nuts mingled with the fragrance of deep-fried funnel cake and candy-coated apples.

"It smells like an indoor county fair," Mrs. Tobias remarked as they lingered in the en-trance, looking over the various vendors separated from each other with chicken wire and particle board.

"I believe Dooley's booth is that-a-way." Attalee pointed down the middle aisle. "But we'll browse for a spell before we make our way over."

Mrs. Tobias gazed up at a collection of T-shirts hanging on a cinder-block wall in a booth by the entrance called Rebel Ware. "Don't be shy. Let it Fly,'" she said, reading the slogans on the shirts. "'Dern tooting I'm a Rebel.' 'If you ain't from Dixie, you ain't spit.'"

A big-bellied man, wearing a faded red bandana on his bald head, noticed Mrs. Tobias and sidled up to her.

"This is just a small sampling of my inventory." He stroked a beard that dangled from his chin like a piece of Spanish moss. "I've got a catalog you can page through. My company will put a Rebel flag on everything from beach towels to underwear to throw pillows."

"Indeed." Mrs. Tobias squared her shoulders. "Don't you know it's inappropriate to display flags on underwear or throw pillows? If you're so enamored of the Confederate flag, young man, you should treat it with more respect."

Attalee seized Mrs. Tobias's elbow and

steered her away from the booth. "Whatcha trying to do, get us kilt?"

"Heritage not Hate' my foot," Mrs. Tobias harrumphed. "What kind of individual displays his so-called heritage on a beer mug?"

"The same kind of yahoo that gets his kicks from lynching loudmouthed little old ladies," Attalee hissed. "Let's move along."

They meandered through a labyrinth of booths, but Mrs. Tobias didn't hold much hope of finding a decent gift for Mavis. The vendors sold drib-drabs of the worst kind of kitsch imaginable. What possible use would Mavis have for a feathery dream catcher or a silkscreen portrait of a sad-eyed coyote?

"I declare," Mrs. Tobias remarked after they left a booth called Kountry Kreations, which carried a collection of driftwood eagle wall clocks and oil paintings of elks on saw blades. "I don't think I've ever seen so many lighthouses, unicorns, and American flags. Everything here is so . . ."

"Classy," Attalee said with a nod. "How can we narrow it down to just one thing? Ye gods and little fishes! We don't have to go any further."

They were standing in front of a vendor

called "Everything Elvis." "Blue Suede Shoes" blared from the speakers inside.

"Mavis is a huge fan of the King," Attalee said. "We're bound to find something good here."

Mrs. Tobias followed Attalee into a narrow stand cluttered with a jumble of Elvis gee-gaws, ranging from Return-to-Sender key chains to polyester replicas of his famous sequined white jumpsuit. Attalee homed in on an object in small glass box. "Have a Hunk of Elvis" read the sign affixed to the container.

She squinted at the price and said, "Three thousand dollars! That's as high as the hair on a cat's back. What is that thing?"

A lumpish woman with brittle black hair glanced up from her copy of *True Crime* magazine. "That's Elvis's toenail. I found it in the Jungle Room when I visited Graceland just after it opened."

"How do you know it ain't the Colonel's toenail, or Pricilla's?" Attalee asked.

"My hands tingled when I picked it up," the woman said with a zealous look in her eye.

"Dang, I sure wish we had more money," Attalee grumbled.

"Enough," Mrs. Tobias whispered. "We're

not getting Mavis a toenail, Elvis's or other- wise. Surely there's something else . . ."

"The Elvis nesting dolls are a popular item," remarked the woman. "So are the King's gold replica sunglasses."

"Real gold?" Attalee asked.

"They're $15.99 a pair. You be the judge," the saleswoman said.

"Fresh little cuss," Attalee said in an aside to Mrs. Tobias. "So what do you think? I'm eyeing those Elvis toilet-seat covers by the door."

Mrs. Tobias sighed and addressed the saleswoman. "Do have anything that's a little less commercial?"

"I've got pen-and-ink drawings of Elvis that I've done myself." She pointed to a wall lined with framed art.

Mrs. Tobias edged past an Elvis beanbag chair to examine the drawings.

"These are beautifully rendered," she said after taking a look. "And the price is right as well. Attalee, why don't you choose one you think Mavis would like?"

Attalee waffled between Vegas Elvis and Jailhouse Elvis but finally chose the drawing of the King garbed in prison attire, saying it would go best with Mavis's striped couch.

"Good," Mrs. Tobias said as she waited for the saleswoman to wrap up the package. "Now we can head back to the civilized world."

"We gotta eat lunch first," Attalee protested. "There's a cold collard sandwich calling my name."

"Must we?" Mrs. Tobias's shoulders drooped. "This shopping trip has exhausted me."

"But you promised you'd have lunch with me and Dooley!"

"Yes, I did, didn't I?" Mrs. Tobias pulled a sterling-silver compact from her purse and glanced at her weary face. "Onward, then."

The two women weaved through a maze of vendor's booths until they arrived at a stall called Knives and Things. An angular white-haired gentleman and a woman with a brown cigarillo dangling between her rubbery lips were chatting inside.

The woman leaned close to the man and whispered something in his ear. He let out a whoop of laughter, and she reached over to give him a sound pinch on his denim behind.

Quick as a bullet, Attalee was at the woman's side with balled-up fists.

"If I've said it once, I've said it a hundred

times. Keep your paws off Dooley, or I'll clean your clock!"

The woman, who was an Irish wolfhound to Attalee's Chihuahua, glanced down at her with hooded eyes.

"You and what army?" she said.

"Ladies." Dooley slipped between the two women. "No call to tussle. Minnie, looks like you got a customer. You might ought to see to her."

Minnie meandered out of Knives and Things, trailing ashes as she went. She manned the booth next door called Heav'nly Treasures, which sold ceramic angels and nativity-scene snow globes.

"How's my gorgeous girl?" Dooley planted a noisy kiss on Attalee's withered cheek.

"Sweeter than a suck of sugar," Attalee said.

"You got that right," Dooley said with a low growl.

Mrs. Tobias cleared her throat.

"Dooley, this here is Mrs. Tobias. Mrs. Tobias, Dooley. You probably remember seeing him at the Sweetheart Dance."

"Charmed." Mrs. Tobias extended her hand to him. Dooley was thin, almost to the point of being skeletal, save for a paunch that protruded over the top of his Levi's like a half-deflated bike tire. His blue eyes, round as gumballs, stared out from behind a pair of trifocal spectacles.

"So, what do you think of his spread?" Attalee said.

Dooley sold knives of every description, from pocket knives emblazoned with John Wayne's image to elaborate daggers with lethal blades. In addition to knives, there was a table littered with cell-phone covers, doo rags, and fuzzy dice, hence the "things" in the name of the booth.

"Pick yourself out a little something," Dooley said to Mrs. Tobias, indicating the "things" table. "On the house."

Since she didn't own a cell phone or have any occasion to don a doo rag, she selected the fuzzy dice.

"They glow in the dark," Attalee said with a grin.

"Y'all ready to get a little greasy around the mouth?" Dooley asked, thumbs in the belt hoops of his jeans.

"I know I am." Attalee rubbed her tiny pooch of a belly.

Dooley fastened a padlock to his stall, and the three made their way to a corner of the flea market where a diner had been set up. After choosing a booth in the back, the group studied menus encased in yellowed plastic. Mrs. Tobias winced at the vase of dusty flowers in the center of the table and the flimsy, discolored flatware. She glanced at the menu, hoping to find something safe to order.

"Broiled squirrel?" she gasped as she read the blue-plate special.

"I'm generally drawn to that, too," Dooley said to Mrs. Tobias. "But Hazel cain't offer squirrel no more. Turns out there's a law against serving customers meat that you've shot in your own yard."

"Hey, ain't that Rusty Williams over yonder?" Attalee pointed at a man in a black leather jacket hunched over the diner's counter.

"Sure as heck is," Dooley said. "Hey, Rusty, come on over, why don't ya?"

Rusty waved and sauntered over to their table. From his perch on the stool, Mrs. Tobias had imagined a much younger man, but as he got closer, she noticed threads of silver weaved through his heavy dark hair and deep furrows etched in his forehead.

"What a co-winky-dink. Rusty's here eating some lunch, and so are we," Attalee said with such exaggerated cheer that Mrs. Tobias raised an eyebrow.

"Why don't you join us?" Attalee continued. "Skooch over some, Mrs. Tobias, so Rusty can have him a seat."

From across the table, both Attalee and Dooley grinned at her like a pair of chimpanzees.

"Certainly, Mr. Williams." Mrs. Tobias shot Attalee a questioning look as she slid closer to the wall.

"I'd be honored to join you," Rusty said. His accent sounded like he came from the deepest southern region of Georgia. Valdosta, or maybe Albany. "Let me tell Hazel I'm moving to your booth."

After he'd departed, Mrs. Tobias spread her napkin on her lap.

"Attalee Gaines, why do I get the impression that running into Mr. Williams was no accident? And that this little lunch is, in fact, a setup?"

"I got no idea what you're talking about," Attalee said, blocking her face with the menu.

"Now dumpling," Dooley said. "I believe Mrs. Tobias is on to our little scheme." He smiled at Mrs. Tobias, revealing a set of poorly fitted dentures.

"We didn't mean no harm, ma'am," Dooley continued. "When Attalee told me she was bringing a lady friend to the flea market, I thought the two of you might hook up. Rusty's single and has a booth catty-corner from mine called Leather Expressions."

"I'm sure Rusty's a wonderful man," Mrs. Tobias said. "And that many women would be delighted to—"

"You bet their britches they would." Attalee yanked down the menu from her face. "Minnie's been buzzing around him like a bee ever since he opened a booth here. Luckily for you, he don't cotton to smokers. Heck, Rusty is the best catch in Aiken County, except for my Dooley of course." She squeezed her boyfriend's arm. "But he's taken."

"Attalee, I wouldn't care if Rusty was Prince Charles himself. The truth is—"

"Shush now," Attalee hissed. "Here he comes."

Mrs. Tobias studied Rusty as he strode toward their table. He *was* uncommonly handsome, reminding her of a weathered Rock Hudson. And he carried himself like the CEO of a Fortune 500 company instead of the proprietor of a booth at a roadside flea market. But it didn't matter if Rusty was a prince or a pauper: She simply wasn't interested in having a paramour.

The vinyl of the booth creaked as Rusty sat beside her, bringing with him the pleasant scents of leather, cedar, and green apples.

"I hope this isn't an intrusion."

"Not at all." Mrs. Tobias kept her eyes fastened on the menu. "I still haven't decided what I want."

"The oxtail soup's delicious," Rusty said. He must have noticed the nearly imperceptible wrinkle of her nose, because he laughed.

"That's what I thought the first time I heard of it, too. But I promise, it's delicious."

A female server, her hair sheared into a raggedy bowl cut, approached the table.

"How you folks today?" she said in an accent as down-home as a mule wearing a straw hat. "Hope yer hungry, 'cause we've been cooking up a gracious plenty in the kitchen."

She set down a large, fragrant basket, which spilled over with buttermilk biscuits, corn bread, fritters, and hush puppies.

"What can I get y'all?" she asked as she

wiped her hands on a dishrag that hung from the pocket of her blue jeans.

"I usually ask Hazel here to bring out whatever she thinks is good today," Rusty said. "Would that suit?"

Everyone nodded, and Rusty collected the menus, handing them to Hazel.

"Don't forget my oxtail soup, sweet pea," he said with a wink.

Hazel lit up like a sparkler, displaying a mouth full of misshapen teeth. She re-arranged the condiments on the table and scuttled back to the kitchen.

Across the booth, Dooley was nibbling on Attalee's ear as if it were an appetizer. Embarrassed by their public display of affection, Mrs. Tobias picked up her fork and examined it for cleanliness.

"Are you a country line-dancing fan?" Rusty asked her.

"Pardon me?" Mrs. Tobias asked.

"The Country Strut, the Watermelon Crawl, or the Tush Push?" Rusty asked.

"No, Mr. Williams," Mrs. Tobias said. "I can safely say I'm completely unfamiliar with the Tush Push."

"It's all new to me, too," he said. "I went to a honky-tonk the other night for the first time in years, and that's the kind of dancing all the kids were doing. It looked so much fun I decided to sign up for some lessons. Do you like to dance at all?"

There'd been a time when she was an accomplished ballroom dancer. She and Harrison would waltz with the best of them during Augusta's cotillion season.

"Now and then," Mrs. Tobias said.

"It's not much fun taking dance lessons on your own," Rusty said. "I don't suppose—"

Hazel arrived at their booth with a tray as wide as a raft. She set it on a collapsible portable stand and plunked down a hot tureen of soup at each place as well as several bowls of steaming food.

"Is sweet tea okay with y'all?" she asked. Hearing no objections, she set down a clear plastic pitcher brimming with beverage and ice. "Holler if you need anything."

Just as Mrs. Tobias was about to dip her spoon into her soup, Dooley removed his cap.

"Shall I say the blessing?"

"By all means," Mrs. Tobias said, bowing her head.

Dooley cleared his throat. "Bless the food and damn the dishes. Let's all eat like sons of—"

"Amen," Mrs. Tobias interrupted.

The oxtail soup was hearty with morsels of silken meat, barley, carrots, and parsnips. At Rusty's urgings, Mrs. Tobias had a nibble of every dish on the table. There were tender crowder peas enlivened with a few shakes of Texas Pete's Hot Pepper Sauce, plump pole beans seasoned with pork, gooey, deep-dish macaroni and cheese, fried chicken that crackled under the teeth, and black-eyed peas tarted up with jalapeños and red wine vinegar.

"Georgia caviar," Rusty declared, as he spooned another helping of black-eyed peas on his plate. The whole table tore through a basket of cathead biscuits with layers so light they melted on their tongues like snowflakes.

"Did ya know," Attalee said, spearing a candied yam with her fork, "that Rusty here is a doctor?"

"Really?" Mrs. Tobias cast an intrigued gaze at her dining companion.

"Now, Attalee," Rusty said. "You gotta quit saying that. I'm not a *real* doctor."

"Are you a Ph.D.?" Mrs. Tobias asked.

"He's an honest-to-goodness doctor," Attalee insisted. "Says so right on his truck."

"Just a little gimmick of mine," Rusty explained. "I clean air ducts in homes and businesses. So I call myself the Duct Doctor."

"I thought you rented a booth here," Mrs. Tobias said. She took a sip of her tea, and a cluster of ice chips bumped her nose.

"I do, but the flea market is only a weekend sideline," Rusty said. "During the week, I clean dirty ducts."

Hazel appeared at the table and surveyed the clutter of scraped-clean plates. "Who's up for a little dessert?"

Dooley groaned. "My belly's tight enough to crack a tick on."

"Then you best have something sweet to fill in the chinks," Hazel said, balancing a row of dirty plates along her pale, skinny arm.

Shortly after, coffee arrived steaming and served in thick-lipped cups. Despite their straining stomachs, they all tucked into the stiff meringue and vanilla wafers of Hazel's banana pudding.

Attalee swiped at her mouth with a napkin and slung her legs into the aisle. "I need to visit the powder room. Maybe you'd like to show me where it is, Dooley?"

"Just go all the way to the back and take a

left," said Dooley as he jiggled a toothpick between his teeth.

Attalee cut her eyes at Rusty and Mrs. Tobias. "I need you to show me."

"Oh," Dooley said, taking the hint and sliding his lanky frame out of the booth.

After they left, Rusty chuckled over the rim of his coffee cup. "Attalee's not exactly the most subtle of women."

"No, she's not." Mrs. Tobias folded her napkin and placed it beside her dessert plate. "Mr. Williams, I understand what Attalee's trying to do, but I'm sorry. That part of my life has been closed for a long while now."

"Understood," Rusty said with a nod. "I wasn't too keen on this meeting myself. I've never thought much of blind dates."

"Thank you for understanding."

"You're welcome, ma'am." He studied her with eyes the color of coffee beans. "You're different from the other ladies I've been introduced to lately."

"Oh?" Mrs. Tobias said.

"Don't know what it is," he said as he opened up his wallet and laid a fifty-dollar bill on the table. "But I'm downright enchanted."

He stood and smiled down at her. "Tell Hazel to keep the change."

A stunned Mrs. Tobias watched him stride out of the restaurant area and when he was out of sight, she peeked at the check on the table. The bill was twenty-eight dollars plus tax for that prodigious feast. Normally Mrs. Tobias thought overtipping was vulgar (her late husband Harrison always tipped precisely fifteen percent no matter what the service), but Rusty's generosity to the odd-looking little waitress seemed somehow more endearing than crass.

**When I married Mr. Right I didn't know
his first name was Always.**
   —Quote of the day in the *Cayboo Creek Crier*

CHAPTER EIGHT

Elizabeth shrugged her shoulders up to her ears trying to drown out the sound of Manny E. the Mozzarella Monkey singing "Happy Birthday" in a jarring off-key tenor. She was surprised she could hear the lyrics over the excited shrieks of children and the ceaseless bings and bongs of the videos games that reverberated throughout the pizza restaurant.

Playtime Pizza was located in Augusta across the Savannah River from Cayboo

Creek. A large flashing sign out front billed it as the "happiest place on the planet." To Elizabeth it seemed like the noisiest place, with a decibel level somewhere between an airport runway and a Metallica concert.

Chiffon Butrell, who was one of Elizabeth's best friends, was hosting a birthday party at Playtime for her six-year-old son, Dewitt. Elizabeth and Timothy had volunteered to attend and help her manage the twelve first-graders that had been invited to the party. Thus far it had been an exhausting responsibility. All the noise and Coca-Cola made the children as wild as an acre of snakes.

When Manny E. finished his uninspired solo and started serving slices of pizza to the party guests, Elizabeth leaned toward Chiffon and said, "I wonder what the 'E' stands for?"

Chiffon, who was beauty-queen pretty with long, wavy blond hair, rolled her eyes. "Expensive, exploitative, and excessive is my guess," she said. "But I didn't have much of a choice. My house is too small to host a party and it was either this or the laser-tag place down the highway."

"Have you heard from Chenille lately?"

Elizabeth asked. Chenille was Chiffon's older sister. She'd been chosen by her school district to teach gifted students in a teacher-exchange program in England for a semester.

Chiffon poked her straw into the remaining ice in her cup. "She called to wish Dewitt a happy birthday. She sure misses everyone. Especially her boyfriend, Garnell."

Elizabeth nodded and glanced at her daughter, who was happily gnawing on a teething ring in her high chair, oblivious to the racket around her. "I'm glad Glenda is too little to care where her birthday party will be."

"Yeah, you have a few years yet." Chiffon snapped a new roll of film into her camera. "Timothy looks happy as a clam."

Elizabeth glanced over at her husband, who was thronged by three little boys watching him twist a balloon into the shape of a wiener dog.

"He does look like he's enjoying himself," Elizabeth said. Instead of appearing frazzled by all the bedlam, Timothy acted as excited as one of the pint-sized party guests.

"Mama!" Dewitt shouted. He was out of breath as he approached Chiffon. "I need more tokens."

"More? You had a whole handful five minutes ago," Chiffon said as she poured a pile of the gold plastic coins into his waiting palm. "After this, you're done. Those darn machines eat up tokens like they were kibble."

Elizabeth ventured a nibble of the pizza slice that the moth-eaten Manny E. had placed in front of her on the sticky table. The cheese was rubbery, the temperature was cold, and the crust was the consistency of cardboard.

A group of Manny E's minions, Doughboy Dan, and the Sausage Sextet got onstage and started singing, "Playtime Pizza is the happiest, happiest place on the planet."

"You got anything for a headache?" Elizabeth shouted to Chiffon. Chiffon nodded and set out three bottles: Extra-Strength Tylenol, Motrin, and Anacin-3.

"Choose your poison," she said. "After last year's party, I came prepared."

Later, after Timothy and Elizabeth had helped drop off half the party guests, Timothy was humming Playtime Pizza's theme song as he pulled up in the driveway of their bungalow.

"Please don't do that." Elizabeth plugged her ears with her fingers.

Timothy chuckled as he put the SUV into park. "I take it you didn't care much for Playtime Pizza."

"It was a train wreck," Elizabeth said, climbing out of the car. "I though Chiffon was going to tear her hair out."

"It *was* kind of loud," Timothy said, opening the back door to release a sleeping Glenda from her car seat. "But I had a lot of fun with all those little kids."

He unlocked the front door and stepped inside the house. "I'm looking forward to the time when we'll have our own tribe of children," he said with a wink.

Tribe! After a long afternoon of herding a pack of rambunctious kids, Elizabeth's patience snapped.

"Timothy Horace Hollingsworth," she fumed as she followed him into the nursery. "I'm your wife . . . not some sort of . . . old woman in the shoe who's supposed to have a parade of children trailing after her."

She hadn't intended to confront him this way; her plan had been to civilly discuss the issue over a glass of Chablis. Too late now: She was spitting like a grease fire.

"What do you mean?" Timothy said as he tucked Glenda in her crib.

"You heard me," she continued. "You keep making remarks about all these babies *we're* going to have. What you really mean is the children *I'm* going to have, because I'm the one who has to do all the work."

"You don't think I help out enough with Glenda?" Timothy said in a wounded voice.

"You lend a hand when you can, but you're not here all day long with a baby." She softened her tone. "You have no idea how isolating that can be."

"But what about your Mommy Time group? Doesn't that give you a chance to hang out with other adults?"

"Mommy Time has been canceled until the weather's warmer. We lost our place to meet, and we can't find another one." She looked at her husband with large, pleading eyes. "Do you have any idea what I'm trying to say?"

"Of course I do, sweetheart. I didn't realize how hard it is to be cooped up with an infant all the time." Timothy curled his arm around her waist. "Have you been keeping this from me for a while?"

Elizabeth nodded, sniffing back tears.

"Tell you what." He smoothed a strand of dark-blond hair behind her ear. "Why don't I get Ferrell to tend the bait shop on Friday afternoons, and I'll come home and look after Glenda. That'll free you up to do a little shopping or have a lunch date with your friends. Maybe you could even treat yourself to a facial or a pedicure. How does that sound?"

"No." She stiffened in his arms. "You don't understand at all. I could care less about clean pores or painted toenails."

"What are you saying, then?"

Tell him, she ordered herself. There would never be a better time than now. She gently broke free from his embrace and faced him. "I want to go back to work."

"Work?" Timothy said, as if genuinely puzzled. "How can you work? Who would take care of Glenda?"

"Timothy, there are people who care for children, nice, decent people who—"

"Strangers," he interrupted. A look of betrayal crossed his face. "You want to put our daughter into the hands of people she doesn't know or trust. We discussed this at length, Elizabeth. We both agreed that the parent is the best person to raise a child. Why even *have* children if you're going to farm them out to other people all day long?"

"Not *all* day long," Elizabeth protested. "I

thought I'd work part-time to start. I called your mother, and she said Hollingsworth Paper Cups could use another marketing executive, especially since they're coming out with those new, insulated coffee cups."

"Are you telling me that you're going to abandon our daughter so you can peddle Styrofoam cups?" Timothy demanded.

Glenda stirred restlessly in her crib and Elizabeth put a finger over her lips.

"Let's go in the living room to talk this out," she whispered. "I don't want to wake her."

Timothy shook his head and dropped down into the rocking chair beside the crib. "I'm sorry, Elizabeth, but there's nothing to talk about. We had an agreement, and you're trying to wriggle your way out of it. As far as I'm concerned, this discussion is closed."

"Come on with me, Timothy, please," Elizabeth rested a hand on his shoulder. "We've always been able to talk things through."

"Not this time," he said darkly. "*You* go into the living room. I'm staying in here with my daughter."

Age is a high price for maturity.
—Sign on the bulletin board at the Senior Center

CHAPTER NINE

With a shy smile, Mavis admired her enhanced silhouette in her full-length bedroom mirror. Yesterday she'd driven to Dilbert's Department Store in Augusta for their annual Foundation Fling, and the saleswoman had talked her into purchasing a Liquid Assets Aqua Bra.

"Oh I don't know," Mavis said as the woman—a little red-haired sprite scarcely out of high school—had extolled the many virtues of the pricey bra.

"It molds to your body's natural shape and temperature," the salesgirl said, handing Mavis the lacy bra on a plastic hanger and ushering her into a dressing room. "And it adjusts to three levels of cleavage."

Once Mavis had tried on the bra, she couldn't get over how shapely she looked. She was used to buying plain A-cup bras on sale, which did nothing to boost her humble little bosom. With the Aqua Bra, her breasts inflated like fireplace bellows, even at the tamest level of cleavage.

A woman's gotta do what a woman's gotta do, Mavis mused as she turned from her mirror and went into the kitchen to check on her chicken divan casserole. She opened the oven and saw the Parmesan cheese on top was golden brown and bubbly. The heavenly fragrance of the dinner wafted throughout her sunny galley kitchen.

As she removed the casserole from the oven, she recalled Attalee's constant hounding ever since Birdie had taken off in the direction of Brewster's house.

"You gonna let Birdie snatch that Brewster from right under your nose?" Attalee had nagged several times. "That gal's got her trotting harness on for your fellow."

"He's not my fellow," Mavis had protested. "Birdie has as much right to him as I do."

Attalee had leveled a bony finger at her. "You saw him first. She knew you were kindling after him."

Later, when Mavis came home to another night of watching old black-and-white movies and munching Healthy Choice popcorn all alone on her sofa, she decided that Attalee was right. She'd seen Brewster first and when she'd confided her interest in him to her friend, Birdie had gone after him like a duck on a June bug. That was mighty underhanded and selfish of her, Mavis huffed. After tossing and turning that night in her narrow single bed, she woke up with a fresh resolve.

Every woman for herself, she'd thought as she flung a leg out of bed. Her new attitude led to her decision to amplify her assets with the Aqua Bra and to prepare a nice, hot dinner for Brewster.

"Perfect," she said to herself as she placed the hot Pyrex dish on the kitchen counter. While it cooled, she reapplied her lipstick and practiced what she was going to say to Brewster when she arrived at his house.

"Brewster, I mean . . . Brew," she said, trying to affect a breezy tone. "I was cooking, and I'm afraid I got a little carried away in the kitchen. Could you use an extra casserole for your freezer?"

Too mealy-mouthed. Plus it sounded like she was trying to pawn off her leftovers on him. The direct approach, though daring, was probably her best tactic.

"Hello there, Brew," Mavis practiced, batting her eyelashes. "I hope you like chicken and broccoli, because I made a casserole especially for you."

She grimaced. Still not quite right. She'd just have to sort out what she was going to say to him when she got there.

Since the day was sunnier than usual, Mavis slipped on her good wool coat to make the short walk from her little cottage on Persimmon Road to Brewster's house on Chickasaw Drive. The warm casserole dish felt toasty against her abdomen, and she liked the sensation of the bracing wintry breeze on her cheeks as she strolled down the sidewalk.

Bluish gray smoke curled from the stout brick chimney of her next-door neighbor's house, and Mavis's nose twitched with pleasure at the intoxicating fragrance. She carefully watched her footing along Persimmon Road, which was lined with ancient oak trees. The mossy roots burrowed from their bases like long, gnarled fingers. She could easily trip over a knuckled protrusion and be sent sailing through the air.

Eloise Jenkins was in her yard inspecting her azalea bushes, and she waved at Mavis and pointed at several burgeoning white blossoms on the bush.

"Those two warm days last week fooled this bush into thinking it's spring," she said. Noting the casserole in Mavis's arms, Eloise asked, "Who's under the weather?"

"Nobody," Mavis said, a hint of irritation in her voice. You could scarcely sneeze in Cayboo Creek without everyone knowing about it. "Just a little hot dish for a friend." Mavis quickened her pace to quell any further questions.

"Seems to be a lot of that going on today," Eloise called after her.

What does she mean by that? Mavis wondered. Thankfully, she managed to make the rest of the walk without encountering anyone else. Rounding the corner, she smiled as she saw Brewster's red car parked in the drive of his house.

She rang the doorbell, her heart knocking against her chest like a woodpecker as she waited for Brew to answer. When he appeared, he tossed her a wide grin and said, "Well, looky here. Today's my lucky day."

Buoyed by his warm welcome, Mavis felt her confidence surge.

"Hello, Brew," she said with a wave of her glove. "I've got something to warm you up on this cold day."

He raised an eyebrow. "Is that a fact?"

Oh dear. That came out a bit more suggestive than she'd intended. Thrusting her casserole dish at him, she said, "I hope you like chicken divan."

"I sure do," he said. "And it looks like I'll be eating a lot of it. Come on in and visit for a spell."

Mavis stamped her feet on the mat while Brewster offered to take her coat. She smelled sawdust and noticed that most of the furniture was shrouded with sheets.

"I hope I haven't caught you in the middle of your work," she said, shrugging out of her coat. "I can only stay for just a—"

"Brew," said a familiar voice coming from the depths of the house. "Who's at the door?"

"It's Mavis, Birdie," Brew replied, hanging Mavis's coat on a hook in the hall. "Aren't the two of you friends?"

Birdie appeared in the hallway, wearing a new red dress with a daring slit up the side. She startled when she saw Mavis.

"Yes," Mavis said, forcing her lips into a smile. "We're the best of friends."

"I thought so," Brew said. "And what a fine coincidence. Birdie just dropped by with her *own* delicious dish of chicken divan."

Using my family recipe, Mavis thought. She and Birdie often swapped recipes, and the chicken divan had come directly from Mavis's collection.

Birdie's eyes fell on Mavis's enhanced bustline.

"You're looking very ro*bust* today," Birdie said, putting her emphasis on the second syllable.

"I'll say," Brewster said, eyeing Mavis with appreciation.

"Thank you," Mavis said with a blush.

"I guess I should dash off," Birdie said. She turned to Brew. "I hope you enjoy the casserole. And if you need to reheat the yeast rolls, put the oven on 375."

Mavis nearly gasped aloud. *Birdie's*

homemade yeast rolls? There were none better.

"And if you don't eat all the blueberry cobbler, it freezes nicely," Birdie added.

Cobbler, was it? Birdie had certainly outdone Mavis's meager offerings.

"Don't let me run you off, Birdie," Mavis said. "I'm the one who needs to be going. I've left Attalee alone in the store."

"Are you sure either of you have to leave?" Brew asked. "I like some company while I eat."

"I guess I could stay a little while, Brew," Birdie interjected. "Sorry you have to run off, Mavis. May I see you out?"

Triumph shone in Birdie's eyes. Apparently she thought the battle was over before it even had begun.

"Not necessary," Mavis said, trying to hide the disappointment in her voice. "I'll just be on my way."

**I can resist everything
except temptation.**
　　　—Message in the Methodist Church bulletin

CHAPTER TEN

Mrs. Tobias ascended the steps to the Cayboo Creek Library, which was housed in a white Craftsman cottage with squatty stone pillars and a generous wraparound porch. As she opened the door, she inhaled the smell of a familiar blend of dried paste, old wood, and heated air from the elderly boiler.

Miss Goodbee, the seventy-five-year-old librarian, teetered on a stepladder, shelving books. She glanced toward the entrance when she heard the thud of the door.

"How do, Mrs. Tobias?" she said. "It's a mite nippish out there." Miss Goodbee's gray eyes looked perpetually surprised, as they swam beneath the thick lenses of her eyeglasses.

"I like the crisp air. It's revitalizing," Mrs. Tobias said, folding her sheared beaver coat over her arm. The librarian stood on tiptoe, revealing two inches of her lace slip.

"Miss Goodbee, your cotton is low," Mrs. Tobias whispered.

"What's that?" Miss Goodbee said, adjusting the knob on her hearing aid.

"Your slip," Mrs. Tobias said, stepping toward her. "It's showing."

"Gracious me." Miss Goodbee tugged her beige pleated skirt down over her knees and alighted from the ladder. "You came on a good day. I just got a shipment of new books in."

Mrs. Tobias browsed the new-arrival shelf, lined with the usual offerings of foil-covered romances and cozy mysteries. Today she was in the mood for something a bit more weighty. "Maybe I should stick with my old standby."

"You're in luck," Mrs. Goodbee said. "*To Kill a Mockingbird* was returned this morning. I've already reshelved it."

"Wonderful," Mrs. Tobias said, heading for the L–M shelf. Once she located the novel, she wandered into the sunny alcove, which served as a reading nook. Settling into a leather wing-backed chair, she positioned the book on her lap and thumbed through it trying to remember where she'd left off. Once she located her place, a folded piece of lined notebook paper drifted from the pages. She opened it to discover a handwritten poem.

Your dark brown eyes. Your cute little
    nose.
You're real special to me, and I hope
    that it shows.
When you tear through the yard, or
    play with your
ball. I cherished those times most of all.
Hap, dear Hap, you're quite a chap,
    and your papa
misses your snore. Come back, dear
    Hap. There
won't be a flap. Your papa will wait by
    the door.

How quaint, Mrs. Tobias thought, smiling at the awkwardly conceived verse. She wondered about its author and whether or not he was looking for his misplaced poem. Mrs. Tobias shook the book to see if anything else might be contained in its pages and a library receipt floated to her lap. She slipped on her reading glasses and looked at the name.

Rusty Williams, I declare! Wasn't that the name of the uncommonly handsome man she'd met at the flea market? Could *he* be the person who'd penned this peculiar little poem? The verse was dated three days ago, during the time when the book was in Mr. Williams's possession, so likely he was its author.

It was such a sincere poem, she'd hate to see Mr. Williams lose it. She'd simply have to alert Miss Goodbee so she could contact Mr. Williams and he could retrieve it.

She went to seek out the librarian, finding her on her knees, arranging magazines on the rack near the circulation desk.

"Someone has desecrated *Crazy for Cross Stitch* magazine, *again,*" Miss Goodbee said as she caught sight of Mrs. Tobias. "They tore out the directions for constructing a pansy bookmark. I planned to make that project myself."

"How inconsiderate!" Mrs. Tobias clucked in sympathy.

"Typical," Miss Goodbee said with a scowl. "Some patrons have no regard for library materials. They take books into the bathtub or scribble phone messages on the covers. Once someone returned a Hardy Boys mystery all scuffed up. Turns out it'd been used as third base in a softball game."

"Shocking," Mrs. Tobias said. "Speaking of books, I found a—" She paused. Why not call Mr. Williams herself? After all, she was the one who'd discovered the poem. The two of them could share a chuckle over the whole incident.

"May I use your phone, Miss Goodbee?"

"Help yourself. There's one in my office," Miss Goodbee said, still shaking her head over the violated magazine.

Mrs. Tobias entered the librarian's cramped office and found the Cayboo Creek phone book tucked underneath a black rotary phone. She leafed through the pages until she found Rusty Williams's name and number. A shiver shimmied down her spine.

Must be a draft in here, she thought as she dialed. She doubted she'd catch him at home in the middle of the day. Likely he was off doctoring dirty ducts.

"Hello," answered a male with a hearty voice.

"Hello, Mr. Williams?" Mrs. Tobias said. "This is Gracie Tobias. We met the other day—"

"At the flea market," he said cheerfully. "How could I forget?"

"That's correct," she said. The chilly office now grew uncommonly warm.

"You won't believe what I came across today," she began. "It's the strangest coincidence."

After she told him about the poem, Mr. Williams laughed with a trace of embarrassment and said, "I'd wondered where it had gotten off to."

"Did you write it?" Mrs. Tobias asked.

"Guilty. I'm no Yeats," he said, mispronouncing the Irish poet's name as if it rhymed with "meats." "But I enjoy turning the odd phrase or two."

"I thought your poem was charming." She paused. "Shall I put it in the post for you?"

"You could do that," he mused. "Or you

could let me buy you a cup of coffee as a sign of my gratitude."

"Coffee . . . I don't know."

"Or tea," he interjected. "Or a grape Nehi if that's your pleasure."

Mrs. Tobias laughed to herself. His earnestness *was* infectious. Surely there was no harm in meeting him for an innocent cup of tea.

"All right then." Mrs. Tobias consulted her watch. "Shall we say the Chat 'N' Chew? In ten minutes. Unless, of course, you have some other pressing obligation."

"Ten minutes will suit me fine," Rusty said.

As Mrs. Tobias maneuvered her Cadillac into the narrow parking space in front of the Chat 'N' Chew, she was jarred by the roar of a motorcycle pulling up beside her.

Gracious me, she thought, *the Chat 'N' Chew is certainly attracting a rough clientele.* She perked her ears for other bikers (she knew they tended to travel in packs), but the only sound she heard was the purr of a motorcycle's engine in the next parking slot.

She noticed a tag on the back of the bike that read "Iron Butt Association." The helmeted hooligan hadn't yet dismounted from his machine, and he appeared to be leering at her.

Oh dear, she thought as she emerged from her car. She'd heard about situations like this in which motorcycle-gang ruffians heckled innocent women. *Stay calm,* she said to herself. *Hurry past him as if you don't even see him.*

The entrance to the Chat 'N' Chew was only steps away and if the situation grew dire, she could always push the panic button on her key chain.

"Mrs. Tobias," the stranger on the motorcycle said. He removed his helmet and sunglasses and smiled. It was Rusty Williams.

"Mr. Williams," Mrs. Tobias said, her heart thumping as fast as a rabbit's. "You gave me a start."

"I apologize if I frightened you. I could tell you didn't recognize me."

"No, I didn't," Mrs. Tobias said. "I had no idea you drove a . . ."

What did motorcyclists call their bikes? She'd heard the term in a movie once.

"Pig?"

He laughed. "I think you mean a hog."

Hog. Iron Butts. Motorcycle lingo was

most unpleasant. Luckily, Mr. Williams wasn't. In fact, he looked quite dashing astride his gleaming machine.

"But this bike isn't a hog," Mr. Williams explained. "That's what people call their Harleys. This baby is a Triumph. They're made in England."

"Are they, now?" Mrs. Tobias said. She approved of most things British, except for the occasional swivel-hipped rock star. She regarded the motorcycle with new eyes. Yes, indeed, his machine looked classier than most.

Mr. Williams hopped off his bike and offered her a leather-clad arm. "Shall we?"

"Yes," she said with a smile. "Let's do."

"Feeling Single, Seeing Double"
—Selection J-2 on the jukebox at the Tuff Luck
Tavern

CHAPTER ELEVEN

⏰ Mavis wove a dejected little path through the brush and brambles of a vacant lot near Chickasaw Drive. She'd decided to take a shortcut back to the Bottom Dollar Emporium from Brewster's house so she wouldn't run into anyone on her return. She was too down-in-the-mouth to make small talk.

Wouldn't you know it? The first eligible bachelor to come into town in ages, and Birdie had managed to wriggle her way into his affections. Mavis sighed as she slipped past the prickly branches of an overgrown rosebush. She had no intentions of trying to compete with her friend for Brew's attention. It was a contest she felt sure she'd lose.

For one thing, Birdie was a much snazzier dresser than she, purchasing nearly all of her clothes from the Career Collection, a specialty shop in Augusta. Mavis, on the other hand, chose comfort over style, favoring roomy polyester separates from Goody's clearance rack.

And Birdie, being a newspaperwoman, could talk intelligently on nearly any subject. She knew what was going on in the Middle East and could keep all those turban-wearing leaders straight. Mavis didn't know Arafat from Sharon, and in fact skipped right over the hard news of the paper to look at Dear Abby and the funnies.

No, Mavis didn't have nearly as much to offer Brew: just warmed-over chicken divan and artificially enhanced cleavage.

As she crossed Main Street, a motorcycle whizzed by. Mavis could have sworn she saw Mrs. Tobias on the back, her arms clasped tightly around the waist of a broad-shouldered driver in a leather jacket. *Must be seeing things, old gal.* When people were as lonely as she, they imagined everyone being part of a twosome.

Mavis pushed open the door to the Bottom Dollar Emporium and heard Attalee talking on the phone.

"Yes, sugar booger," she cooed, wrapping the cord around her fingers. "I love you, too." She made a loud smacking sound into the hand piece before she hung up.

"I've got some boxes to open in the back," Mavis said, brushing past Attalee. She wasn't up to hearing about Attalee's latest exploits with Dooley. It was hard to believe an eighty-six-year-old soda jerk had such a lively love life.

"Hold up, gal," Attalee said, grabbing her elbow. "Why's your chin dragging the ground?"

Her eyes widened when she saw Mavis's chest. "Forget your chin; look at your chest. June is busting out all over."

Mavis turned away. "I don't want to talk about it."

"You don't have to," Attalee said. "I'm getting the picture loud and clear. You must have crashed and burned over at Brew's house."

"How did you know?"

"Victoria spilled her secrets," Attalee said, pointing to Mavis's bustline. "I reckon you didn't wear that bra to buy ham hocks at the Winn-Dixie."

Mavis hastily buttoned her sweater to hide her cleavage. "This Aqua Bra is going into retirement starting today. It's back to Maidenform for me."

"Ain't nothing wrong with treating a fellow to some eye candy. I'm just surprised the Brew boy didn't bite." Attalee scratched her head. "You don't suppose his plumbing's gone rusty?"

"You'll have to ask Birdie that." Mavis strode to the checkout counter and snatched open the cash-register drawer. "She was at his house, plying him with chicken divan, yeast rolls, and blueberry cobbler."

Attalee let out a low whistle. "That gal's bringing out the heavy artillery. Still, your Aqua Bra ain't exactly a popgun."

"Could we just forget about my bra?" Mavis said, counting bills to prepare a deposit.

"I got it!" Attalee clapped her hands. "Hustle over there with your world-famous sweet-potato casserole. It'll make her offerings seem like homemade paste."

"I'm not about to start a pie war over a man. Birdie's my friend, and if she's keen on Brew then she should have him."

"What kind of cockeyed reasoning is that? You spied him first, and—" Attalee gasped as she gazed out the front window. "Speak of the devil. Here comes that double-dealing dame right now. She's got a heck of a nerve."

Mavis held up a finger. "Don't you be ugly."

The bell overhead jingled and Birdie stepped inside, a sappy grin plastered on her face. "Toodles, ladies. I thought I'd nip in for a cherry phosphate and a little bite. I'm famished."

"Stealing other folk's sweeties works up an appetite," Attalee mumbled. Mavis shot Attalee a warning glance.

"What's that, Attalee?" Birdie shucked off her jacket and pulled out a heart-backed chair at the wrought-iron table in the soda fountain area.

"I says, do you want an extra spritz of seltzer in your phosphate?" Attalee asked, slipping behind the soda fountain.

"However you usually make it is fine." Birdie folded her hands on her lap and looked at Mavis. "Do you have time to join me?"

"Wouldn't miss it." Mavis picked up an opened package of Lorna Doone cookies from the break table. They were Birdie's favorite snack.

"So good to see Brew again, isn't it?" Birdie said as Mavis joined her at the table. "The memories came flooding back."

"And a bird starts circling around." Attalee placed the phosphate in front of Birdie.

"Attalee, what are you muttering about? I can't hear a word you're saying," Birdie said.

"Sorry, Buzzard. I mean, Birdie," Attalee said.

"Didn't I see a lot of dirty glasses behind the soda fountain this morning?" Mavis asked Attalee in a tight voice.

"Nope," Attalee said. "I spiffied them up when you were out."

"You were so right about Brew," Birdie said, clasping her hands together. "He looks incredible for his age, and so fit. And what a charmer!"

"Not to change the subject," Attalee said, plopping down across from Birdie. "But a few Sundays ago Reverend Hozey had a sermon about coveting thy neighbor's fellow."

"I don't remember that sermon," Mavis said sharply.

Attalee leaned back in her chair and eyed Birdie. "It was a powerful sermon, all right. Turns out, on Judgment Day, coveters are sent to the innermost rings of hell."

"What are you trying to say, Attalee?" Birdie asked in an insulted tone.

Attalee jumped up from her chair and loomed over Birdie. "I'm trying to say that Mavis got dibs on Brew first. She stood right here and declared her intentions."

"What's this all about?" Birdie turned to Mavis, eyes wide with innocence. "Are you upset with me, Mavis?"

"Course not." Mavis tucked into the bag of cookies. "Attalee. Stop this nonsense right now."

"Yes, Attalee. Please do." Birdie jutted her chin in the air. "Brew and I go way back. We were lab partners in high school. I was merely paying him a neighborly visit." She giggled. "Although, I must confess. I think he might be sweet on me."

"They used to whup horse thieves," Attalee said. "And at our age a fellow's a lot more valuable than a horse."

"Attalee! That's enough," Mavis said. She forced herself to smile. "I'm tickled that you and Brew are getting along so well."

"And I thought I was done with beaus," Birdie sighed. "Who'd have guessed? Sometimes you have to walk by a bakery to know you're hungry for a Danish."

"But you're not supposed to go inside the bakery, pry the Danish from the baker's hand, and scuttle off like—"

"Attalee!" said Birdie and Mavis in unison.

Birdie shook her head and chuckled. "We shouldn't scold her, I suppose. Attalee's just being loyal and that's touching, even if it is misguided. I know you, Mavis. It's not in your nature to get upset about a thing like this. And besides . . ." Birdie took a dainty sip of her phosphate. "Brew isn't your type."

"To get all worked up would be pure foolishness, and—" Mavis paused. "Not my type? What do you mean?"

"I just mean that you prefer salt-of-the-earth men, like your dear, sweet Arnold. Brew, with his matinee-idol looks and flashy sports car, isn't exactly your speed."

"Are you saying Arnold wasn't nice-looking?" Mavis asked.

"Of course not." Birdie reached out to pat Mavis's hand. "He was a very *interesting*-looking man. The two of you suited each other to a tee."

"Meaning that *I'm* also interesting-looking?" Mavis asked, pointing to herself.

"Well, I—" Birdie said.

"And *interesting*-looking people should stick with their own kind? Is that it?" Mavis rose from her seat.

"Not exactly—"

"Interesting-looking women should just step aside and let grabby women have all the good-looking men." Mavis's face turned red. "Isn't that what you're *really* saying?"

"Mavis!" Birdie bolted up from her chair.

"You tell her, sister!" Attalee said, hopping up and down.

"And for your information, Attalee was right. I *am* upset," Mavis said. "I confided my interest in Brew to you, and before I know it, you're over there like a robin to a worm. Next thing I know, you're trying to win him over with *my* chicken divan recipe."

"Ha! At least I was tempting him with food rather than trying to titillate him with my . . ." Birdie pointed an incriminating finger at Mavis's chest. "Ta-tas," she whispered.

"I can't believe you said that." Mavis reared back. "Specially since you're wearing a skirt cut so high it'd make Britney Spears blush."

Birdie's face turned pink as a flamingo's. As she opened her mouth to make a retort, her cell phone chirped.

"Birdie Murdock," Birdie barked into the phone. "Okay. I'll be right there."

She snapped her phone shut. "There's been an accident on Highway One. A Dinty Moore truck overturned."

"Anyone hurt?" Mavis asked.

"No, but traffic's backed up to Graniteville, and there's tins of beef stew all over the road." Birdie slipped into her jacket, refusing to meet Mavis's eye. "I have to rush over and take some photographs for the paper."

"I'm partial to their chicken and dumplings," Attalee said. "You mind picking me up a can or two?"

Birdie shot her a poisonous look, hitched her pocketbook on her arm, and marched out the front door.

Always remember you're unique just like everyone else.
—From the Baptist Ladies' League newsletter

CHAPTER TWELVE

For two days and nights after Elizabeth told Timothy she wanted to return to work, the couple didn't exchange as much as a "good morning" or a "please pass the coffee creamer." And although they still slept in the same queen-sized bed, the space between them seemed wider than the Savannah River.

About four on the morning of the third day, Elizabeth couldn't sleep, so she tiptoed into the kitchen to microwave a package of kettle corn. After preparing her snack, she went into the living room to read. She pawed through the stacks of *Child* and *Parent* on the coffee table until she unearthed what she was looking for: a *Working Mother* magazine she'd bought at the supermarket a couple of weeks back.

Wistfully, she scanned the magazine's table of contents: "Fun Meals in a Flash," "Surviving Morning Mania," and "Carpool Time Can Be Quality Time." The lives of working mothers were frantic and full of verve, so different from her own. Only yesterday, she'd spent a full ten minutes in the Winn-Dixie, pondering pear varieties.

Bosc or Bartlett? Sometimes her life felt like it had the leisurely pace of the boats in the "Small World" ride at Disney World. How she longed for the surge of adrenaline that came from deadlines and client demands! She was tired of drifting around in a tame rowboat; she wanted to board the rocket ship in Space Mountain.

Elizabeth shoved the magazine between the cushions of the sofa. As much as she'd like to rejoin the corporate world, it wasn't worth the breakup of her family. The two days of coldness between her and Timothy had seemed more like two hundred.

It's time for a reconciliation, she thought. Before he left for work this morning, Elizabeth decided she would prepare Timothy's favorite breakfast—French toast with cinnamon— as a peace offering. Then she'd promise to rededicate herself to being a full-time mother.

It wouldn't be so bad. Some of the members of her Mommy Time group were avid scrapbooking fans. Maybe Elizabeth could crop and paste her way to contentment. Or she could take a greater interest in home decor. The local community college had recently advertised a continuing education course on feng shui that sounded interesting.

Her eyes watered as she yawned and stretched her arms. She wanted to catch another hour of sleep before Glenda began her early-morning babbling. Elizabeth pulled a mohair throw over her bare legs and was reaching for the lamp switch when she heard the creak of the floorboards in the hallway.

Timothy stood in the threshold of the living room wearing only a pair of gray sweatpants. His features, which had been all sharp, angry angles for the last two days, now looked soft and muted by sleep.

"Do I smell popcorn?" He swept his hand through a chaos of dark curls.

"There's plenty left." Elizabeth indicated the earthenware bowl on the coffee table. Her husband sat beside her and balanced it on his knees. Elizabeth surrendered a portion of the throw and tucked it around his legs.

"Tastes good," Timothy said, as he reached for a handful of popcorn. Several pieces escaped his grip and tumbled to the carpet.

Elizabeth bent down to retrieve the errant popcorn, but Timothy caught her hand and said, "Don't worry about it. Maybelline will find it in the morning."

He continued to hold her hand, squeezing it at odd intervals while he munched on popcorn.

"I was thinking," Timothy said, in a voice still thick with sleep. "Maybe you *should* try going back to your job. We could see how it works out."

Elizabeth pulled herself up to a sitting position.

"Are you sure?"

"No," Timothy said softly. "But I know I can't live through another day of silence."

"Oh honey!" she squealed. Suddenly she felt wide awake. "It's just part-time. It'll be okay. You'll see."

He continued to chew his popcorn. "I hope so."

Later in the morning, after Timothy had showered and was seated at the breakfast nook and Glenda was banging a rattle against the tray of her high chair, Elizabeth placed a plate of French toast in front of her husband.

"I thought I'd visit day-care centers in Augusta today. Get a feel for what's out there," Elizabeth said.

"Why Augusta?" Timothy cut a piece of toast with his fork. "Why not Cayboo Creek?"

"There's more choices there, and I'd feel better if Glenda's day care was close to the paper cup plant. In case anything happens."

"What would happen?" Timothy's fork stopped in midair.

"Nothing!" Elizabeth said. "It's just comforting to be nearby."

Timothy shook out his napkin and placed it on his lap. "I'll go with you. I want to check out these places for myself. Ferrell can handle things at the Bait Box."

Reluctant to cart Glenda all over town, the couple arranged to drop her off at Great-grandma Tobias's house. When they rang the bell, Mrs. Tobias opened the door wearing a red cashmere sweater and a pair of freshly pressed blue jeans.

"I've never seen you wear blue jeans before," Elizabeth said. "What are you doing? Cleaning out the basement?"

"No, I'm just sampling a new look," Mrs. Tobias said as she took Glenda from Elizabeth's arms. "Don't look so shocked. They're Ann Taylor, not Old Navy."

"You look like a teenager," Timothy said.

"You old flatterer." Mrs. Tobias kissed both of them on the cheek. "Don't forget to be back by five. I've got an engagement this evening."

"Garden club meeting? Bridge game?" Elizabeth said, handing her Glenda's diaper bag.

"Something like that," Mrs. Tobias said with a carefree laugh.

"What was up with *her*?" Timothy said later, as they pulled out of his grandmother's driveway. "She seemed kind of giddy. You don't suppose she's been nipping at the sherry."

Elizabeth's nose was in the telephone book, reading over the day-care listings. "Who knows? Maybe she's just letting her hair down for a change."

Elizabeth stood in front of an institutional brick building with a merry string of multicolored paper dolls hung over the entrance. "Lads and Lasses Child Care. That's a cute name." She pushed opened the glass door and was assaulted by the collective shrieks of at least a dozen children, as well as the stench of dirty diapers.

"It sounds kind of hectic in there. Maybe they're having a bad day." Elizabeth whirled around. "What's next on the list?"

"Why are those kids screaming?" asked Timothy, who was inching up the steps outside. "What are they doing to them?"

"It's probably close to naptime. Let's move on," she said, hustling him along so he wouldn't get a whiff of the place. "We have at least ten more to visit."

The morning wore on, and none of the centers seemed any more promising than Lads and Lasses. A facility called Kinder

Corral had rows of grim-faced tots pasting dry macaroni to cardboard while a German-accented teacher named Dagmar paced in front of them, issuing orders in a staccato voice.

After Kinder Corral, they visited a day care called Little Sprouts. Unfortunately, the facility lived up to its name. The building smelled damp, and Elizabeth saw a colony of mildew climbing up the wall in the hallway. Elizabeth and Timothy exited before the tousled-haired director, wearing a stained teddy-bear smock, could approach them.

Kid Kingdom seemed promising from the street. The building looked like a tiny castle and the banner stretched across the façade read "We treat children like royalty." The infant room, however, was a scene straight out of a Romanian orphanage. Two frazzled employees were trying to care for ten squalling babies.

"You've caught us short-handed," said an exhausted-looking woman who was juggling three babies on her lap. "One of our teachers is out with the flu."

"They treat kids like royalty all right," Timothy said after they'd returned to his truck. "Like the peasants treated Marie Antoinette."

"There's only one place left on our list," Elizabeth said, a note of panic in her voice.

Posh Playcare resembled a miniature Georgian mansion on the outside, with classical-style columns and ornate roof balustrades. Timothy and Elizabeth strolled along the stone walkway that cut through a large swath of neatly trimmed rye grass.

They entered the building and took in the black-and-white tiled foyer, the high ceilings, and the elaborate moldings along the walls. Timothy let out a low whistle. "Pretty fancy for a child-care center."

"Actually, Posh Playcare is a child *development* center." A thin woman, who'd been seated behind a row of security monitors, stood up.

"I'm Cynthia Dare, the headmistress." She approached them and extended her hand. "Care' is much too minimal a term for what we do here at Posh Playcare. If you sent your youngster to Harvard, you wouldn't call it student care, now would you?"

"Of course not," Elizabeth said as she introduced Timothy and herself. She approved of the woman's gray wool suit and her calm, composed manner.

"Would you care for a tour?" Ms. Dare asked.

"Absolutely." Elizabeth gave Timothy's hand an excited little squeeze.

"We're very proud of our facility," Ms. Dare said, striding down the hall in a sleek pair of designer shoes. "To your right is the bibliothèque. We boast a healthy five thousand volumes."

"Bibliothèque?" Timothy asked.

"Library," Ms. Dare said with a toss of her Veronica Lake hairstyle. "Next door is our state-of-the-art computer center and foreign-language lab. Shall we have a peek?"

"Ms. Dare," Timothy said, "our daughter is only ten months old."

"Which is the ideal age to learn conversational Mandarin," Ms. Dare said.

"Maybe," Timothy said. "If we could just see the baby room . . ."

"Ah, the Petite Suite!" Ms. Dare clapped her hands together. "It's our crown jewel at Posh Playcare."

They followed her down a hallway covered with Berber carpeting and decorated with a row of framed Impressionist prints.

Elizabeth eagerly sniffed the air. "What's that heavenly smell?"

"Lunchtime," Ms. Dare said. "Chef is preparing coq au vin today."

The headmistress stood outside the classroom, which had a pink elephant cutout on the door. "Here we are. Baby Nirvana!"

She opened the door to a room awash with sunlight. The sounds of a Mozart symphony played softly in the background as two pink-cheeked babies gamboled happily on a plush ABC rug. An attendant, wearing a starched white uniform, scooped up a giggling little girl in a pink onesie and carried her to the window.

"See the cardinal. Look at the red cardinal," the attendant crooned. A feeder and bath had been positioned outside the window, and several varieties of birds were splashing in the water or nibbling on suet.

Elizabeth noticed a row of wooden cribs with blue-and-white toile bedding and shelves filled with cloth books, stuffed animals, and other new toys. An armoire, handpainted with plump, wooly lambs, held stacks of clean diapers, powders, and lotions.

"It's gorgeous," Elizabeth said.

"You're in luck," Ms. Dare said. "We have one opening. We keep our ratios at one teacher for every three babies. Young children need constant attention and nurturing, and they get it here in the Petite Suite. Not to mention a full curriculum."

"Curriculum?" Timothy said with a sharp laugh. "What? In teething skills?"

"You're very droll, Mr. Hollingsworth," Ms. Dare said. "Here at Posh Playcare we keep up with the latest studies in infant development and adjust our program accordingly. With our youngest charges, we concentrate on creative movement, eye-hand coordination, vocabulary development and, our parents' favorite, rest-room readiness. We're quite comprehensive."

"I love it here, Timothy," Elizabeth said, her eyes shining. "Where do we sign up?"

"You've not seen the solarium or the mini water park," Ms. Dare said.

"I've seen enough to know that my daughter belongs here," Elizabeth gushed.

A few minutes later, as they sat in Ms. Dare's office, she pushed a brochure across her massive cherry desk.

"I've circled the weekly tuition amount,"

Ms. Dare said. "The application, supply, and athletics fee are separate, naturally."

"Athletics fee?" Timothy said.

"The babies utilize a fully equipped gymboree," Ms. Dare explained.

Elizabeth studied the brochure and sucked in her breath. "This figure can't be right. Glenda wouldn't be enrolled full-time."

"Exactly," Ms. Dare said. "I circled the correct amount for half-time enrollment."

Timothy peered over Elizabeth's shoulder. "Elizabeth, this is more than your salary!"

"So it is," Elizabeth said with a jittery laugh. She glanced back at the brochure. "I don't suppose scholarships are available?"

"I'm afraid not." Ms. Dare drummed her manicured nails on the glossy desk while Elizabeth glanced at Timothy.

"I guess we'll have to discuss this at home," she said.

"Fine." The headmistress sprang up from her chair. "Keep in mind that openings in the Petite Suite are snapped up very quickly."

Timothy and Elizabeth made the ride to Great-grandma Tobias's house in silence. After they retrieved Glenda, they drove back to Cayboo Creek. Elizabeth kept her face turned to the window as she doodled circles in the condensation on the glass.

"I don't think there's anything to talk about, Elizabeth," Timothy said finally. "How could we justify the expense of that place?"

Elizabeth thumped her back against the passenger seat in frustration. "But it's the only place we liked."

"Who can afford that kind of money for child care?" Timothy shook his head. "It's crazy."

"We should think of the tuition fees at Posh Playcare as an investment in Glenda's educational future," Elizabeth said. "She's certainly not going to pick up conversational Mandarin from me."

Timothy jerked the gearshift into park after he pulled into their garage. "Glenda's not even a year old. She needs her mother much more than she needs Mandarin. I don't understand why you can't see that."

"And I don't understand why you can't see that I'm going crazy being cooped up with a baby all day long."

He turned off the engine and sighed. "We can't afford Posh Playcare, and all the other places we visited were terrible. I think we're running out of options here, sweetie."

Elizabeth didn't respond and instead kept squeaking her finger against the window.

"It's only five years of your life, Elizabeth, just until Glenda starts kindergarten," Timothy said. "That's all I'm asking."

Elizabeth turned to him. Long streaks of mascara striped her cheeks. "Just five years, you say. I don't know if I can last five weeks."

**When Blondes Have Fun
Do They Know It?**
　　　　　　　—Sign outside the Dazzling Do's

CHAPTER THIRTEEN

Mrs. Tobias twitched her hips and snapped her fingers to the song "California Dreaming" as it played on the stereo in her bedroom.

"All the leaves are brown, and the sky is gray," she sang in a soprano voice. She parted her brocade curtains for a peek at the weather outside. The bare tree branches in her yard looked stark against a sky heavy with low-bellied clouds.

The day was indeed gray and dreary, but

Mrs. Tobias's mood didn't match the season. She felt as sunny as a Palm Beach summer.

Her phone jangled on its stand, and she dropped the curtains and hastened to answer it.

"How's the most fascinating woman south of the Mason-Dixon line?" rumbled a male voice.

"Rusty! You're such a character." She dropped down onto the cushioned stool of her dressing table.

"Is that the Mamas and the Papas I hear in the background?" he asked.

"It is. I fear you're wearing off on me."

"Is that such a terrible thing?"

"I'm beginning to think it's a grand thing." She removed the stopper from a crystal perfume bottle on her vanity and dabbed a drop of Joy behind each ear.

"I'm tickled to hear that," Rusty said. "So, can I pick you up at the usual time?"

"I'll be waiting," Mrs. Tobias said. She paused. "Any hints on the nature of our outing?"

"You'll just have to wait and see," Rusty said in a teasing voice. "Why don't you slip into that cute pair of jeans you wore on our last date."

Mrs. Tobias hung up the phone, laughing. No telling what kind of plans Rusty was brewing up. Last week they'd gone roller-skating, two nights ago they'd noshed on Thai food, and last night they'd floated along the moonlit canal in a canoe.

Mrs. Tobias's mind drifted back to their very first date at the Chat 'N' Chew. As she sat across from Rusty at the scratched Formica table, he'd instantly put her at ease. It turned out he'd read *To Kill a Mockingbird* almost as many times as she, and they'd enjoyed a lively discussion of their favorite characters and scenes.

From their conversation, Mrs. Tobias discovered that Rusty was a study in contradictions. With his leather bomber jacket and faint razor stubble, he was one of the most rugged-looking men she had ever seen. Yet that afternoon at the diner, he'd admitted to a weakness for baking and claimed to take enormous pride in the flakiness of his piecrusts.

He also relished 'sixties music. The CD playing on her stereo was borrowed from his collection. Ever since they'd met, he'd been gently trying to indoctrinate her in his musical tastes. She'd turned up her nose at Jimi

Hendrix and Jefferson Airplane, but enjoyed the upbeat sound of The Mamas and the Papas. And while she didn't share his fervor for all flower-power music, she discovered they both adored opera, Doris Day and Rock Hudson movies, and barbecue.

"I really must go," Mrs. Tobias had said that very first afternoon after she looked at her watch and discovered she'd been at the Chat 'N' Chew with Rusty for nearly three hours. It felt more like three minutes.

"Do you have to?" His dark eyes clouded over with disappointment.

"I almost forgot." Mrs. Tobias sorted through the contents of her handbag and withdrew a folded piece of paper. "The poem you left in the library book. You must love this Hap very much. Is he your grandchild?"

"No." His jaw tightened. "Hap's my dog. He ran away about a week ago."

"Oh dear." Mrs. Tobias put down her handbag. "I'm so sorry."

"I've had him fifteen years, since he was weaned from his mama. Hap's always had some wanderlust in him." A tear grazed his cheek but he made no move to wipe it away. "But he's never stayed gone this long before.

I'm afraid something's happened to him. He's not a pup anymore."

Mrs. Tobias had never seen a man cry before, and certainly not over a dog. All the other men she'd known in her life were stoic in the face of tragedy. When their daughter Lily died in a car accident over twenty-five years ago, her late husband's eyes had remained dry. At the time, she'd respected Harrison's control over his emotions since she'd been brought up to believe that men who openly wept were weak.

But Rusty's tears unexpectedly moved her. Here was a strong, strapping man unabashedly grieving over an animal. It was touching.

Without thinking, Mrs. Tobias got up from her side of the booth and scooted next to Rusty. She gently squeezed his arm as he continued to cry softly over his empty coffee cup.

Mrs. Tobias didn't leave the diner for another hour and when she did depart, it was on the back of Rusty's motorcycle.

"Who are you?" she now asked the lively-eyed woman staring back at her in the vanity mirror. Up until last week, there would have been a simple answer to that question: widowed matriarch. President of the Augusta Garden Club. Upstanding, dignified, and proper.

All her life she'd done everything to the letter, from the details of her debutante ball to the flowers at Harrison's funeral. She didn't ride in canoes; she'd never gone roller-skating, and she most certainly did not hop on the back of motorcycles.

Yet when she was with Rusty, such activities seemed more exciting than inappropriate. He'd unearthed facets of herself that she'd been unaware of until now. Who knew she could be so spontaneous, or that she had such a lusty appetite for adventure?

Mrs. Tobias got up from her dressing table and changed into her blue jeans. Just as she was slipping into a pair of loafers, her doorbell sounded and she hastily fluffed her caramel-colored bangs.

She went to the door to find Rusty standing on her front porch, a beribboned package in his hands.

"What do you have there?" she said, ushering him in.

"It has to do with our outing tonight," he said with a wink. "Open it."

She tore off the wrapping paper and lifted the lid off the box. "Shoes?" she asked in bewilderment. They were white athletic shoes with pink lacings.

"They're bowling shoes," Rusty explained. "I thought we'd go cosmic bowling at the Bowl-A-Rama. And I couldn't ask a classy gal like yourself to wear other people's shoes."

"Oh, Rusty." She held up a shoe to examine it. "They're lovely. I'll be the belle of the bowling alley."

He eyed her with a wide grin as she tried on the shoes. "That, my dear, is an understatement."

Cosmic bowling was a surreal experience involving psychedelic lights, thick billows of fog, and loud, pulsating music. The pins at the end of the lanes glowed in lollipop shades of pink, yellow, and green, while Mrs. Tobias and Rusty were bathed in an eerie blue laser light. Mrs. Tobias enjoyed herself, despite the fact that her ball rarely made contact with a pin.

Later, as they relaxed in a booth in the bowling alley's coffee shop, Rusty shook his head and smiled at her.

"I can't believe you've never been to a bowling alley before."

"That accounts for all those sewer balls of mine," Mrs. Tobias said, stirring her tea.

Rusty laughed. "You mean gutter balls." He touched his mug to hers. "What do you think about antiquing?"

"It's one of my favorite pastimes. Why?"

"Tomorrow's Saturday. I thought it'd be fun for the two of us to poke around in a few of the shops around here."

"What about the flea market?" Mrs. Tobias picked up her cup. "I thought you worked there on Saturdays."

"Not tomorrow. The roof's been leaking, so management is closing it down for a couple of months." He grinned. "So how 'bout it?"

"Antiquing sounds delightful." She took in the strong planes of his jawline and admired his almond-shaped eyes. Fearing that she was staring, she transferred her gaze to the salt and pepper shakers. "You're constantly surprising me, Mr. Williams."

"I aim to please."

She'd never imagined that a man could make such a satisfying companion. Looking back on her marriage to Harrison, she realized that she and her husband rarely spent leisure time together. He had his golf game and skeet-shooting, and she preferred bridge and gardening. Occasionally he'd sit through a Puccini opera with her, but he'd treat such an outing as if it was an enormous sacrifice on his part.

From previous conversations she knew that Rusty loved the performing arts, and now he claimed to enjoy antiquing as well. He was almost too good to be true!

Rusty laughed, snapping her out of her private thoughts.

"Those guys crack me up," he said.

"What guys?" Mrs. Tobias asked.

"Those guys on *Queer Eye for the Straight Guy.* There's a TV behind you."

"I'm not familiar with that show." Mrs. Tobias turned around to glance at the screen mounted above her and watched for a moment.

"My," she said, turning back to face Rusty. "Those men seem rather . . . effeminate, wouldn't you say?"

"That's one way of putting it. They're gay. All five of them. It's funny stuff. I catch the show when I can."

"I see." Mrs. Tobias shifted in her seat.

"By the way, tomorrow when we go antiquing, I know of a little bistro about twenty miles south of here. Serves a delicious shiitake mushroom quiche."

"Quiche?" Mrs. Tobias said.

"Yeah." Rusty downed the rest of his coffee. "I'm a big quiche fan."

Suddenly it dawned on her why Rusty seemed so different from other men she'd known. Was it possible that Rusty was gay? And this was his subtle way of telling her?

Mrs. Tobias tried to mask her dismay. She didn't want Rusty to think she was judging him.

"I don't care what anyone says," Mrs. Tobias said, trying to recover her composure. "Quiche is a perfectly lovely dish."

"I'm glad you think so," Rusty said. His attention had once more wandered to the television suspended above her head.

What a pity, Mrs. Tobias thought. Rusty was the first man she'd felt any attraction to since Harrison's death. It would hardly be fair if he turned out to be a homosexual.

What if the Hokey Pokey Is Really What It's All About?
—Sign in the break room of the Bottom Dollar Emporium

CHAPTER FOURTEEN

Mavis sat in the break area of the Bottom Dollar Emporium nibbling on a stale Lorna Doone cookie and listening to the crop bulletin on the AM radio station.

"Soybean and sorghum harvest are completed," said the male announcer through a flurry of static. "Overall pecan poundage was good, but quality was poor."

Mavis leaned over to snap off the radio and glanced up at Attalee, who was sweeping the tile floor near the soda fountain.

"I've made my decision. I'm going to call her, and I'm going to apologize," Mavis said.

"Stay away from that phone." Attalee looked up from her broom. "She's the one in the wrong, not you."

Mavis's knee joints creaked as she rose from her chair. "I don't care. Birdie hasn't come in for days, and I miss her. We've known each other since elementary school, and I'm not going to ruin our friendship because of a—"

The bell jingled over the door, and Brewster Clark entered the store wearing a gray overcoat and a forest-green muffler that complemented his eyes.

"Hey there, Mavis." He wiped his feet on the mat just inside the door. "Do I smell a pot of coffee perking?"

"Brew!" She brushed cookie crumbs from her chin and the front of her candy-striped uniform. "Long time, no see."

"I know." Brew removed a felt Indiana Jones–style hat from his head. "I kept saying to myself, 'Brew, get yourself over to the Bottom Dollar Emporium and have a visit with that pretty filly of an owner.' So here I am."

"I'm delighted to see you." Mavis was already pouring him a cup of coffee in the only mug without any chips. "How do you like your java?"

"Black as a gypsy's heart, m'lady," Brew said.

"Coming right up."

Attalee stole out from behind the soda fountain and grinned at Brew.

"Brew," Mavis said. "I'd like you to meet Attalee Gaines, my dear friend and employee."

"You're a vision, madam." Brew leaned down to kiss Attalee's gnarled hand.

"Thank you kindly," Attalee said, with a provocative flick of her sausage curls. "Must be my new lip gloss. Nude pink. When I wore it at the picture show last night Dooley couldn't keep his hands to himself."

"Dooley is Attalee's boyfriend," Mavis explained.

"That's right, tiger," Attalee, said showing off her toothless gums. "I'm taken. But Mavis here is free as a bird."

Mavis cast an annoyed look at Attalee.

"Whoopsie daisy." Attalee covered her mouth. "I forgot. Birds are a ticklish subject 'round here."

"Don't you want to finish your sweeping?" Mavis said in a small voice.

"You don't have to hit me on the head with

a two-by-four," Attalee said. "I can take a hint. I'll finish my sweeping so you two can finish your sparking."

Once Attalee had disappeared into the back of the store, a pink-faced Mavis handed Brew a coffee cup.

"Sorry, Brew. Attalee can be a handful at times. Don't take her seriously."

"She's a character all right," Brew said with a smile.

"Would you like to have a seat in the break room?" Mavis asked.

"I'd love to, but I'm expecting a lumber delivery at my house in a few minutes. But while I'm here, I wanted to run an idea by you. What do you think about having a high school reunion? We're coming up on our forty-fifth year since graduation."

"A reunion?" Mavis leaned against the checkout counter. "I don't think we've had one since our twentieth. Glady Hobbs used to organize them all, but she moved to Knoxville about ten years back."

"I've been thinking a lot about our high school days," Brew said, stroking his beard. "Wouldn't it be great to relive them?"

"Well, maybe." Mavis's high school days

hadn't been all that memorable. She'd fretted constantly over blemishes and was forced to purchase her poodle skirts from the chubbette department.

"Bottom line is this," Brew said. "What with working on my aunt's old house I just don't have the time to put together a reunion all by myself. I need a right-hand woman. Someone with the organizational skills to tackle a project like this. And someone who can pull it together fast, since I don't know how much longer I'll be here."

"Me?"

"Exactly. But I warn you." He laid a hand on her shoulder and gazed into her eyes. "We'd have to work pretty closely together. I don't know if you'd mind being around me so much. Just the two of us." His voice dropped to a lower pitch. "Alone."

All Mavis could think about was the pressure of his hand on her shoulder and the masculine smell of his lime-scented aftershave lotion. How long had it been since she'd felt a man's touch?

"Sounds wonderful," she stammered.

"Great. Why not come to my place tomorrow night, and we'll discuss it over dinner?"

He stuffed his hands in his pocket. "Not that I'm much of a cook. Scrambled eggs are my specialty."

"Nonsense," Mavis tutted. "I'll fix dinner for you at my house. Are you a fan of rib-eye steaks?"

He chuckled. "Darling, you're playing my song."

The bell over the door jingled once again and an agitated-looking Mrs. Tobias bustled inside. She wore a double-breasted jacket and a pair of blue jeans.

"Mavis, I was wondering—" Mrs. Tobias stopped short. "Oh, forgive me. I didn't notice you had a customer."

"I'm not a customer." Brew clamped his hat back on his head. "I'm more like family. Call you later, Mavis?"

"Yes, Brew," Mavis said with a good-bye wave.

"My goodness, who was *that*?" Mrs. Tobias said after Brew had exited through the front door.

Attalee popped up from behind a display of cast-iron pots.

"That was Brew. Mavis's main squeeze."

"You were spying," Mavis said.

"'Course I was." Attalee put her hands on

her hips. "I needed to stay close in case he got fresh." She eyed Mrs. Tobias. "Creation! You're wearing dungarees."

"I don't see what the fuss is all about," Mrs. Tobias said, pulling her jacket down over her hips. "I simply want to be comfortable in my dotage."

"Dotage jeans, are they?" Attalee said, looking them over. "I ain't never heard of them. I wear Wranglers, and nothing comes between me and my—"

"Attalee." Mavis sighed. "It's much too early in the day."

"So you have a new beau, Mavis?" Mrs. Tobias asked, settling into a chair in the break area.

"Well—" Mavis began.

"She and Birdie were feuding over that feller," Attalee said. "But it looks like Mavis won by a cup size."

"Gracious," Mrs. Tobias said. "I've been away from the Bottom Dollar Emporium for only a few days, and I've missed all the scuttlebutt."

"You've haven't missed a thing." Mavis sat next to Mrs. Tobias. "Brew and I went to high school together back in the dark ages. We're just friends."

"But she's angling for more," Attalee said.

"He's quite handsome," Mrs. Tobias remarked. "You never can tell. Maybe those friendly sparks will burst into flame."

"I'm not betting the farm on it," Mavis said. "But I wouldn't mind a little male attention now and again."

"Speaking of males," Mrs. Tobias said, "there's a gentleman I've been seeing—"

"Who?" Attalee demanded.

Mrs. Tobias held up her index finger. "I'd prefer to be discreet about his identity for now."

Mavis dragged her chair closer to Mrs. Tobias. "I thought you were done with dating. Isn't that what you said at the Sweetheart Dance?"

"I did, and I genuinely believed that part of my life was over. But then I met this man." Mrs. Tobias let out a long exhale of breath.

"Good-looking?" Attalee inquired.

"Absolutely," Mrs. Tobias said. "But his appeal goes far beyond his appearance. He's witty, kind, and sensitive." She bit her lip and scanned Attalee and Mavis's attentive faces. "There is one *small* problem, however."

"I've been in your shoes, ma'am." Attalee draped an arm around Mrs. Tobias's shoulder.

"And whoever says size don't matter can't tell their huckleberries from their scuppernongs."

"Attalee Gaines!" Mavis said. "If you can't behave yourself, I'm sending you home."

Mrs. Tobias was so distracted she didn't react to Attalee's comment.

"I'll just come out and say it." Mrs. Tobias gritted her teeth together. "I think my new beau is . . . gay."

"Oh my," Mavis said. "What makes you say that?"

"There's several things," Mrs. Tobias said. "He enjoys cooking and antiquing. And quiche. Isn't a fondness for quiche a dead giveaway these days?"

"I'm not so sure," Mavis mused. "I've heard there's something telling about track lighting. And listening to Barbra Streisand records."

"None of them things matter anymore," Attalee interjected. "Nowadays, it's perfectly normal for menfolk to act like a pack of pansies. I read it in *Cosmo*. They're called mezzosexuals."

"Heavenly day," Mrs. Tobias said with a raised eyebrow.

"I saw something about that on *Entertainment Tonight*," Mavis said. "Only I think the word is metrosexual."

"Mezzo, metro. Nowadays its plum hard to tell if a man's a Bambi or a bull," Attalee said. "Luckily, there's still the fingernail test."

"The what?" Mrs. Tobias asked.

"The fingernail test," Attalee explained patiently. "You ask a man to take a gander at his fingernails. If he bends his fingers and stares at them close up, he's a Mickey. If he stretches his arm and looks at his fingers from a distance, he's a Minnie."

"That doesn't sound very reliable," Mavis said.

"It's based on scientific fact." Attalee flounced up from her chair to make another pot of coffee.

Mrs. Tobias shook her head. "Who would have imagined courting in the twenty-first century would be so complicated?"

If God Is Your Co-Pilot, Switch Seats.
—Sign outside the Rock of Ages Baptist Church

CHAPTER FIFTEEN

Elizabeth and her friend Chiffon sat beside each other in the Dazzling Do's beauty parlor waiting to get their nails manicured.

"I'm torn between Mocha Mauve and Feisty Fuchsia," Chiffon said, surveying a row of nail polish bottles on the manicurist's tray. "What are you going to get, Elizabeth?"

"Parchment Paper," Elizabeth said in a pinched voice.

Chiffon made a sour face. "That's beige.

Why in the world would you want beige fingernails?"

"They'll match my mood."

"I thought you sounded dejected on the phone. That's exactly why I suggested this outing." Chiffon extended her hand for the manicurist. "There's nothing like pretty painted fingernails to cheer a girl, and Dazzling Do's has a two-for-one deal on Wednesdays."

"What color have you selected?" the white-coated manicurist asked Elizabeth.

"She'll have Hothouse Pink." Chiffon turned her head to her friend. "So are you going to tell me why you're so blue, or do I have to wheedle it out of you?"

Elizabeth sighed. "It has to do with Timothy."

Chiffon snorted. "I could have guessed that. Whenever a woman has a problem, there's always a man at the root of it."

"You're just cynical these days," Elizabeth said. Chiffon had separated from Lonnie, her wayward husband of fifteen years, and had been in the man-bashing mode for months. "Besides, it isn't technically Timothy's fault that we can't find decent, affordable day care for Glenda. But I know he's secretly pleased."

"What? Are you thinking about going back to work?" Chiffon asked.

Elizabeth wrinkled her nose as the manicurist swabbed at her nails with the acrid-smelling polish remover.

"I was. *If* I could find a good arrangement for Glenda."

"I know what you mean," Chiffon said. "I day-care-hopped for ages with Gabby. Nothing seemed right, and every place I liked kept raising their prices. I was lucky to find dear, sweet Mrs. Pirkle. She loves kids and doesn't charge an arm and a leg."

"Who's Mrs. Pirkle?" Elizabeth asked.

"She's the sweetest old lady you've ever met. Hey!" Chiffon snapped her fingers "She's got an opening. Little Frankie Morgan's family moved to Macon a week ago."

"How many kids does she keep?"

"Just Gabby now. She won't take on more than two. Ever since I found her, my child-care worries have been over. I've got Emily and Dewitt enrolled in an after-school program, and Gabby is in the loving arms of Mrs. Pirkle."

"She sounds perfect." Elizabeth yanked her hand away from the manicurist and stood. "I'll call her right away."

"What about your manicure?" Chiffon asked.

"I don't want Mrs. Pirkle to fill her opening with another child." She grabbed her coat from the chair and slipped into it. "What's her number?"

"Good grief. I'm sure it will keep through your manicure, Elizabeth." Chiffon studied her friend's anxious face. "All right. You must be itching to go back to work. Her number's 555-9991."

"Thanks, Chiffon." Elizabeth jotted it down on the back of a grocery receipt. "You may have saved my life. Sorry about the manicure."

"It's all right. Oh, wait a minute. I almost forgot." Chiffon rummaged through her bag and handed Elizabeth a sealed white envelope.

"What's this?"

"Emily's birthday invitation. The party's next Saturday."

Elizabeth tucked the invitation into her purse. "It's not another Mozzarella Monkey party, is it?"

"Fraid so," Chiffon said with a sheepish grin. "And quit making that face. My house is too small to have a birthday party, and that hairy ape's the only game in town. Wait until

Glenda gets old enough for a kiddy party. Then you'll see."

When Elizabeth called Timothy and told him about Mrs. Pirkle, she could tell he wasn't thrilled.

"Mrs. Pirkle? Who's that? I've never heard of her," he said.

"I know you haven't, honey. I just spoke with her and she told me she's new to Cayboo Creek. But I'm going to meet her today at four P.M. and—"

"I'm coming, too," Timothy interrupted. "I'll close the bait shop early."

That afternoon, she and Timothy pulled up to Mrs. Pirkle's white-brick ranch house in the Camellia Estates subdivision. After Timothy put the SUV into park, Elizabeth opened the backseat door to get her daughter.

Timothy stood in the front yard waiting for them. When they approached, he pointed to a small sign lodged in the soil.

"Look at this," he said in a low voice. "This grass has been treated with chemicals. Read it. It says 'hazardous to small children and pets.'"

"I see." Elizabeth hoisted Glenda higher in her arms. "But I'm sure Mrs. Pirkle won't let

Glenda play in the front yard. If the children go outside at all, it will likely be in the back."

"If she treats the front yard with chemicals, she probably treats the back," Timothy said, sputtering like a motorboat. "This is a grave matter. What kind of person spreads pesticides all over her yard? Not the kind I want to have watching my child."

"We'll ask her about the yard, okay?" Elizabeth adjusted the strap of her diaper bag. "Let's just go inside."

They followed the pansy-lined fieldstone leading up to the house. Mrs. Pirkle was a collector of lawn ornaments. She had a kissing Dutch boy and girl, three ceramic geese, two stone bunnies, and a plastic gnome, all placed at various points in her yard. Her doormat featured a picture of a Boston terrier carrying a basket of flowers in its mouth.

"Kind of cutesy, isn't it?" Elizabeth cast a sidelong glance at her husband.

"Extremely deceptive considering her yard is a toxic-waste dump." Timothy's hands were shoved into his pockets, and he was kicking at a collection of pebbles on the front step.

Elizabeth rang the doorbell. "Let's not bring that up right out of the gate, okay?"

Timothy didn't answer. He burrowed his neck into the collar of his jacket.

"Hello there," said a musical voice as the front door flung open. The woman who answered had white hair, curled into tight springs. She wore a bright red sweatshirt that said "Nana is another word for love."

"I'm Mrs. Pirkle," she said. "And you must be the Hollingsworths." Mrs. Pirkle was portly, but in a pleasant, grandmotherly way. The smell of freshly baked peanut-butter cookies drifted out into the cold afternoon.

"Come on in. It's much too nippy out today," she said, beckoning them inside. The pair advanced into a cozy living room with blond wood paneling and periwinkle drapes tied back with pink satin ribbons. Mrs. Pirkle squealed when Elizabeth pulled Glenda's knitted cap from her head.

"Look at this wee one. What a picture! May I?" she said, holding out her arms. Glenda bicycled her legs as Elizabeth handed her to Mrs. Pirkle. Mrs. Pirkle pointed to a curved-back sofa with a multi-colored afghan draped across the cushions.

"Make yourself comfortable on the davenport," she said. "Oh, the dear wee one has a runny nose. Let me get a tissue." She indicated a plate on a glass coffee table. "Also, please help yourself to a cookie. They're hot out of the oven."

As Mrs. Pirkle ambled down the hall with Glenda in her arms, Elizabeth turned to Timothy to give him an enthusiastic thumbs-up. He didn't see her; he was too busy peering at something behind the couch.

"What are you doing?" Elizabeth whispered.

"Checking to see if her electrical outlets are covered."

"And?"

"They are. In *this* room."

"All better," Mrs. Pirkle said, returning to the room with a babbling Glenda.

The rocking chair across from the couch squeaked as Mrs. Pirkle arranged her plump frame on its wooden bottom. Glenda was perched on her lap, staring up at her with large, quizzical eyes the size and color of robins' eggs.

"I'm sure you have a million questions for me," Mrs. Pirkle said. "On the lamp table there is a typed summary of my background, along with a host of references. But to give you a short overview, I worked as an RN in a hospital nursery for fifteen years. I also have a master's degree in child development, but I think my most important qualification is that I just love little children." She nuzzled Glenda's cheek. "Isn't that right, wee one?"

Glenda let out a joyful gurgle in response.

Elizabeth picked up Mrs. Pirkle's résumé and read it. "This is so impressive. Look, honey." She handed the paper to Timothy, who gave it a cursory glance.

"I know you'll want a tour of the house," Mrs. Pirkle continued. "I keep two brand-new cribs in my guest room, so there's no need to bring a porta-crib. I also have two high chairs in my kitchen, and I—Mr. Hollingsworth, you look like you have a question?"

Timothy stood up and cleared his throat. "You're painting a very pretty picture, Mrs. Pirkle," he said, with an accusatory voice, "but how do you explain the deadly poisons in your front yard?"

"Timothy!" Elizabeth flew up from the couch.

"Poisons?" Mrs. Pirkle looked puzzled.

"Mrs. Pirkle," Elizabeth began. "There was a sign in your front yard saying your grass had been treated with lawn chemicals, and Timothy was concerned—"

"As he should be," Mrs. Pirkle said with just the right touch of outrage. "What kind of person puts pesticides on their yard when there are young children and unsuspecting animals in the neighborhood? I'm so sorry, Mr. Hollingsworth. That sign was left over from the previous occupants of this house. The ground's been so hard this winter I haven't been able to budge it from the yard. Regardless, your precious little daughter won't be anywhere near that grass. I have a sunny playroom, filled with toys, where she can crawl."

"See, honey," Elizabeth said with a nervous grin. "Everything's okay."

"Mr. Hollingsworth," Mrs. Pirkle said. "I can see you're a diligent father, and I commend you for it. Let me know if there's anything I can do to put your mind at ease."

They toured Mrs. Pirkle's tidy, one-story house and Timothy scrutinized each room, using the childproofing checklist that he'd downloaded from the Internet. He poked his nose in her kitchen cabinets and looked under beds. But despite his thorough search for lurking dangers, thus far, Mrs. Pirkle's house was above reproach. There were corner bumpers on the edges of the furniture and locks on all the toilets. Cleaning products and sharp objects were placed well out of reach of curious little hands.

Noting the furniture straps anchoring a dresser to the wall, Elizabeth elbowed Timothy. "This place is safer than ours," she whispered.

Timothy ignored her and pointed to a white flowering plant on top of a television.

"Is this a lily of the valley?" he asked Mrs. Pirkle.

Mrs. Pirkle blinked behind her wire-rimmed glasses. "I do believe it is."

"Did you also know it's an extremely dangerous plant?" Timothy said with the self-righteous tone of a trial lawyer. "Eating its leaves or flowers can cause local irritation of the mouth and stomach, followed by vomiting, pain, and diarrhea. Mental confusion may also ensue."

"How astute, Mr. Hollingsworth!" Mrs. Pirkle said. "If other fathers were as concerned as you, there'd be far fewer tragedies in the world."

She turned the plant upside down and examined the bottom of the vase. "Fortunately this was made in China. Isn't it amazing what they're doing with plastic plants these days?"

Timothy didn't even have the decency to blush and continued his arduous (and embarrassing) inspection of Mrs. Pirkle's home. Finally, after he'd scrutinized every room as carefully as a police detective at a crime scene, he said, "I think I've seen enough."

The couple made their way to the living room and stood near the door. Readying to leave, Elizabeth spoke.

"Mrs. Pirkle, I don't think I could hope for a better care-taking situation, and I'm sure my husband agrees with me. So I think—"

"That we need to go home and mull this over," Timothy interrupted as he took Glenda from Mrs. Pirkle's arms. "Thank you for your time."

"All right, Mr. and Mrs. Hollingsworth," Mrs. Pirkle said. "Take care of the wee one for me, and I'll wait to hear from you."

Once they were outside, Elizabeth glared at her husband. "What could possibly be wrong? The price is right. Glenda already loves her. It's an ideal situation."

"Are you seriously thinking about leaving your child in that woman's hands without running a criminal background check on her?" Timothy said, fumbling in his pocket for the car keys. "Who knows what kind of skeletons Mrs. Pirkle, if that's her real name, has rattling around in her closet. She's not even from Cayboo Creek. She could be Lizzie Borden's great-aunt for all we know. I'll stop by the sheriff's office tomorrow morning and get the goods on her."

"I think you're being an alarmist." Elizabeth sighed. "But okay, we'll run the check. However, if she's clean, we hire her. Agreed?"

Timothy toed the grass with his work boot. "Agreed," he said. "But with extreme reservations. You didn't think there was something kind of shifty about her?"

Elizabeth laughed. "She's about as shifty as Mr. Rogers." Then she cuffed his arm. "Come on, Timothy, everything's going to be all right. I promise."

Timothy shook his head. "I wish I were as optimistic as you are."

**Five days a week my body is a temple.
The other two it's an amusement park.**
—Graffiti in the ladies' room of the Chat 'N' Chew

CHAPTER SIXTEEN

Mrs. Tobias stood in front of a painting of an oversized magnolia. "This would go well over my fireplace," she remarked to Rusty. "I like the artist's bold strokes."

He pulled out his wallet from the back pocket of his jeans. "Let me buy it for you."

"Absolutely not. It's much too much money." Mrs. Tobias moved on to the next painting, a voluptuous nude reclining in a bathtub.

"Can I get you a glass of wine?" Rusty asked. "They've got a jug in the back."

"That would be lovely," Mrs. Tobias said. She watched his muscular leather-garbed back disappear into the swarms of gallery-hoppers. It was First Friday in Augusta, a monthly event where the art studios downtown fling open their doors for the evening to serve wine and cheese.

Mrs. Tobias had never attended the event before, and she was having a pleasant time. Peddlers lined the sidewalks hawking clay bowls, silver jewelry, and crocheted handbags. Families maneuvered strollers through the crowds, trailing popcorn and helium balloons. Performers, their grease-painted faces gleaming like moons underneath the streetlights, sang songs or danced along the perimeters of the aging storefronts.

Despite her jovial mood, Mrs. Tobias was still plagued with concern about Rusty's sexual orientation, and she couldn't think of an acceptable way to broach the topic. If he admitted to being a homosexual, would she be able to hide her dismay? Or what if he was one of those fellows who lusted after both women and men? Could she continue to keep company with someone who might, at any moment, steal off with a bewhiskered stranger?

Rusty returned with a plastic cup filled with an overly sweet Chardonnay, and they finished viewing the rest of the paintings in the gallery.

"Let's stroll a bit, shall we?" Rusty said.

"But I've not finished my wine," Mrs. Tobias said.

"Take it with you." Rusty grasped her hand. "Come on, it's just a big street party."

"All right," Mrs. Tobias said. Well-bred ladies most definitely did *not* drink in the streets, but she was too distracted by the squeeze of Rusty's big, warm hand to protest.

The night air was bracing, and Mrs. Tobias pulled up the collar of her beaver coat. A group of teenagers were prowling the streets, their open jackets flapping in the breeze like bat wings. Mrs. Tobias noticed one young man wearing a red wool hat with a University of Georgia logo.

"Are you a football fan?" Mrs. Tobias asked Rusty.

"Not particularly," Rusty said. A spicy aroma drifted from a corner restaurant that twinkled with a string of jalapeño-shaped red lights.

"I could go for a burrito about now," Rusty said, steering her toward the restaurant. "How about you?"

"Basketball? Or hockey?" Mrs. Tobias continued. "I understand Augusta has its own hockey team. Perhaps you attend some of the games?"

"Too violent for me. All that fighting." Rusty gazed at the chalk menu posted on the wall. "The Baja burrito is tasty. It's made with mahi-mahi and potatoes."

"Baseball then?" Mrs. Tobias asked over the jerky rhythms of music that blared from a pair of speakers above their heads. "It is one of the more civilized sports."

"Not as civilized as figure skating," Rusty said. "Now that's a sport I actually like to watch."

A young man, his head wrapped in a multicolored yarn turban, approached the counter. Thick, snakelike rolls of hair slithered out of his head covering. "Help you folks?" he asked.

"I'll have the Baja and a margarita," Rusty said. "Gracie?"

She hadn't even bothered to look at the menu. *Figure skating?* The evidence was stacking up like planes over Atlanta's Hartsfield International Airport. Her new beau was almost certainly gay.

"Perhaps a nice Cobb salad?" Mrs. Tobias said.

"I don't see that on the menu," Rusty said. "The nachos are fairly decent."

"Nachos it is." It didn't matter what she ordered, since her appetite was waning.

They sat down at a high-top table in the back, waiting for their order. Rusty bounced his knee to the beat of the music and winked at her from across the table.

"You're wearing a new outfit, aren't you? It's very flattering."

That clinched it. Heterosexual men never noticed women's new clothes. Harrison certainly never had. Mrs. Tobias searched Rusty's face.

"It's okay." She paused. "I *know*."

"You know what?" Rusty said, his forehead wrinkling.

"About your . . . preferences. And it's fine. We can still be friends." She reached across the table to stroke the back of his hand. "I do so enjoy your company."

"I'm lost," he said with a shrug.

"Figure skating. Antiquing. Quiche. It all adds up."

"To a big old mystery. What are you talking about, Gracie?"

Mrs. Tobias winced. "Look at your finger-nails, Rusty."

"What?"

"Indulge me. Just take a quick peek."

"Okey doke." Rusty curled his fingers and examined them. "Looks like I could use a sound scrubbing."

"Wait a minute," she said, shaking her head. "That's not what I was expecting. I'm confused now."

"What's wrong? Tell me."

Mrs. Tobias grasped the sides of the table and took a deep breath. "Rusty, are you gay?"

He considered her question for a moment as Mrs. Tobias sat wide-eyed and waiting. Then he hopped off his stool, sauntered over to her side of the table and planted a tender kiss on her lips.

Once he was finished, he whispered into her ear.

"Does that seem like the kiss of a gay man to you?"

No, she thought, as a thousand pleasure neurons fired simultaneously in her brain. It certainly did not.

Go braless. It will pull the wrinkles from your face.

—Magnet on Attalee Gaines's refrigerator

CHAPTER SEVENTEEN

Mavis whistled as she thumbed through her recipes. She'd brought her plastic box of index cards to the Bottom Dollar Emporium so she could plan the meal she was going to serve Brew on Saturday night. She'd already prepared chicken divan, steaks, and salmon croquettes for him. What about country-style pot roast? She plucked the card from the box. *Perfect.* She'd make it with her special sour-cream gravy.

Smiling, she recalled how Brew rubbed

his belly after every meal she'd prepared for him. "I'll be lucky to squeeze out of your front door," he'd say, which was a silly exaggeration since Brew's midsection was as trim as a teenager's.

After three official dates at her house, Mavis was beginning to think of herself as part of a couple. Brew would devour her home-cooked meal, and then they'd linger at the supper table over coffee. He'd often talk about his progress with his aunt's house on Chickasaw Drive.

"Don't know what I'm going to do with that place once it's finished," he'd said on their last date. "Maybe I'll live in it myself and settle down in Cayboo Creek." Then he smiled at her in a meaningful way. "Who knows what might happen between now and then?"

Mavis had shivered with delight. She hoped he was implying that she might play a part in his future plans.

Over dessert, they'd discussed the high school reunion. Even though it was short notice, they'd decided on a date in early April. Mavis had secured the high school gymnasium for the evening. Now she was engaged in the arduous task of finding and contacting her far-flung classmates. Though the work was time-consuming, it was also gratifying to share a project with Brew.

Their dates always ended in the same way. Brew would yawn and sneak glances at his watch, muttering something about the early bird catching the worm. Then he'd slowly lumber to the door. Mavis always wished he'd stay longer. The other evening she'd even rented a couple of action movies, but he begged off. She hadn't pressed the point. She knew he was working hard on his aunt's house and needed his rest.

The only downside to her budding relationship with Brew was her rift with Birdie. Birdie still hadn't set foot inside the Bottom Dollar Emporium since their argument, and she was deliberately avoiding Mavis. Yesterday she'd crossed Main Street and ducked into the Book Nook when she saw Mavis walking in her direction.

Most likely, Birdie was eaten up with envy. In a small town like Cayboo Creek, it was impossible to keep anything secret, so Birdie probably knew that Brew was keeping regular company at Mavis's house. And now she was punishing Mavis for it by ignoring her. Mavis's old friend had always been something of a poor loser.

Still, Mavis missed her and hoped they could make amends. She suspected it would be up to her to make the first move; Birdie could be as stubborn as a blue-nosed mule.

Mavis heard footsteps behind her. Looking up from her recipe file, she saw Elizabeth coming through the front door carrying Glenda.

"Elizabeth!" she said, scurrying over to greet her. "What a treat! It's been much too long. And would you look at that dear, little baby. I swear she's grown since I've seen her last." She held her arms out. "May I?"

"Of course," Elizabeth said, handing a wriggling, snow-suited Glenda to Mavis. Elizabeth squinted into the back of the store where the soda fountain was located. "Where's Attalee?"

"Not here yet. Ever since she's been stepping out with Dooley, she slinks in twenty minutes late every morning." Mavis pointed to a chair in the break area. "Come on. Take a load off. We've got some catching up to do."

"I'll do that." Elizabeth paused by the coffeepot to pour herself a cup. "I've got big news."

Mavis jiggled Glenda on her knee. "You

look like you're bursting with something. Let's hear it."

"Yoo-hoo!" Mrs. Tobias called out from the front of the store. "Anybody home?"

"We're in the break area," Mavis said. "Join us. You're just in time for Elizabeth's announcement."

"I thought that was your car parked outside," Mrs. Tobias said, pecking Elizabeth's cheek. "And there's my great-grandchild."

"You'll have to fight me for her." Mavis hugged Glenda closer to her chest.

"Five minutes and then it's my turn." Mrs. Tobias unbuttoned her coat, revealing a patterned beaded shawl, flirty, flared skirt, and high, shiny black boots.

"Wow," Elizabeth said. "Aren't you the fashion plate!"

"Thank you," said Mrs. Tobias. She tugged on the fringe of her shawl. "It isn't too young, is it? I don't want to look silly."

"It's up-to-the-minute, but in a very classy way," Elizabeth said.

"Talbot's in Augusta was having its winter clearance sale, but then I noticed a Chico's right next door." Mrs. Tobias smoothed her skirt with her hand. "I'd never been in that boutique before. I went a little crazy."

"I've been hearing rumors about you," Elizabeth said with a knowing smile. "Is it true there's a new beau in your life?"

"Maybe. Maybe not," Mrs. Tobias said. "Let's not talk about me. I want to hear *your* news."

"I'm going back to work!" Elizabeth exclaimed, jumping about in her seat. "Just part-time, but I'm so excited."

"Back to work?" Mrs. Tobias sat across from her. "What about Glenda?"

"That's the best part," Elizabeth continued. "I found a wonderful, dear woman named Mrs. Pirkle to look after her. Her references were all glowing, and she passed her criminal background check with flying colors. But I knew she would. How could such a motherly looking woman possibly be a criminal?"

"Criminal background check? What's this?" Mrs. Tobias asked with alarm.

"Timothy insisted on running a check on Mrs. Pirkle. The only mar on her record was a jaywalking rap," Elizabeth explained. "Even that set him off. He said, 'Jaywalking implies a certain carelessness on her part.' I said, 'I think you're making a mountain out of a molehill.' It took a lot of back-and-forth, but I finally wore him down."

"I know Mrs. Pirkle," Mavis said. "She comes in the store every once in a while. What a sweetie!"

"Are you and Timothy having financial problems?" Mrs. Tobias reached for her purse on the floor. "If so, I'll write you a check this instant."

"No. Everything's fine. I just want to go back to work." Elizabeth shrugged. "I miss it."

"I suppose things are different these days," Mrs. Tobias said after a moment. "Young people have so many choices. And being cooped up with a child all day can be wearing."

"So you understand?" Elizabeth asked. "I've had a heck of a time convincing Timothy."

"I do understand, my dear," Mrs. Tobias said. "And you have to remember Timothy's background. I'm afraid he seldom saw his parents as a child, so he often felt neglected. But you're a much more attentive parent, very different from his mother, Daisy. Timothy will come to understand that."

"I hope so," Elizabeth said. "It's the only thing we've ever disagreed about."

"Disagreements make for spicy relationships." Mrs. Tobias winked.

"Speaking of relationships—" Elizabeth began. "I still want to hear about this new beau of yours."

"Stop the presses!" shouted Attalee. She bounded into the break area, eyes sparkling and a skip in her gait. "Want to know why I'm grinning like a possum with a mouthful of persimmons?" she asked once she reached the other women.

"Knowing that you and Dooley drove to the drive-in movie in Monetta last night, I'm afraid to ask," Mavis said.

"Shoot, there wasn't a whole lot of hanky-panky going on betwixt us. Just kissing and a couple of feel-ups," Attalee said.

"Enough!" Mrs. Tobias held up her hand.

"Anyhoo, I've decided I want to save myself." Attalee thrust out her hand. "For our wedding night."

"Oh my gosh." Elizabeth looked at Attalee's finger. "You're engaged!"

"It was so romantic," Attalee said, wiping a tear from her eye. "After the drive-in, we went to the Chat 'N' Chew. Dooley had the cook bury the ring in the meatloaf. I thought I'd bit into a piece of gristle. Imagine my surprise when I spat out a diamond ring on my plate!"

"How quaint," Mrs. Tobias said, scrutinizing Attalee's tiny diamond.

"Congratulations." Mavis hugged her friend's skinny frame. "When's the big date?"

"Soon as I can plan a wedding," Attalee said.

"A wedding?" Mrs. Tobias pursed her lips in disapproval. "Wouldn't it be simpler to elope?"

"I eloped when I married my late husband Burl and I've always dreamed of a fancy wedding." She touched Mrs. Tobias's sleeve. "Since you're such a proper lady and know what's fitting, I'd like you to help me plan it. There's a mess of decisions to make. What flavor of Cheez Whiz to spread on the crackers? Should our names on the matchbooks be embossed with silver or gold? What color bridesmaids' dresses to get?"

"Bridesmaids?" Mavis said.

"That's right." Attalee nodded her head. "I want all of you here to be my bridesmaids, and Mavis, I'd like you to be my matron of honor."

"I'm flattered," Mavis said. "But Attalee, a big wedding is so expensive."

"I've got me a little nest egg that I inherited when my cousin Cornelia choked on a pork-chop bone six months ago," Attalee said. "I was planning on using it for a few nips and tucks, but now that I've hooked me a fellow, I think I'll blow it on a wedding instead."

"This is big news." Elizabeth grasped Attalee's wrist. "I'm very happy for you."

"There is one bug in the ointment," Attalee said with a frown. "What am I going to do about Birdie? I want her to be one of my bridesmaids, but she and Mavis ain't speaking."

"What's this?" Elizabeth said.

"Nothing." Mavis adjusted the bow in Glenda's hair. "Just a little bump in the road. It happens with all friendships if they last long enough. We'll straighten it out before the wedding."

"She and Birdie were tussling over the same man," Attalee explained. "But Mavis won out."

"Do you have to broadcast everything?" Mavis asked.

"We're all family here, ain't we?" Attalee asked in a wounded voice.

"I'm sorry, dear," Mavis said in a softer

tone. "This a very exciting day, and I'm so happy for you."

Attalee glanced at her watch. "Hell's bells, it's late. I best get the soda fountain ready for business."

"There must be something in the water," Elizabeth said after Attalee hurried to the stock room. "First Grandma Gracie is seeing a beau, then Attalee gets engaged, and now Mavis has a fellow. By the way, Mavis, I wouldn't worry too much about Birdie. I drove by her house the other evening, and I saw this handsome man get out of a little red sports car and go inside. Sounds like she's sought out greener pastures."

"What night was that?" Mavis asked, knitting her brow.

"It was last night. Why?" Elizabeth said.

"No reason. Just curious." Mavis got up from her chair and handed Glenda to Mrs. Tobias. "I best get back to work myself. The candy bins need filling."

"So are you going to tell me about this new fellow of yours?" Elizabeth asked her.

"Not much to tell." Mavis tore open a bag of Red Hots with her teeth. "He's just a man. Deep voice. Facial hair. What you'd expect."

"That doesn't tell me diddly." Elizabeth turned to Mrs. Tobias. "How about you? Are you going to be closemouthed about your beau as well?"

Mrs. Tobias glanced at her watch and rose from her chair. "Oh my goodness, I'm late for a hair appointment. Good luck with your job, Elizabeth."

Elizabeth took Glenda from Mrs. Tobias's arms.

"Used to be you could get a little gossip around here," she grumbled. "Now, when there's finally something to talk about, everyone clams up."

Mrs. Tobias hugged Elizabeth good-bye. "In good time, my dear. Bye all! See you soon."

Elizabeth followed her to the front of the store.

"Mavis?" Elizabeth said.

"I don't want to jinx things," Mavis said over the rattle of hard candies being poured into a wooden bin. "You'll be the first to get the dish. I promise."

"Fair enough." Elizabeth zipped up Glenda's snowsuit. "Tell Attalee good-bye for me."

After Elizabeth left, Mavis stared out the

window watching a stray leaf scrape across the expanse of asphalt in the front parking lot. Unless there were two handsome men with little red sports cars in town, Brew had obviously been visiting Birdie.

But why? She'd assumed that she and Brew were established as an item. Was he two-timing her?

Do not play leapfrog with a unicorn.
—Message in fortune cookie at Dun Woo's House
of Noodles

CHAPTER EIGHTEEN

Elizabeth peered at the clock on her computer. Eight-thirty A.M. If she were at home she'd be lying on the couch in her terry-cloth bathrobe, flipping through television channels like a zombie. Instead she was sitting in a corner office at Hollingsworth Paper Cups, wearing a crisp white blouse with a boiled-wool burgundy jacket and matching skirt. Her blond hair was slicked back with styling gel, and she wore gold earring bobs and a herringbone necklace.

When she'd scrutinized her reflection that morning, she almost cried.

"I'm myself again," she said to the clear-eyed, professional woman who stared back at her with a satisfied smile.

"Knock, knock," Daisy Hollingsworth said as she breezed into Elizabeth's office bringing in the flowery scent of Chanel No. 5.

Daisy wore a fitted black silk jacket with a pencil skirt. A string of knotted cultured pearls hung around the slender stalk of her neck, and her golden hair was styled into a gleaming chignon.

"So good to have you back, Elizabeth," she said. "Hope you're enjoying the flowers."

"Who wouldn't appreciate a dozen white roses?" The flowers were displayed on the corner of her desk. Elizabeth inhaled deeply to take in their sweetness. "Thank you so much."

"And your office." Daisy pulled up the window blinds. "I think you have a better view this time around."

"It's great." Elizabeth's office window overlooked a small park with sloping hills and a wooden bridge stretching over a stream.

"Soon the dogwoods and Japanese magnolias will be in bloom." Daisy turned her back to the large window. Her silver bangles jingled softly as she pressed her hands together. "Elizabeth, if there's anything you need, just ask. You know my extension?"

"I do."

"One more thing." Daisy touched the top of Elizabeth's brand-new Macintosh. "If, after a while, you find that this job isn't the right fit for you, I'll understand. It's not easy being a working mother."

"Thanks. But I think everything's going to be just fine." Elizabeth leaned back in her swivel chair. "Timothy's finally accepted that I'm going back to work. He even gave our baby-sitter, Mrs. Pirkle, a mantel clock as a gesture of goodwill. I was so proud of him."

"I'm delighted to hear it." Daisy flashed a smile. "By the way, speaking of Glenda, do you have any recent photos of my gorgeous grandchild? I need new ones for the top of my piano."

"I'll bring in a few tomorrow," Elizabeth said.

"Wonderful. See you at this afternoon's meeting."

After Daisy left, Elizabeth inhaled the smell of her Italian leather chair. God, how she loved being back in the office! The stutter of the fax machine, the aroma of roasted coffee beans, the hum of her computer as it booted up—all of it soothed her senses.

She spent the morning huddled over a legal pad, brainstorming ideas for the summer campaign. Warm weather was a big season for paper cups what with all the picnics, outdoor parties, and barbecues that went on. She noticed sales were down in the drinking-straw division. Just as she was trying to devise a strategy to beef up those figures, the phone beside her computer buzzed. Elizabeth picked it up. "Elizabeth Hollingsworth."

A strangled sob came over the line. "Mrs. Hollingsworth. I'm so sorry."

"Mrs. Pirkle, is that you?" Panic seized Elizabeth's voice. "Is there something wrong with Glenda?"

"She's just fine. I guess." Mrs. Pirkle said in between sobs. "Your daughter's with your husband. He just left here."

"Timothy has Glenda? Why? What's going on?"

"You know that clock your husband gave me as a gift? Well, it was much more than that." Mrs. Pirkle's voice caught in her throat.

"It was something called a Nanny Cam. It had a film camera built inside."

"No!" Elizabeth wrapped the phone cord so tightly around her fingers they turned blue.

"Yes. I put the babies down for their naps, and I sat down to watch my favorite television talk show," Mrs. Pirkle said. "I wasn't doing any harm, Mrs. Hollingsworth. I had the baby monitor on the sofa next to me so if either of those two dear wee ones made so much as a peep, I'd hear them."

"Yes, yes, and then—?"

"And then, your husband banged on my front door. Turns out he'd been spying on me with the Nanny Cam. He wanted to know why I was watching trash TV instead of keeping an eye on his daughter. I don't know why he was so upset, Mrs. Hollingsworth. Am I expected to stand over Glenda's crib while she's napping?"

"Of course not, Mrs. Pirkle. I am so sorry. I'll talk to my husband about this incident immediately."

"I'm sorry, too, Mrs. Hollingsworth." She paused. "You seem like a fine couple, and your daughter Glenda is precious, but I won't be treated as if I'm some sort of criminal."

Elizabeth's mouth went dry. "What are you saying?"

Mrs. Pirkle took a deep breath. "I'm saying that you need to make other child-care arrangements, Mrs. Hollingsworth."

When Elizabeth got home, the first word out of her mouth as she slammed her car keys down on the coffee table in the den was, "Why?"

Timothy, who was seated on the couch bottle-feeding Glenda, held up his palm. "Before you start in on me, you need to hear my side of the story. I guess you've spoken with Mrs. Pirkle?"

"Yes. She told me what happened." Elizabeth dropped into the chair across from her husband. "Through her tears."

"She was crying?" A pained look crossed Timothy's face. "I didn't mean to make her cry. But she did leave Glenda all alone."

"While she was taking a nap!"

"We don't pay her to watch television while Glenda's in her care, asleep or otherwise. Did she tell you what show she was watching?"

Elizabeth propped her feet on the ottoman. "Some talk show."

"Not just *some* talk show." Timothy lowered his voice to a whisper. "It was *Jerry Springer.*"

"So?" Elizabeth threw up her hands. "I admit that's a crass show but that doesn't mean—"

"The show was about the Midget Klu Klux Klan! Tiny little munchkin people in white hoods. Is that the kind of thing you want your daughter exposed to? And what does it say about Mrs. Pirkle?"

"It says that she's a voyeur, like ninety-five percent of all Americans," Elizabeth said, kicking off her high heels. "His show's like a car wreck; it's hard to pry your eyes from it. I've caught a couple of *Jerry Springer* programs myself. Does that mean I'm an unfit mother?"

"No," Timothy said softly.

"And speaking of voyeurs, how could you secretly film her?" Elizabeth rubbed her hand over her forehead. "What were you thinking?"

"Maybe I overreacted," Timothy said. He patted Glenda's back to burp her. "I just want the best for our daughter."

"Here. Let me have her," Elizabeth said. "I haven't seen her for a few hours."

Timothy got up from the couch and placed Glenda on Elizabeth's lap.

"Hi, sweetie. How's Mama's little girl?" Elizabeth cooed softly to her sleepy-eyed daughter. "Did you miss me today? Well, don't you worry. Mommy will be here from now on."

Timothy knelt beside his wife. "What do you mean by that?"

"What do you think I mean? I quit my job." Elizabeth gave her husband a sharp glance. "Mrs. Pirkle refuses to watch Glenda anymore, and I don't have any other child-care alternatives. My career at Hollingsworth Paper Cups was over before it even began."

Timothy turned pale. "I'm so sorry, Elizabeth."

"You are not. Don't even pretend that you are. You hoped this would happen."

"Not like this. I swear." He swallowed. "How can I make it up to you?"

"You can't," she snapped. "What you have done today, Timothy Hollingsworth, is completely unforgivable."

**The secret of a happy marriage
remains a secret.**
> —Sign outside a divorce lawyer's office

CHAPTER NINETEEN

"It's a nice day for a white wedding gown," Attalee lip-synched to the Billy Idol song playing on the tape deck in Mrs. Tobias's car.

"Could you turn that down just a tad?" Mrs. Tobias shouted to Attalee over the din.

"Sorry." Attalee snapped off the music and ejected the cassette. "Just trying to get in the mood for wedding planning."

Mrs. Tobias steered her Caddie into a shopping center off Washington Road in Augusta. "Here it is. Wedding Warehouse." She stared at the massive boxy building. "Are you sure you want to shop in this place? It looks like a Home Depot."

"That's because it used to *be* a Home Depot." Attalee unbuckled her seat belt. "Their slogan is 'all your nuptial needs under one roof.'"

The two women got out of the car and strolled across a parking lot the size of a football field. When they reached the entrance the double glass doors of the store swooshed open, and a male greeter in a black plastic top hat and bow tie handed them both a sales flier.

"Welcome to Wedding Warehouse," he chirped. "A reminder, ladies. There's a boutonnière bonanza in the florist department. Order ten boutonnières and your next two are absolutely free."

"Thank you," Attalee said to the greeter. She glanced at the piece of paper in her hand. "Let me take a look at the map on the back of this flier. I'd like to go to the wedding-dress aisle first."

The song "I'm Getting Married in the Morning" was being piped in through the store's speakers. A forklift zoomed by carrying boxes of plastic champagne flutes.

"I'm not so sure about this concept," Mrs. Tobias said, following Attalee.

"I'm with you, gal," Attalee said. "All this bridal stuff in one place. It's almost too darn romantic. Ah, here we are. Wedding dresses. A sea of white loveliness."

Attalee tugged on the skirt of a satin monstrosity hanging on one of the many racks. "I like this one, but the sleeves need to be puffier, and the train needs to be longer."

"Ahem, Attalee," Mrs. Tobias said. "Those dresses are suitable for first weddings." She sorted through several of the gowns and withdrew one from the rack. "Look at this. A lovely tea-length dress in antique beige."

Attalee stared at the garment in Mrs. Tobias's hand. "Where's the train and the seed pearls and the long white veil? Plus are you color-blind, Mrs. Tobias? That thing ain't even white."

"Attalee, you have five children, twelve grandchildren, and nineteen great-grandchildren. And you're eighty-six."

Attalee planted her hands on her hips. "Your point is?"

Mrs. Tobias shook her head. "I don't even know why you asked me to come along."

"This one is right pretty," Attalee said, pulling a lacy gown from the rack. "Oops. My mistake. It's a maternity wedding gown. See? It's got a built-in tummy panel."

"Things have certainly changed since my day," Mrs. Tobias said with a shake of her head.

Attalee tried on several wedding gowns, modeling them all for Mrs. Tobias. She finally settled on one that made her look like an oversized, sequined marshmallow.

"Now, about the bridesmaids' dresses," she said.

"Oh, Attalee, aren't we all a little long-in-the-tooth for that?" Mrs. Tobias said.

"No. If you want a proper wedding, you gotta have bridesmaids," Attalee said with a pout.

They sorted through several different styles of dresses. Attalee finally selected a capped-sleeve, bow-studded gown in iridescent eggplant.

"This dress is so fancy y'all might steal some of my glory," she said.

"What's next on the list?" a fatigued Mrs. Tobias asked.

Attalee methodically made her way through the store, ordering all manner of items for her upcoming nuptials. From the personalized champagne glasses (with tiny stuffed bears clinging to the side) to a blinking garter belt with matching "Kiss me" thong underwear, Attalee's wedding purchases went from bad to worse on the tacky scale.

After sorting through a selection of tuxedos (Attalee remarked she was leaning toward the baby blue to match Dooley's eyes), Mrs. Tobias felt completely shopped out.

"Attalee, I'm swaying in my shoes," she said. "Could we possibly save the rest for another day?"

"I'm feeling kind of meager myself," Attalee said with a yawn. "Let's make tracks."

They left the store to a recording of the Dixie Cups singing "Chapel of Love."

"Thanks so much for lending a hand, Mrs. Tobias," Attalee said as they reached the sidewalk outside. "I'm going to tell everyone you were my wedding coordinator."

"No, please." Mrs. Tobias touched Attalee's sleeve. "I don't want anyone making a fuss over me."

"Gracie!" Someone was waving at her from several shops down.

"Rusty?" Mrs. Tobias said, recognizing her beau as he walked toward her. She noticed Attalee looking at her with a naughty gleam in her eye, and her voice immediately assumed a formal tone.

"Mr. Williams. How are you today?"

"Fine," said Rusty, shooting her a puzzled look due to her use of his surname. "I was next door at the Pet Palace. They got some real dirty ducts in that building. Lots of dog and cat hair."

Mrs. Tobias had never seen Rusty in his work clothes before. He was wearing a blue shirt with "Duct Doctor" embroidered in red thread on the pocket. Crescent-shaped sweat marks seeped from underneath his arms, and his fingernails were dark with grime.

"Hi, Attalee," Rusty said. "I ran into Dooley yesterday afternoon. I understand congratulations are in order."

"Thank you kindly," Attalee said. "I done picked out my dress and everything."

"Good for you," Rusty said. "By the way, Gracie, I left a message on your machine. I may be a half-hour late for our date tonight. Hope that won't inconvenience you too much."

"Not at all," Mrs. Tobias said.

"I'll be there as soon as possible." He glanced at his watch. "Gotta run. I'm late for my next job. See you, ladies."

After he hurried off to his truck, Attalee hooted. "So Rusty is your new fellow. I knew y'all were perfect for each other."

Mrs. Tobias sighed. "Attalee, we're just friends. And I'd appreciate it if we didn't discuss this at the Bottom Dollar Emporium with the others. I'm just not ready yet."

"Mum's the word," Attalee said with a wink. "But, regarding the 'friend' part, I didn't take any chemistry classes in school, but I know it when I see it. You two 'friends' have enough of it to power a nuclear reactor."

"Pish-posh. You have a vivid imagination." Mrs. Tobias waved her off. "Now where did I park my car?

As they searched for her Caddie, Mrs. Tobias couldn't blink away the image of Rusty in his work shirt. She'd always known he was a laborer, but actually seeing him garbed in blue-collar attire had proved to be more unsettling than she'd expected.

Snob. The bitter word floated up from her subconscious. She'd never regarded herself as an elitist before, despite an upbringing by an extremely pretentious mother.

NOKD. *Not our kind, darling.* That's how her late mother would dismiss Rusty and his Duct Doctor shirt. She wouldn't bother to take into account his humor, integrity, and sensitivity. Trouble was, when Mrs. Tobias saw Rusty in his work clothes, for a brief moment, it had blotted out all of his good qualities.

Was it possible that she was more like her mother than she thought?

Wanted: Meaningful Overnight Relationship
—Graffiti in the men's room in the Tuff Luck Tavern

CHAPTER TWENTY

"Dang, Mavis. That was some good eating." Brew crumpled his napkin and placed it on top of his dinner plate. "I could live off that feast for two weeks."

"Glad you liked it." Mavis cleared a stack of dishes from the table and took them into the kitchen, just off her small dining area. "I thought it might be nice to take an after-dinner walk. It's not as cold as usual, and there's a full moon."

"Maybe," Brew said. "I was just wondering,

have you gotten any more RSVPs from our classmates?"

"I got several in the post yesterday. I made a list for you. Would you like to see it?"

"Yeah." Brew leaned back in his chair. "If it's not too much trouble."

"Not at all." Mavis wiped her hands on a plaid dishtowel that hung on her refrigerator door. Then she withdrew the list from the drawer beneath her telephone and went into the dining room to give it to Brew.

He muttered to himself as he read the list. "These are all the people coming so far, huh?"

"Yes."

He tapped the paper with his index finger. "And you were able to find everyone except—?"

"Dolores Montgomery."

"Who?"

"Remember, I said she used to be treasurer of the stamp-collecting club. Cat-eye glasses, a bit stout—?"

"Yeah, yeah, I remember now." Brew folded the list and stuck it in his shirt pocket. "It probably wouldn't hurt to call some of those people who haven't responded. Just to make sure their invitations didn't get lost in the mail."

"I'll do it," Mavis said. "Now, Brew, I was thinking about the decorations for the gym and the refreshments. I have some ideas—"

"That's my department, sugar. I've gotten it all taken care of." He unfolded his sizeable frame from his chair. "We're a team, remember?" He eyed her as she stood in the door frame leading into the kitchen. "How did I ever overlook a pretty filly like you? I must have been blind in high school."

Mavis relished the compliment for a moment but quickly remembered that Brew's use of flattery was often a prelude to his departure for the evening.

"You aren't running off just yet, are you?" she said, trying to keep the disappointment out of her voice. "How about a quick stroll around the block?"

Brew shook his head with regret. "Much as I hate to leave your company, darling, I gotta go. Big day tomorrow. Got a crew of painters coming in at seven sharp."

"Wait one minute. There was something I wanted to discuss . . ." She stared down at the hooked rug underneath her feet. "That is . . . I was wondering about . . ." She glanced up quickly. "Birdie."

He raised an eyebrow. "What about Birdie?"

"There's been some talk around town. Is it true that you've been seeing . . ." Mavis avoided Brew's eyes, and her voice grew softer. "Both of us?"

"Are you jealous, m'lady?" Brew's lip curled in amusement.

"Of course not, I just—"

"You tell that pretty, little green-eyed monster of yours to take a powder," Brew said. "There's not a thing between Birdie and me."

"It's just that . . . people have seen your car outside her house, and—"

"I know." Brew shrugged on his sports coat. "Call me old-fashioned. I just can't ignore a damsel in distress."

"Birdie's been in distress?"

"You could say that. You know how things around a house get out of sorts. Faucets drip. Toilets run."

"I see." Mavis also knew Birdie was perfectly capable of making her own simple home repairs. In fact, she prided herself on her handiness with tools, and even owned a soldering iron.

"She calls me over there, and I just can't say no," Brew said. He touched her chin with one finger. "But you're my special gal. I thought you knew that, Mavis."

"Are you sure?"

"Does a hound dog have fleas?" Brew chuckled. "See you on Thursday."

Her heart fluttered as she watched Brew walk out the door. *I'm such a lucky woman,* she thought. Mavis could hardly blame Birdie for trying to steal Brew away from her. Instead of feeling angry toward her friend, she felt a twinge of sympathy. Poor dear Birdie. Reduced to out-and-out chicanery in an attempt to win Brew's affections. How lonely she must feel!

The next day after work, Mavis stopped by the Winn-Dixie to shop for her upcoming dinner date with Brew. The weatherman had warned that Cayboo Creek could expect a hard frost, so she thought a hearty bowl of chili and a skilletful of cornbread would be just what the doctor ordered. She turned her buggy down the baking aisle to get a bag of cornmeal when she saw Birdie reaching for the White Lily Flour.

"Hi, Birdie," Mavis said. "Long time no see."

Birdie gasped and immediately backed away.

"Wait, Birdie," Mavis said, following her. She figured Birdie was fleeing because she was ashamed of her recent actions. "Can't we patch things up? Does it have to be like this between us?"

Birdie paused beside the cake mixes. "Yes. It does, Mavis. You've made that choice."

"I don't understand."

"Ha!" Birdie cocked her hip against her buggy. "You understand perfectly. I'm referring to this latest business you've been pulling with Brew. I *know* what you've been up to."

"I figured you'd hear sooner or later. And I'm sorry. But, after all, I did see Brew first, and—"

"Mavis, this isn't primary school. You can't call dibs on a man and think he's yours."

"I know that, but—"

Birdie shook a finger at her. "And if you have any hopes of saving our friendship, you must stop this nonsense with Brew immediately."

Mavis opened her mouth but no words came out. "It's not fair of you to ask me that," she said, finally recovering her voice. "I'm sorry, Birdie. But that's the one thing I won't do."

"Of all the nerve! I never imagined you could stoop this low." Birdie swung her buggy around. "Go on, then, make a fool of yourself. I simply don't care."

She stormed down the aisle, leaving behind a stunned and shaken Mavis.

Do vegetarians eat animal crackers?
—Sign outside Boomer's Butcher shop

CHAPTER TWENTY-ONE

Elizabeth's eyes sprung open as streaks of lemon-yellow sunlight slanted in the bedroom through the blinds. Glenda! Something had to be wrong. Her daughter was as regimented as a boot-camp recruit, always rising at six A.M. or earlier. But, judging by the amount of sunlight filtering into the room, it had to be at least seven o'clock.

She flung off the covers and was about to tear off to the nursery when her nose picked up the smell of perking coffee. She also heard the sizzle of bacon in the cast-iron skillet. Timothy had obviously gotten Glenda out of her crib and was now making breakfast.

Yesterday he'd brought home an oversized box of Godiva chocolates. The day before, it was a bag of yogurt-coated pretzels. If Elizabeth didn't forgive Timothy soon, her walk was going to turn into a waddle.

She slipped her feet into a pair of fuzzy mules lying beside the four-poster rice bed and padded into the kitchen. There she stood in the hallway, silently watching Timothy feed Glenda a baby-food jar of peaches.

"Zoom!" he said to Glenda, whose chin was sluiced with orange goo. He twitched the spoon inches in front of her pursed rosebud lips. "Come on, into the hangar."

Timothy wore a cable-knit sweater that made his eyes look as blue as the hydrangeas that bloomed outside the back door in the summer. Dark bangs loped over his forehead as he leaned down to refill his spoon with peaches. Elizabeth found herself holding her breath.

He could still do it to her. Still make her palms sweaty, still speed up the percussion of her heart. She'd always love him, even if he infuriated her.

"That bacon I smell had better be crisp," Elizabeth said as she perched on a stool at the breakfast nook.

Timothy dropped the baby's spoon and it clattered on the tray of Glenda's high chair. "Elizabeth, you're talking to me?"

"Only because I'm hungry." She banged her fist on the counter. "Where's the chow?"

"Elizabeth, I'm so sorry. It was wrong of me. I shouldn't have ever bought that Nanny Cam. I promise you—"

Elizabeth covered her ears with her hands. "Enough. I've heard it a million times. Last night I think you were even apologizing in your sleep. Let's put it behind us. Okay?"

"Deal," Timothy said with a relieved smile. "The queen will get her breakfast as soon as the princess is fed."

"Thanks, by the way, for getting Glenda up. I don't think I've slept that long since she was born."

"I could do it more often. I don't mind—"

"No," Elizabeth said. "It's my job. I'll get up with Glenda like always."

Later, after Timothy left for work (lingering in the foyer, blowing kisses until she had to shove him out the door), Elizabeth tried on a half-dozen pairs of too-tight pants before she settled on a burgundy corduroy jumper that she could pull over her ever-widening hips.

There'd be no lollygagging on the couch today. Yesterday she'd gotten a call from Patsy Dinkins, who lived behind the house Elizabeth had inherited from her grandmother.

"Your renters packed up every stick of their furniture and left in the dead of the night," Patsy reported. "Maybe you'd best check on the house."

Ever since she'd acquired Meemaw's old house, Elizabeth had struggled to keep it rented. Tenants came and went, and the aging home was always in need of some kind of repair. Elizabeth wasn't cut out to be a landlord, but she didn't want to sell the place. She'd been raised by her grandmother and had spent the first eighteen years of her life in that house. The hardwood hallways were scuffed with her shoe marks, and the walls bore traces of her crayon scribblings.

Still, she dreaded the task of trying to find new tenants. The people she'd rented it to last, a couple called the Hendricks, had seemed stable enough. They'd come to Cayboo Creek to work at the kaolin company just outside of town, and their rent payment always arrived on or before the first of the month. They were also relatively undemanding tenants. In six months they'd called her only once, to complain about an ant infestation in the kitchen.

When Elizabeth had accompanied the exterminator to the house, all the beds were made and the aging appliances in the kitchen gleamed from good, old-fashioned elbow grease. She'd begun to regard the Hendricks as ideal tenants. What would cause them to steal off like thieves in the middle of the night?

Half an hour later, Elizabeth pulled into the driveway of Meemaw's old house. The 'forties-style brick ranch was located on the outskirts of a subdivision called Dogwood Village, and several commercial establishments were encroaching on the once-sleepy residential area. A florist was setting up shop across the street, and two blocks down an auto insurance office had opened up next to a dry-cleaning establishment.

Elizabeth studied the house's façade for a minute before going inside. Nothing had changed since her last visit, except the spacious picture window out front was now bare of curtains. Pine straw had collected on the striped metal awnings above the door and windows, causing them to sag from the weight. She made a mental note to hire someone to get on the roof with a rake.

Holding Glenda in her arms, Elizabeth trudged up the concrete driveway, noticing several dark splotches. Hadn't she once heard that pouring kitty litter on oil stains would soak up the grime? Maybe she could do that herself before she rented the house again.

A few pieces of mail were stuffed in the aluminum box just outside the front door. Elizabeth collected the envelopes and turned her key in the lock, almost expecting Pierre, Meemaw's bedraggled poodle, to jump up on her legs as soon as she entered. But there was no Pierre to greet her as she stepped inside. There was only the steady hum of the refrigerator and the stuffy, closed-up odor of the house.

Her eyes searched the large, sunny living room, looking, as always, for reminders of her childhood. There was a shiny swatch of pink ribbon entangled in the brass chandelier above her head where her granddaddy—

whom she called Peepaw—had hung balloons for her sweet-sixteen party.

She smiled up at it as she left the empty
living room and went down the hall, where
there was a small built-in shelf for the telephone. Elizabeth searched until she spied a
faint phone number, written in blue ballpoint,
crawling up the wall beside the alcove.

It was Clip Jenkins's number, her high-
school sweetheart. She'd doodled it nearly
twelve years ago as she sat on a swivel stool
in the hall talking on the phone.

Drifting into the kitchen, she could almost
hear the clang of pots and skillets over the
hulking gas stove and smell the piquant
aroma of fatback and black-eyed peas
simmering over blue flames on the black
iron burners. She could practically taste
Meemaw's oatmeal-raisin cookies, so crisp
they'd snap when you broke them in half.

Now, besides the appliances, the kitchen
was stripped bare. Elizabeth could see the
ghostly outline of pans on the wall where
they'd once hung from hooks. She poked her
nose into the pantry and found shelves
dusty with flour and cornstarch. An opened
package of saltines and a couple of cans of
beets were the only things left behind by her

former tenants. Equally empty was the Frigidaire. A squashed-in bottle of mustard lay on its side on the wire shelves of the refrigerator, and the icebox contained a freezer-burned bag of mixed vegetables.

Elizabeth set the mail down on the counter, thinking how sad it was to see Meemaw's kitchen so empty. It had been a beehive of activity when she was a child.

Glenda was getting restless, squirming and making discontented grunting noises. Everything looked in order. Her tenants may have fled without warning, but at least they hadn't damaged the house or left it a mess.

Elizabeth decided to glance into the bedrooms, sort through the mail, and head home. Then she'd place a "house for rent" ad in the *Cayboo Creek Crier.*

A knock sounded on the door. Elizabeth crossed the recently installed blue carpet of the living room and peered out one of the three diamond-shaped windows that were lined up vertically in the front door.

"Boomer!" She swung open the door. "This is a surprise."

"Hi, sugar bean. What's shaking?" He wore a big, puffy coat with a fur-lined hood that made him look like a bald, wide-eyed

Eskimo. When he gathered her up in an enthusiastic hug, she felt like she was being mauled by a bear.

"Boomer, I think you might be smooshing the baby," Elizabeth said in a muffled voice.

Boomer dropped his embrace and closely eyeballed Glenda, who stared back at him with a cautious gaze. "You smooshed, kid? Don't fret. If your Uncle Boomer made a dent in you, it'll pop right out."

"If you say so," Elizabeth said with a smile. Boomer was not really Glenda's uncle. He'd been Meemaw's beau before she'd died of a stroke two years ago.

"So, I see Bonnie and Clyde have fled the hideout." Boomer stepped inside and glanced about the living room

"I guess so. Meemaw's neighbor Patsy called me and told me the Hendricks took off in a U-Haul about two this morning."

"Patsy called me, too. I was here earlier, and so was the fuzz."

"Fuzz?"

Boomer's eyes narrowed. "The man, the coppers. The long arm of the law."

"What were the police doing here?" Elizabeth asked with alarm.

"Asking questions. Turns out there was

some moolah missing from the till at the kaolin plant. The local Mounties think your tenants might have sticky fingers."

"The Hendricks?" Elizabeth said in surprise. "Gosh, they seemed like such a nice, average couple. Last time I was here, they had a game of Boggle spread out on the kitchen table."

"Gangsters have to get their jollies, too, sister," Boomer said in the whispery tones of a film-noir private eye. He was clearly enjoying all the intrigue.

"I guess the police will want to talk to me," Elizabeth said.

"I gave them your number. They'll most likely be calling you," Boomer said. "But that's not all. I have more news."

"Isn't that enough?" Elizabeth shifted Glenda to her other shoulder. "I wonder if having former crooks as tenants will make this place harder to rent."

"Not necessarily. Families might get spooked, but businesses won't care." He grinned. "That's the news. The city council recently zoned this side of the street for limited retail business."

"Really? Do I *have* to rent to a business?"

"No. Either an individual or a business. It's

still zoned for residents, too. But you can see what direction this street is going. You'd be smart to get a thriving company in here. The city should have sent you a letter."

"I saw an official-looking piece of mail in the box today. Maybe that's it." Elizabeth took a step in the direction of the kitchen. "I'm going to grab the mail, and then I gotta go home. Glenda's overdue for her nap."

"Glenda," Boomer said, his gaze softening. "I keep forgetting you named your daughter after your meemaw."

"Yes. Meemaw would have loved her grandbaby."

Boomer's eyes misted over, and he hastily rubbed at them with the back of his hand. "Enough of that. Gotta move on. That's what I keep telling myself. If you don't let go of the old, you'll have no room for the new. Your meemaw used to say that all the time, you know."

"I remember," Elizabeth said, startled for a moment as if Meemaw had spoken through Boomer.

"A wise woman," he said. He zipped up his coat and bugged his eyes at Glenda, who let out an amused shriek. "I best be going. Nice to see you, sugar bean, and your cute little ankle-biter. Let's hope baby Glenda grows up feisty and pretty, just like her namesake."

"Thanks, Boomer."

"Sayonara," he said with a jerky salute. The screen door thwacked him in the backside on his way out.

Elizabeth laughed. "Sayonara, Boomer."

Give Satan an inch and he'll be a ruler.
—Sign outside Rock of Ages Baptist Church

CHAPTER TWENTY-TWO

"It's celebration time!" Rusty had said to Mrs. Tobias over the phone. "Put on your best stepping-out clothes."

She dressed in her funky new outfit from Chico's and gave her hair a soft curl, thinking the looser style made her look younger. If she squinted while she gazed at her reflection in her full-length bathroom mirror, she could almost imagine a forty-something woman staring back at her.

"Not too shabby for a senior citizen," Mrs.

Tobias said to herself as she heard the door-bell chime.

Rusty stood on her porch, wearing his ever-present black leather jacket. Underneath she saw a spotless white shirt and a blue silk tie.

"This *is* a special night," she remarked, touching the uneven knot of his tie. Clearly he wasn't accustomed to dressing up.

"It surely is," he said, as the two strolled to his Honda Civic parked in the drive. He opened the passenger door of his car with the flourish of a footman helping her into an elegant carriage.

Tonight they were celebrating the return of his dog, Hap. The wayward hound had finally found his way back to his master.

"There he was, sitting in my garage, when I got home yesterday afternoon," Rusty said. "Except for a few ticks and burrs, he's the same old Hap. I hope the two of you can meet soon."

"I'd be delighted," she said, tickled at the idea of being introduced to a dog. The momentary blip of distaste she'd experienced earlier that day upon seeing Rusty in his work clothes seemed silly. She relaxed into the passenger seat, listening to The Byrds on the

CD player and enjoying the pleasant weight of Rusty's arm slung over her shoulder.

Then Rusty pulled into Savoy Center, an affluent shopping center in west Augusta, and Mrs. Tobias's back stiffened.

"Where are we going?" she asked.

"The best restaurant in Augusta. Jacque's. I told you we were celebrating." Rusty reached over to squeeze her shoulder.

"Is Jacque's even open now?" Mrs. Tobias glanced at the clock on the dash. Besides the county club, Jacque's had been Harrison's favorite restaurant. When he was alive, they'd dined there at least once a week.

"Yes." Rusty went around to the passenger door to let her out of the car. "They open at five for the sunset dinner specials."

Mrs. Tobias's fingers fumbled with the latch of her seat belt. Most likely she wouldn't see anyone she knew during early-bird hours. Only prom couples and little old ladies dined at such an unfashionable time of the evening. And what if she did run into her old friends? Did she actually care what they thought? A few months after Harrison died, they'd dropped her completely. There was no place for a widow in their chummy circle of couples.

Drizzle stained the blacktop of the parking lot, so the pair sprinted from the car and ducked under the familiar black canvas awning in front of Jacque's. Rusty held open the cumbersome oak door for Mrs. Tobias and followed her inside. The two stood blinking in the foyer, adjusting to the pale light of the restaurant.

"Table for two?" asked a bored-looking hostess garbed in a short black dress.

"I had reservations. The name's Williams." Rusty's south Georgia accent sounded more pronounced than usual in the hushed, refined atmosphere of Jacque's.

The hostess didn't bother to consult her book. Reservations weren't necessary at such an early hour, and insiders knew that.

"Follow me, please." She led them all the way to the small tables in the back as Mrs. Tobias knew she would. Harrison and her group of friends used to call them the riffraff tables. Mrs. Tobias didn't mind the insult. She'd prefer to be sequestered from prying eyes, but Rusty wouldn't have any of it.

"What about those high-backed booths in the front room?" he said as the hostess indicated a minuscule round table near the flapping kitchen door. He grinned. "This is a real special night for me and my date. We've got a lot to celebrate."

Mrs. Tobias cringed at Rusty's chattiness with the hostess, which was a no-no at Jacque's. You didn't get familiar with the staff unless you were a regular, and even then there were certain boundaries that were never crossed.

"This way, please," the woman said, her young, impassive face revealing nothing.

They were seated in a booth up front and handed thick, brown menus. No frou-frou foliage, faux waterfalls, or chrome for Jacque's. The restaurant resembled an exclusive men's club with its dark wainscoting, starched linen tablecloths, and oversized leather furniture. The menu also reflected the staid sensibilities of the decor. It featured simply prepared chops, steaks, and seafood, leaving the mango tuna tartare and duck-leg confit to more adventurous establishments.

The waiter, who wore a stiff white shirt and black bow tie, approached the table. Jacque's hired male servers exclusively. The management associated waitresses with tight pink uniforms and greasy diners.

"Hey there, fellow," Rusty said. "I don't see

the sunset dinners on this menu. Am I missing something?"

The waiter's lips twisted in an unfriendly
way. "They're not on the menu, sir. The sunset dinners include a choice of roasted
chicken, broiled flounder, or a petite seven-
ounce New York steak."

"That's petite all right. Sounds more like
shrimp than a steak," Rusty joked. "None of
those dinners sound interesting. Let's just go
whole hog, Gracie, and forget these boring
sunset choices. But first I want a bottle of
champagne. This one here." He pointed at
his selection in the wine list.

"Very good, sir," the waiter said.

"You okay?" Rusty asked Mrs. Tobias after
the waiter departed.

"Fine." Mrs. Tobias spread her napkin over
her lap.

"You don't look fine," Rusty said. "Is this
place a bad choice? I know it's kind of stuffy."

She softened at his concern. Rusty was always so considerate of her. If Jacque's was
stuffy, her attitude was making it even stuffier.
What was wrong with her? Who cared what
Jacque's' uppity wait staff thought? She was
here with Rusty, a very dear man, to celebrate the return of his beloved pet.

She smiled at Rusty and felt herself loosening up just as the champagne arrived in a gleaming, silver bucket. After the waiter poured, Rusty held up his glass.

"It's meant the world to me to spend time with you these past few weeks," he said. "When Hap came home, you were the first person I wanted to tell."

They drank their champagne and gradually inched closer together in the roomy circular booth. Rusty ordered lobster and Mrs. Tobias ordered veal shanks, and they shared their entrées with each other, all the while talking and laughing.

There were so many things to discuss: music, books, art, and travel. The dark-paneled walls of Jacque's seemed to open up as they conversed. Mrs. Tobias could never remember discussing such topics with her late husband. Harrison's world was so narrow: golf at the country club, Glenlivet Scotch on the rocks, and classical music in the study.

"Would you like a nibble of my dessert?" Rusty cracked the surface of his crème brûlée with a spoon. "I can't believe you didn't order some."

"I have to watch my figure," Mrs. Tobias

said with a girlish titter. The champagne was going to her head.

"Just a taste," Rusty beseeched. She shook her head and continued to laugh.

"Why not taste it here?" Rusty touched his mouth and leaned into her.

He pressed his warm, sweet lips against hers. When he pulled away, she said in a soft voice, "You're right, Rusty. That was absolutely delicio—"

"Gracie!" a voice said. "Is that you?"

Mrs. Tobias glanced up at a woman hovering beside their booth. It was Cecilia Tobias, Harrison's mother. Beside her was her husband, Phillip. He was in his late eighties and looked even more shrunken and ancient than Mrs. Tobias remembered.

Cecilia, however, hadn't withered in the slightest. She wore a red couture suit with white piping and a matching boater hat, and her carriage was as upright as a debutante's. She took in all the details of her daughter-in-law's table with her alert green eyes.

"Mother Tobias and Mr. Tobias. What an unexpected pleasure!" Mrs. Tobias rose from the table to air-kiss Cecilia's cheek. "May I present my companion, Rusty Williams."

She continued with the introductions as Rusty struggled up from the booth, bumping his knee on the table. "Nice to meet y'all," he said.

Cecilia did not change her expression as she studied Rusty's leather jacket, her daughter-in-law's smeared lipstick, and the empty champagne bottle on the table. Her head strained from her neck like the carved face on a ship's prow.

"Delighted to meet you, Mr. Williams," she said.

Cecilia's eyes rested on Mrs. Tobias's face. "It's been far too long, Gracie. You must come and visit me."

"I agree," Mrs. Tobias said, smoothing her hair with her hand. She felt like a teenager who'd been caught necking on her parents' sofa.

"Lovely. How about tomorrow at three? I'll have Ernestine prepare a tea."

"Three o'clock? I suppose I could—"

"Good. I'll see you then," she said, turning to her husband. "Come along, Phillip. Our table is ready." She nodded at Mrs. Tobias and Rusty. "Good evening to you both."

Don't be so open-minded your brain falls out.
—From the Methodist Church bulletin

CHAPTER TWENTY-THREE

"Here comes Elizabeth," Mavis said to Attalee, who sat in the break area of the Bottom Dollar Emporium wolfing down a sausage biscuit. "She's probably feeling punk because her job didn't work out. So don't say anything about it or Mrs. Pirkle, because I don't want her even more upset." Mavis paused and considered her friend for a minute. "Matter of fact, maybe you shouldn't speak at all. Pretend you have laryngitis."

"Hey!" Attalee glowered. "Are you implying I ain't got no tact?"

Before Mavis could respond, Elizabeth bounced in the door pushing Glenda in an umbrella stroller and pulling Maybelline on her leash.

"What a beautiful morning!" Elizabeth sang out. She wore a pink velour sweat suit with a matching wool hat, and her face was lit up with a dazzling smile.

"Hmpph, if that's being punk, let me have it," muttered Attalee.

"Elizabeth you look wonderful," Mavis said, giving her a hug.

"Thanks. I'm feeling better," Elizabeth said.

"Hallelujah," Attalee said. "Considering you had to quit your you-know-what be-cause you-know-who was watching *Jerry Springer.*"

"Attalee!" Mavis said.

"I didn't say a thing," Attalee said, blinking behind her glasses.

"I'm trying to put that all behind me," Eliza-beth said. "I want to move on, and my first step is to lose some of this baby weight. I walked all the way here from my house."

"Your pooch looks a little winded," Attalee said, pointing to a panting Maybelline.

"I know," Elizabeth said. "Can I get a drink for Maybelline?"

"Of course," Mavis said, going into the restroom off the break area to fill a bowl with water.

"Have you gotten fitted for your bridesmaid's dress yet?" Attalee asked Elizabeth.

"Yes, I did. That's one reason I'm going on this diet. I looked like a big satin zeppelin when I tried it on."

Mavis returned with the water and placed it in front of Maybelline, who immediately stuck her black snout inside the bowl and started lapping it up.

"I've put Maybelline on a diet, too," Elizabeth said in a low voice. "She hates her Portly Pet dog food. She keeps spitting kibble out at my feet, but I'm hanging tough. I don't want her to have a heart attack in her prime."

"It is so nice to see you happy again, Elizabeth." Mavis knelt beside Glenda's stroller. "And I love seeing this sweet baby."

Elizabeth smiled down at Mavis. "A couple more cheek pinches, and then we've gotta

go. I need to take Maybelline back home, because Glenda and I are going to Kinder-
musik at the Methodist Church this morning."

"All right." Mavis kissed the top of
Glenda's silky head and reluctantly got up
from the floor. "Don't forget the Business
Person of the Year Banquet Saturday night."

"Wild horses couldn't keep me away. I've
already hired a baby-sitter," Elizabeth said.
"Thanks for the water, Mavis. I really have to
go now."

"So have you asked Brew to be your date
for the banquet?" Attalee asked after Elizabeth left.

"Not yet. I will tonight, though." Mavis ran a
feather duster over a shelf lined with jars of
jams and jellies.

"Where y'all going?"

"Nowhere. Just dinner at my house."

Attalee scrunched up her forehead.
"That's what you always do. Doesn't the man
ever take you out on the town?"

"He likes home cooking."

"Not much fun for you, though. 'Course,
you probably like what goes on after dinner."
Attalee grinned at Mavis. "On the sofa."

"Nothing goes on," Mavis said.

"Now Mavis. I'm your oldest friend. Spill a

little for me. What kind of kisser is he? Lots of slobber, or a desert mouth?"

"Neither. I mean, I don't know." Mavis colored. "I've never kissed him."

"Tarnation! Why not?"

"I'm not sure." She laid down her feather duster. "Maybe he's too much of a gentleman, or he's too shy. All I know is I've chewed a lot of Tic Tacs after supper for nothing."

Attalee banged the armrest of her chair with her fist. "In that case, you're just going to have to make the first move. Put a Barry White record on the hi-fi, and swoop in for the pucker."

"Oh, I don't know if I can—" Mavis's eyes widened as she glanced out the window. "Goodness, there he is. He's coming up the walk."

"I'll scoot to the back room so you can have a little privacy," Attalee said, as she scampered off. "Don't forget to ask him about the banquet."

Mavis took a quick glance at her reflection in the bottom of a copper pot hanging in the kitchenware department. Her lipstick had worn off, but there was no time to reapply it.

"Ollie, Ollie oxen free!" Brew called out as he came inside the store. "Anybody home?"

"Here I am, Brew," Mavis said, stepping into the center aisle.

Brew smiled. He wore a college sweat-shirt and blue jeans covered with plaster dust. "There's my pretty filly."

"You've been busy, I see." Mavis walked to the front of the store. "What can I do for you?"

"Just had me a yen for a Yoo-Hoo and a licorice whip. And a chat with a gorgeous woman."

Mavis laughed. "You're a caution." She slid open the glass drink cooler by the cash reg-ister and presented him with a bottle of chocolate Yoo-Hoo. "Just pick out any candy you want from the bins."

Brew twisted off the cap and took a big swig.

"Can you believe our class reunion is one week from Saturday?" he said after he'd swallowed. He swiped at a trace of chocolate mustache on his lip with his sleeve. "We sure pulled it together fast. I couldn't have done it without you."

"Thank you, Brew." She had worked hard, all that mailing and calling of former class-mates and reserving a block of rooms at the Cozy Night Inn on the Aiken-Augusta Highway. But at least she hadn't had to worry about the refreshments and decorations. Brew was handling all of that.

"There's still a few folks who haven't responded, right?" Brew asked.

"Yes," Mavis said. "I've left several messages on Connie Bradshaw's machine. She's never called me back. Hank Bryson's phone just rings and rings. And Prissy Stevens . . ."

"Yes?" Brew leaned over the checkout counter with interest.

"I've let two messages with her housekeeper. She assured me she'd passed them on to Prissy."

"Maybe you should try calling *one* more time." Brew stroked his beard.

"Brew," Mavis said, picking at the sleeve of her uniform. "About Prissy. Y'all were such an item in high school. I just wondered . . ."

"If there might still be some leftover feelings?" Brew asked.

Mavis nodded.

"Don't you fret," Brew said. "Prissy's probably got a few double chins by now. Besides, we haven't heard from her, so likely she's not even coming to the reunion." He tilted up her chin with his thumb and forefinger. "Who's my best girl now?"

"Me?" Mavis touched her collar.

"That's right, m'lady."

"So kiss her already!" came a voice from the back.

"What in Sam Hill?" Brew turned his head in the direction of the sound.

"That's Attalee," Mavis said covering her face with her hands.

"Sounds like a tempting idea," Brew said with a smile. "Under the right circumstances, of course."

"I'm sorry, Brew. Attalee is—"

He put a finger over her lips. "She's a romantic. Just like me. So, how about dinner Saturday night? Maybe then we can do something about that kiss."

"Saturday night is the Business Person of the Year Banquet at the Wagon Wheel. It starts at six," Mavis said, her eyes dropping to her shoes. "I'd love for you to be my escort."

"Oh, well, I—I'm flattered . . ."

"But?" Mavis asked. She braced herself for his refusal.

"I'd be honored to be your date," Brew said in a rush of words.

"Really?" Mavis said.

"But it would be best if I met you there. I'm

driving out to Columbia that day to buy some bathroom fixtures, and I don't want to make you late if I get delayed."

"Just come to the honoree table. I'll have a seat reserved for you," Mavis said. She felt like whooping out loud. Everybody who was anyone in Cayboo Creek would be at the banquet, and they'd all see her with Brew on her arm. They would be announcing their status as a couple to the community.

"I best be going." Brew laid down a couple of bills near the register. "See you soon."

Mavis hugged herself after he left, letting pleasant daydreams of Brew play through her mind. Then she frowned suddenly.

"Birdie," she said aloud.

"What about her?" Attalee said, stealing out from behind a wall column.

"She'll be at the banquet to photograph the winner," Mavis said. "It'll upset her to see me there with Brew. I told you what happened at the Winn-Dixie."

"Tough tamales," Attalee huffed. "She's been a real sore loser about this. Let her squirm."

"She has been difficult," Mavis said. "But my happiness over Brew is bittersweet because it comes at her expense." She glanced at Birdie's empty chair in the break room. "I miss her. I wish we could straighten this all out."

I just got lost in thought. It was unfamiliar territory.
—Bumper sticker on Taffy Polk's Trans Am

CHAPTER TWENTY-FOUR

Elizabeth was flat on the floor of her living room sweating to a Butt Blaster video when the phone rang.

"Ouch, that smarts." Her derrière muscles burned as she scrambled up from the exercise mat to answer the phone in the kitchen.

"Hello," she said trying to catch her breath.

"Did I interrupt something?" Elizabeth recognized the honeyed voice of her step-mother, Taffy Polk. "You and Timothy having yourselves a little afternoon delight?"

"No, Taffy." Elizabeth wiped the perspiration from her forehead with a hand towel. "I was just working out. Trying to burn off some baby fat."

"Hmmm. You had that baby nearly a year ago. Sounds more like *bakery* fat to me. I've seen the way you tear through biscuits and bagels."

"Could be," Elizabeth asked, anxious to do more butt-blasting before Glenda woke from her nap. "What's going on?"

"Brace yourself," Taffy said. "I have terrible news. Your uncle Ray's in the hospital. He was driving a souped-up all-terrain vehicle and flipped over a big rock. Now he's in intensive care."

"That's awful," Elizabeth said. Ray was her daddy's older brother. "How's Daddy?"

"Dwayne's all broke up. He idolizes Ray, you know. Poor thing didn't even go into work today."

Elizabeth's daddy owned the Bargain Bonanza, a rent-to-own furniture business located on the highway between Augusta and Cayboo Creek. He was known as "Insane

Dwayne" from his obnoxious television commercials.

"I'm so sorry," Elizabeth said.

"It's touch and go for Ray. Your daddy and I were planning to drive to the hospital in Dry Branch first thing in the morning, and we'd like you to come with us."

"This is so sudden," Elizabeth said. "There's the baby to consider—"

"It would mean a lot to your daddy if you went with us, considering Lanier can't go. He's still wearing his ankle bracelet and isn't allowed to leave the county."

Lanier, Elizabeth's half-brother, had the unfortunate habit of hot-wiring cars and taking them for joyrides. Currently, he was on house arrest.

"Let me see if I can find someone to look after Glenda," Elizabeth said. She didn't look forward to being cooped up in a car with her daddy and Taffy for several hours, but she felt obligated to go. Ray was her daddy's only sibling.

After hanging up with Taffy, she called Timothy at the Bait Box and told him the news.

"That's a tough break," Timothy said. "I'll

just get Ferrell to look after the shop, and I'll stay home with Glenda."

"Are you sure?" Elizabeth asked. "We'll end up staying over. You've never had the baby alone for an entire night before."

"I'm her father," Timothy insisted. "I can handle it."

Across the river, in Augusta, Mrs. Tobias stood in front of the stylish brick condominium that was now the home of Mr. and Mrs. Phillip Tobias. The senior Tobiases had recently sold their enormous clapboard-sided Queen Anne home. The twisting staircases and basketball-court-sized rooms of the mansion were now too strenuous for Harrison's father, Phillip, who had trouble walking more than a few feet. It was Mrs. Tobias's first visit to her in-laws' new residence, and she wondered how Cecilia was adjusting to her much-reduced quarters.

She rang the bell and it was answered, as usual, by Ernestine, the Tobiases' ancient housekeeper, who wore a black uniform with crisp white cuffs and matching pleated apron. Forty some years ago, when Gracie Tobias had been a young bride, Ernestine had been recruited to teach her the ins and outs of making flaky, Southern-style biscuits. Even then Ernestine had seemed old to her.

"Good afternoon, Mrs. Tobias. The missus is expecting you," Ernestine said.

Mrs. Tobias followed the housekeeper through the small foyer, noticing a silver calling-card dish by the door and freshly cut white gladiolas in a Waterford crystal vase displayed on a marble pedestal table. Apparently, Cecilia was maintaining the same level of formality she'd enjoyed in her larger home.

Ernestine paused outside a Florida room where Cecilia was seated in a cushioned wicker chair, thumbing through the latest issue of *Town and Country.*

"Mizz Tobias. Your daughter-in-law is here," announced Ernestine. She waited a moment for further instructions and when none were forthcoming, hobbled off to parts unknown in heavy orthopedic shoes.

"Gracie, how nice to see you! Would you mind if we took our tea in here? It's a bit casual for a proper tea, but the light is so beautiful."

"That's fine with me." Mrs. Tobias sat across from Cecilia and peered out the windowed room into the backyard. She spotted

Jamison, the Tobiases' longtime gardener, laying down pine straw in the flower beds. The grounds surrounding the home were so tiny she wondered how he kept busy all day. The same could also be said for Ernestine. Surely the upkeep on the small condo didn't fill a forty-hour week.

Cecilia was dressed in a grosgrain tweed suit trimmed with pink piping. Mrs. Tobias had never seen her wear slacks, even on the family's yearly excursions to Hilton Head. Her gray-blond hair was pulled back in its customary bun, held in place by a floppy pink bow.

"You take yours with lemon, right?" Cecilia asked.

Her severe hairstyle stretched her skin, making the netted planes of her face seem as taut as a painter's canvas. When Cecilia took her hair down before bed, Mrs. Tobias wondered if her face would fall along with it.

"Lemon's fine," Mrs. Tobias said just as Ernestine entered the room.

"Mail's in, ma'am," she announced.

"Put it on the sideboard, Ernestine," Cecilia said, handing Mrs. Tobias her tea in a bone china cup. "I'll sort through it later."

As Ernestine set down a thick stack of

mail, Mrs. Tobias spotted several colorful envelopes that were almost certainly invitations. Despite her advanced age, Cecilia still led an active social life, marked with luncheons, dinner parties, and charity events hosted by what Harrison used to call Augusta's "biddyocracy."

It had been a long time since Mrs. Tobias had received her own collection of invitations. After Harrison's death she was dropped from many guest lists, and when she had been invited, she'd frequently sent her regrets. These days the only Augusta functions she attended with any regularity were garden club meetings. When her grandson Timothy had married Elizabeth and moved to Cayboo Creek, she'd gotten close to the women who frequented the Bottom Dollar Emporium. With Mavis, Birdie, and Attalee, she'd found a certain earthy genuineness that had been missing from her past friendships.

"We had a lovely evening at Jacque's last night," Cecilia mused. "Although I did have to send back my scallops. They'd been overcooked." She peered at Mrs. Tobias over the top of her teacup. "How was your evening, Gracie?"

"Very nice, thank you."

"Champagne always livens up a meal."

Mrs. Tobias crossed her ankles and sighed. "Why don't we just be frank with each other, Cecilia? You're curious about my dinner companion. Isn't that why you asked me here this afternoon?"

Cecilia fingered her pearls. "I'm just looking after your best interest, dear. He was a handsome gentleman. You seemed to enjoy each other's company."

"NOKD," Mrs. Tobias said.

"Pardon me?" Cecilia asked.

"Nothing. Just something my mother used to say." Mrs. Tobias took a sip of her tea. "Please continue."

Cecilia clasped her hands together in her lap. "I admit it gave me a start to see you with another man. I suppose I shall always think of you as Harrison's wife. I'm also aware it's been several years since my son's been gone, and I don't expect you to wear your widow weeds forever. In fact, it's probably high time you found a male companion . . ." She paused for a moment. "Of the right sort."

"And Rusty didn't pass muster," Mrs. Tobias said. "What did you object to most, Cecilia? His leather jacket? His pronounced south Georgia accent?"

Cecilia reached for a macaroon from the selection of store-bought baked goods displayed on a gold-rimmed china plate on the coffee table. "A woman of your means has to be alert to fortune hunters."

"Rusty isn't like that," Mrs. Tobias said.

Cecilia cocked her head. "One can never be sure now, can they?"

"I am."

"But you're missing the most important consideration, my dear—"

"What will other people think?" Mrs. Tobias interrupted. "I'm sixty-four years old, and I no longer care what others think. Besides, I've made a new set of friends since Harrison died. They'll think Rusty is wonderful."

Cecilia fixed her pale green eyes on Mrs. Tobias's face. "That might very well be true, but the important question is what do *you* think? When I saw you with your companion last night, you looked as if you wanted to dive under the table. Can you honestly say you're comfortable with a man who is so different from yourself?"

Mrs. Tobias remembered her distaste upon first seeing Rusty in his Duct Doctor shirt.

Then there was her initial discomfort in Jacque's. A feeling of shame rushed over her.

"I suppose there have been some awkward moments, but—"

"They will only get more frequent. I can assure you of that," Cecilia said with a definitive nod of her chin.

"Forgive me, Cecilia, but how could you possibly know that?"

"I wasn't always a dried-up old woman. I've had experiences with this precise situation." Cecilia leaned in closer to Mrs. Tobias and spoke in a hushed tone. "Decades ago, before I met Phillip, I was enamored with a butcher's son. We were engaged for a time. My parents were appalled of course, but I dug in my heels and insisted I was in love.

"It was a magical time," she continued with a faint smile. "But after a while, I grew weary of his clumsiness in social settings, and he felt diminished by my family's money. Inevitably, our differences parted us. It was a painful exercise for all concerned."

"But you were so young. Maybe if you'd been older and more mature—"

"On the contrary, youth was on our side," Cecilia said. "As people get older they tend to become less tolerant and more entrenched in their identities, if they'd only admit it."

The women sat across from each other in silence, save for the clicking of Jamison's hedge clippers as he trimmed the camellia bushes outside.

"Thank you for your concern," Mrs. Tobias finally said, picking up her handbag. "I should be going."

"Sorry to see you rush off." Cecilia rose from her chair at the same moment as Mrs. Tobias did. "I've always been fond of you. That's the only reason I called you over here today."

"I understand."

She leveled her gaze at Mrs. Tobias. "Like it or not, Gracie, you are a Tobias, a name that implies wealth and privilege in this community. Why not save yourself and that handsome gentleman the unnecessary heartache that comes from a mismatched relationship?"

**Wrinkled is not one of the things I
wanted to be when I grew up.**
                    —Sign outside the Senior Center

CHAPTER TWENTY-FIVE

Mavis stood in front of the full-length mirror in her bedroom, viewing her new ruffled polka-dot dress from every angle. It was the evening of the Business Person of the Year Banquet, and tonight the winner would finally be announced.

Although she'd love to win the coveted Bizzie, she was most excited about making her first public appearance on Brew's arm. She'd spent hours fussing with her hair and perfecting her lipstick. Just before she'd slipped the new dress over her head, she'd unearthed her Aqua Bra from the bottom of her lingerie drawer and put it on.

The bra was now set to the first level of cleavage, which gave her bust a flattering fullness. Mavis couldn't help but wonder what would happen if she went to the highest level so, plunging her hand down her dècolletage, she made the necessary adjustment.

Vavavooom! She marveled at the swelling of bosom blossoming from her scoop-necked dress. Did she dare? She imagined Brew's eyes popping out from their sockets when he saw her. Chuckling to herself, she kept the cleavage at level three. She did indeed dare!

Mavis picked up her wool shawl from the bed and wrapped it around her shoulders, imagining Brew's strong arms around her. Tonight would be the night he'd kiss her for the very first time. She could feel it in the air.

After one more glance in the mirror, she left the house and drove to the site of the banquet. When she pulled into the parking lot of the Wagon Wheel, Mavis noticed a commotion in front of the restaurant. She teetered up the sidewalk in her high-heeled pumps and saw Prudee Phipps, wearing a full-length evening dress, standing on a "red carpet"—actually a long, fuzzy burgundy bath mat—greeting people as they came through the door. Mavis had forgotten that the chamber of commerce was adopting an Academy Awards theme for the event.

"Here comes one of our nominees now," Prudee said, into a Mr. Microphone. "Mavis Loomis, owner of the Bottom Dollar Emporium. Hi, Mavis. You look dressed to the nines. Who are you wearing tonight?"

"Who?" Mavis said, in a perplexed voice.

"Your dress. Where'd you get it?" Prudee prompted.

"Oh. This is a Lane Bryant creation." Mavis twirled for the onlookers while Mello Vickery, president of the chamber, peered through a disposable camera and took her photograph.

"And your jewels?" Prudee asked.

Mavis tugged on her silver-plated earrings. "Goodie's, maybe? Or was it Target?"

"I got the cutest broach at Target the other day," Prudee said. "And it was seventy percent off."

"Prudee, here comes another nominee," Mello said. Prudee hurried over to Jerry

Sweeny with his date, Reeky Flynn, on his arm. Mavis went inside the restaurant just as the taxidermist told Prudee that he was wearing Sears khakis and a shirt from the Boots and Spurs Palace.

Once inside the restaurant, Mavis was greeted by Chiffon, who was passing out name tags and directing people to the Sirloin Banquet Room.

"You look gorgeous tonight," Chiffon said, handing Mavis a name tag with a red ribbon affixed to it to signify her status as a nominee.

"We don't see much of you at the store anymore," Mavis said.

"I know," Chiffon said, blowing her bangs out of her face. "My photography business is running me ragged. I miss everyone."

"We miss you, too. Chiffon, my escort should be arriving any minute. Will you direct him to the honoree table?"

"Escort?"

"An old classmate of mine," Mavis said. "He's tall, dark, and bearded. His name is Brewster Clark." She experienced a tingle of pleasure just saying his name aloud.

"I can't wait to meet him," Chiffon said. "I'm doing freelance photography for the newspaper tonight, so I'll take a picture of the two of you together."

If Chiffon was taking photographs for the *Crier* maybe Birdie wouldn't show up at the banquet at all. Her absence could be a blessing. If Birdie saw her old friend was out on a date with Brew, it would just strengthen their dreadful feud.

Chiffon led her to her seat at the honoree table, which had an empty place next to it reserved for Brew. Mavis was the first nominee to arrive, and she felt conspicuously alone at the big round table. Luckily, moments after she sat down, Reeky and Jerry joined her.

Reeky wore a simply cut royal-blue dress that made her pale skin appear translucent in the soft candlelight of the table. Jerry was his usual rangy self, in cowboy boots and a Western shirt.

"I'm so proud of Jerry for his nomination," Reeky said, clinging to his bicep. Jerry owned the Stuff and Mount Taxidermy Shop. "He deserves it for all the work he does on the Christmas parade."

"Behind every good man is a loving woman," Jerry said, squeezing her hand. "Reeky's been taking a real interest in the art of taxidermy. She finished her first piece this week."

"It was just a squirrel," Reeky said with a modest dip of her head.

"Yes, darling," cooed Jerry. "But you've got a real eye for detail. I half expect that critter to wriggle its nose. Next she's taking on a beaver."

"How are things at the Book Nook, Reeky?" Mavis asked. "I keep meaning to stop in and get the new Nora Roberts."

"Awful." Reeky pushed her glasses farther up her pointed nose. "The new Harry Potter is out, and the Baptists are in an uproar." She glanced at the empty place beside Mavis. "Who's sitting there?"

"My date, Brewster Clark. He's new to town." Mavis consulted her watch. "He said he might be running a little late."

Jewel Turner, wearing a green dress that emphasized her considerable curves, sat down next to Jerry.

"I just announced to everyone on the red carpet that I got my dress from Goodwill Industries," Jewel said with a scowl. "I bet that never happens to Nicole Kidman."

"There's no shame there," Mavis said. "The Goodwill carries lots of nice, name-brand things. Congratulations on your nomination, Jewel. The Chat 'N' Chew's done so well since you've taken over."

"Thanks, Mavis," Jewel said, still flustered by her interview on the red carpet. "I should have worn a sign on my back that says 'My other dress is a Versace.'"

Dun Woo from the House of Noodles sat down at the nominee table, as did Boomer from the butcher shop. All the places were now occupied except for Brew's. A waitress approached Mavis and asked, "Will you be needing this seat, ma'am? One of the other tables is short."

Mavis dropped her pocketbook on the chair. "Sorry, it's taken. My guest should be here any moment now."

Attalee and Mrs. Tobias arrived and stopped by the honoree table.

"We're so proud of you, Mavis. In honor of this auspicious occasion, we'd like to present you with a little gift," Mrs. Tobias said, handing her a wrapped package. "It's from all the Bottom Dollar Girls, Attalee, Birdie, Elizabeth, and myself."

"Birdie?" Mavis said in a hopeful voice.

"She pitched in before the two of you started fussing," Attalee said, surveying the table. "Where's Brew? In the little boy's room?"

"He said he might be late." Mavis tore open the package and gasped when she examined the contents. "An Elvis print! I'm a huge fan. Y'all were so sweet to do this."

"You're welcome, Mavis," Mrs. Tobias said, taking a small sideways step to get out of the path of a waitress with a large tray. "It looks like they're starting to serve. We should go back to our seat, Attalee."

Mrs. Tobias started in the direction of her table, but then suddenly turned back to Mavis. "I almost forgot. Elizabeth called on her way to Dry Branch. She told me to say 'good luck' and that she wishes she could be here with you."

"I hope her uncle's going to be okay," Mavis said. Then, after Attalee and Mrs. Tobias went to their table, she trained her eyes on the door. Any minute Brew would come sauntering through it.

An iceberg lettuce salad with a tomato chunk and ranch dressing was placed in front of her, but there was still no sign of her date. A few minutes later, the next course, a hamburger steak and a side of string beans, was left untouched as Mavis kept glancing at her wristwatch.

After a dessert of lemon meringue pie arrived, Birdie strutted over to the honoree table with her camera and started snapping pictures.

"Smile wide, all of you nominees. Your picture's going to be in the paper," she said, avoiding Mavis's eyes.

"Where's Chiffon?" Reeky asked. "I thought she was taking photos tonight."

"Her youngest daughter's running a temperature, so she got called away," Birdie said. "Dun Woo, could you scoot over a smidge? I'm just getting your left ear in my viewfinder. That's perfect."

"I think I blinked in that last one," Jewel said after Birdie took a few photos.

"It's okay. I've got several good shots," Birdie said. "Good luck all." Her eyes rested briefly on Mavis. "I hope you get exactly what you deserve."

The dishes were cleared away from the tables, and Mello Vickery, who was mistress of ceremonies, had taken her place at the podium. Mavis had quit staring at the door and was now tugging distractedly at the fringe on her shawl. *Where was he?* She didn't know whether to be worried or angry. At this point she just wanted the evening to be over with so she could crawl under her bedcovers and hide from the world.

Get it over with already, she thought as Mello droned on about how all of the nominees deserved to win. Personally, Mavis thought Dun Woo was a shoo-in. When chamber meetings ran long, he'd always brought the attendees free cartons of chow mein.

Just before the announcement was made, Prudee appeared at Mavis's elbow. "A friend of yours named Brewster Clark just called," she whispered. "He said he got stuck in Columbia with a flat tire, and he apologizes for missing your big night. He said, and I quote, 'Knock 'em dead, gorgeous. Hugs and kisses, Brew.'"

"Kisses?" Mavis said. "He said kisses?"

Prudee nodded and Mavis touched her lips. It wasn't a real kiss, but it was almost as good.

"And the Bizzie goes to . . ." Mello said, pausing as she pulled off the wax seal affixed to a long white envelope. "Mavis

Loomis, owner and operator of the Bottom Dollar Emporium."

"Hot damn!" Attalee shouted out from across the room. Mavis was so startled she sat motionless in her seat, blinking with surprise.

"Go on and get your award," Jewel whispered to her. Mavis stood on unsteady legs and advanced to the podium, where Mello gave her a gold-plated statuette of a figure holding a briefcase, the coveted Bizzie.

"This is so unexpected," Mavis stuttered, standing too close to the microphone, causing it to squeal. She backed away, startled, and Mello made a minor adjustment and indicated for Mavis to continue.

"There's so many people to thank," Mavis said in a quavering voice. "Elizabeth Hollingsworth, who helped save the Bottom Dollar Emporium from bankruptcy. My soda jerk and right-hand woman, Attalee Gaines."

A piercing wolf whistle came from Attalee's table.

"I'm also grateful to the rest of the Bottom Dollar Girls, and to all the people of Cayboo Creek who have supported the Bottom Dollar Emporium all of these years," Mavis said.

She paused for a moment, her cheeks warming at the thought of Brew calling her gorgeous. Although he wasn't with her in body, he was definitely there in spirit.

"And finally," she said, the words spilling out as if they had a momentum of their own, "thanks to my new, dear friend Brewster Clark, who just makes me feel special. Thanks so much."

Mavis held up her award for the crowd and returned to her seat to enthusiastic applause. As soon as she reached her table, people crowded around her, offering their congratulations.

"Make way for the press," Birdie said, maneuvering her way through the crush of well-wishers until she reached Mavis's side.

"Mrs. Loomis," Birdie said, her head bent over her reporter's notebook, not looking at Mavis. "How do you feel at this moment?"

"I'm surprised, of course," Mavis began. "It's hard to say how I feel."

"Elated?" Birdie offered, and then she looked up from her pad and glared at Mavis with cold blue eyes. "Or maybe you have mixed emotions," she said in a much lower voice meant for Mavis alone. "Like shame or humiliation, seeing how you made a spectacle of yourself up there."

"Birdie?" Mavis glanced nervously around. No one seemed to have heard her comments. "This isn't the time or place."

"Where do you see yourself in the next five years?" Birdie asked. "Not with Brewster Clark," she continued in a ragged whisper. "I can assure you of that. He's just being polite to you. You're going to be a laughingstock if you keep this up."

"Why are you doing this?" Mavis whispered back. *If anyone's going to be a laughingstock it will be you,* she wanted to retort, but she choked back the unkind words. Her old friend was clearly going off the deep end, first luring Brew to her house with phony repair jobs and now trying to shame Mavis into breaking off with her new beau.

"Birdie, please calm down," Mavis continued. "I shouldn't have publicly thanked Brew. It upset you, and I apologize. I just got carried away with the moment."

She tried to touch her friend's shoulder, but Birdie dodged out of reach. In the process, Mavis's shawl slid from her shoulders to the restaurant floor. People around were starting to notice the unfolding drama.

"I think your emotions are getting in the way of your sense of fair play," Mavis said, leaning down to pick up her shawl.

With an open mouth, Birdie wheeled around to face her friend. When she looked down and saw Mavis's level-three cleavage, her eyes narrowed to slits, and she pointed her fountain pen at Mavis.

"How dare you talk to me about fair play when you sashay around here like a *Playboy* bunny?" Birdie said.

Suddenly conversation in the room ceased, and all eyes were on Birdie and Mavis.

The next incident—which would be told and retold for weeks afterward in the diners and barber shops of Cayboo Creek— seemed to happen in slow motion. Attalee emerged from the depths of the crowd of on-lookers, jostling Birdie in the process. Birdie tipped forward, losing her footing, the pen still grasped in her hand. It made an arch in the air, and like a guided missile, zeroed in on its target.

"It reminded me of a raft springing a leak," recalled Jerry Sweeny much later as he related the tale on his favorite stool in the Chat 'N' Chew.

"It was like a fountain, just spewing water," Jewel Turner said, the day after, to the teller while cashing a check at the credit union.

The moment would be played over and over in Mavis's head as she twitched and groaned under her electric blanket later that evening. With a sickening despair, she knew that no one in town would ever forget the night that Mavis Loomis sprung a leak in her Aqua Bra.

To you it's a six-pack. To me it's a support group.
—Bumper sticker on Dwayne Polk's pickup truck

CHAPTER TWENTY-SIX

As Mary Chapin Carpenter wailed, "Sometimes you're the windshield, sometimes you're the bug" over Taffy's car radio, Elizabeth was feeling a kinship with the bug.

The family had traveled only ten miles out of Cayboo Creek when Elizabeth's daddy and Taffy started a squabble over which radio station to listen to. Dwayne wanted Metal Rock 107, because it interrupted songs like "Highway to Hell" with regular NASCAR updates.

When Dwayne changed the channel during the song "Strong Enough to Be Your Man," Taffy screeched, "That was Travis Tritt, you nitwit," and twisted the knob back to KIX Country. Currently Taffy was winning the battle of the airwaves, and was twanging along to her country songs in an off-key voice.

Elizabeth tried to block out her family's bickering by staring out the backseat window at the passing landscape, but the highway out of Cayboo Creek wasn't particularly scenic. She had already counted seven businesses selling manufactured homes—all with flapping banners advertising liquidation sales—and five car lots.

As they traveled closer to the coast, the land gradually flattened out and became more rural, but not necessarily prettier. Rundown farmhouses, bristling with lightning rods, were plunked in the middle of scrubby fields. A handmade cardboard sign advertised "Collards, sweet potatoes, and boiled peanuts, three miles ahead." Barren trees, choked with trails of dead kudzu, stood in stark relief against the diluted gray sky.

"It's the Prize Pack!" screeched Taffy, her lacquered blond hair barely stirring as she bounced up and down in her seat. "We can win the entire Toby Keith CD catalog if we're the fifth caller. Where's the dang cell phone?"

Dwayne unhooked his phone from his belt and handed it to his wife, but Taffy couldn't get through to the station in time.

"I'll keep this phone from now on," she snapped at Dwayne.

"Those contests are always rigged anyway. The station manager's daughter probably won it," Dwayne said, changing the radio station just as Classic Rock 107 announced the beginning of their Hairball Weekend. The band Twisted Sister screamed, "We're Not Going to Take It Anymore."

After ninety minutes on the road, Taffy and Dwayne were more listless than combative.

"Florence, S.C." Taffy yawned while reading a billboard. "Home of Maytag Appliances." She emitted a loud snort and her head lolled against the window. Dwayne, his camouflage hunting hat low on his head, made a whistling sound through his nose.

"Daddy, you awake?" Elizabeth asked with alarm.

"I'm as alert as a pit bull guarding a ham

bone," Dwayne responded, rolling down the window and spitting. "Look ahead, it's the first of the Sparky's signs."

Taffy jolted awake. "Sparky's? Can we stop, Dwayne?"

"I suppose so. I wouldn't mind picking up a gift for Ray," he replied.

Sparky's was an enormous roadside store on Highway 501 just outside of Dry Branch. According to the Day-Glo orange signs that were posted every few miles, Sparky's had it all, from live hermit crabs to fireworks to pecan logs.

Taffy grew more excited with every passing sign.

"Exotic seashells," she said, reading the latest one. "Dwayne, we're so close to Myrtle Beach. It's a shame we can't have a mini holiday."

"Don't forget what this trip is about," Dwayne said in a solemn voice. "Ray may be darkening death's door, and you're thinking about beach vacations."

Taffy slid down her seat and sulked for a while after her husband's admonishment, but perked right up when she saw the next Sparky's sign.

"Saltwater taffy!" she shouted out.

After twenty miles and several more signs, Sparky's was finally in sight and even Elizabeth was antsy with anticipation. As soon as Dwayne parked the car, the trio tumbled out onto the blacktop pavement outside the store and headed for the entrance.

Sparky's was stuffed with the usual touristy junk: seashell nightlights, painted coconuts, and rock candy.

Dwayne chuckled over a display of fossilized shark droppings. "Ray will get a big kick out of this," he said.

Taffy rolled her eyes and said, "You're going to give petrified poop to a dying man?"

"I'll give it to him when he's better," Dwayne said, his black eyes flashing. "And don't say he's dying. You don't know Ray. He's strong as a bull."

Taffy meandered away from Dwayne to consider a display of pickled Vidalia onions and hot sauces of various strengths. Elizabeth went into the sweets department to buy a package of peanut brittle for Timothy.

After she made her purchase she wandered around the store, looking over the bins filled with sand dollars, conch shells, and shark's teeth, until Taffy grabbed her elbow and said, "Come help me tear your daddy away from the firecrackers."

She followed Taffy to a large room spilling over with fireworks packaged in bright, cheery colors usually reserved for children's toys.

"This is creepy," Elizabeth remarked. "You could blow up half of South Carolina with this stuff."

"I think that's what your daddy intends," Taffy said. "Or, at the very least, a sectional sofa."

Dwayne liked his explosives. As a gimmick, he blew up various pieces of furniture on his television commercials to advertise his rent-to-own business.

When they reached him, Dwayne was talking to a short man with a droopy gray mustache.

"How much is this one?" Dwayne asked, pointing his thumb in the direction of a large, round package the size of a bicycle tire.

Taffy read the label. "Dwayne, what on God's green earth would you do with sixteen thousand cherry bombs? Haven't you blown up enough things?"

"I'm getting it for the boy," he said. "Lanier

gets bored sitting around the house all day with that ankle bracelet."

"Then he shouldn't steal people's cars," Taffy said. "He's spoiled rotten through and through."

Dwayne ignored her and addressed the salesman. "Cherry bombs *are* kind of limiting. How much for that Genghis Khan variety pack?"

"Only $299," said the salesman. "But you also get the mushroom-cloud assortment free with purchase."

Taffy seized her husband's arm and yanked him out of the room.

"What the—" Dwayne snarled.

"The last thing your son needs is explosives," Taffy said. "If you have to get him something, buy him some champagne poppers or a box of sparklers."

"Those are wuss fireworks," Dwayne grumbled, but he allowed her to lead him out of the store.

The trio got back in the car and proceeded down the highway to Dry Branch, which was only ten miles away.

"What's the name of that hotel we're staying at?" Taffy asked.

"The Presidential," Dwayne said.

"Sounds fancy." Taffy put on a pair of pink-tinted sunglasses. "You think they might have some cute antique shops in Dry Branch?"

"This isn't a shopping spree, Taff," Dwayne said with a grunt.

"Geeze Louise, I'm just asking." Taffy pulled down the mirror on the visor and reapplied a coat of bright red lipstick.

"We're here." Elizabeth pointed to a sign and read it aloud: "Dry Branch is a great place to live."

"Let's hope so, for Ray's sake," Taffy said, teasing her bangs with a comb.

"Can I borrow your cell phone?" Elizabeth asked. "I want to tell Timothy we arrived safely."

Taffy handed her the phone and Elizabeth dialed the number, feeling a pang of concern when it rang seven times without anyone picking up.

Finally, on the eighth ring, Timothy answered.

"What are you doing? I was beginning to think you were out," Elizabeth said.

"No, we're right here," Timothy said. "Having a blast."

"What are you doing?"

"Bonding. Daddy-and-daughter time. It's great."

"Good for you. I just wanted to let you know we're now entering Dry Branch." She shifted the phone to her other ear. "Everything's going okay then?"

"Hon. You've only been gone . . . what? Four hours? Of course everything's okay." He paused. "When are you coming back?"

"Late tomorrow. We'll probably spend the whole day at the hospital. Kiss Glenda for me, and I'll talk to you soon. Love ya."

"Love ya, too," Timothy said.

Elizabeth glanced out the window, looking for familiar landmarks. She'd been to Dry Branch several times as a child to visit her uncle and she used to explore the town with her cousin Dorrie, who was the same age as Elizabeth. Dorrie was something of an anomaly in the Polk family. Instead of getting married and having a couple of babies after high school, she'd studied law and was now a practicing attorney in Atlanta.

"Don't know why she went traipsing off to school for seven years when she could have had a perfectly decent job in Dry Branch," Uncle Ray had said after she left. He owned Co-Zee Heating and Air Company and had hoped Dorrie would be his secretary.

"Do you think Dorrie will be here?" Elizabeth said. She hoped to see her, even though she knew she'd feel something of a failure around her ambitious cousin.

"Why wouldn't she?" Dwayne said. "She's lived here for going on two or three years now."

"What? I thought she lived in Buckhead." Elizabeth poked her head between Taffy and her daddy's seat. Buckhead was a moneyed area of Atlanta.

"She did, but then she married a local boy, and they set up housekeeping in Dry Branch," said Dwayne. "Seems to me Ray said she's got a young 'un now."

"Are you sure?"

During Elizabeth's rare visits, Dorrie had always insisted that as soon she graduated high school she was going to wipe the red clay of Dry Branch off her Keds and never come back.

"Sure as spitting," Dwayne said, easing on the brakes as they passed a thirty-five-mile speed limit sign.

The interior of the car alternately darkened and lightened as the sun slipped through the pine trees. Elizabeth was trying to imagine her tomboy cousin with a child. Dorrie had never cared for dolls and once when she got a Barbie for Christmas, she gave the fashion doll a buzz cut, dressed her in trousers, and stuck her behind the wheel of a Tonka truck.

"This town is a pit," Taffy frowned as she stared out the window.

They passed a rusting trailer where a speckled hound howled in the dirt yard. Old hulks of cars slumbered underneath an oak tree, and sunlight bounced off a row of bullet-shaped propane tanks. Dwayne had to swerve to avoid an old sofa that was turned on its side and spilling its innards of springs and foam onto the road.

"We're getting into the commercial section now." Dwayne flipped down his visor to shade his eyes from the midday sun.

They passed E-Z Tax service, a Super 10 store, and a unisex salon. A dingy, windowless building advertised itself as Sister Soul Food Diner.

"They serve some darn good country-fried steak as I recall," Dwayne said.

Taffy lowered her sunglasses and peered at the small restaurant. "*You* eat there. I'm not getting citronella poisoning."

"Salmonella," he corrected. "And that place is so clean you could eat off the floor."

"I only eat in chain restaurants; you know that, Dwayne," Taffy said. "But I bet there isn't an Olive Garden within miles of this country-bumpkin town."

"Sandpit Road," Dwayne said, noting a street sign in front of a rusting tin water tower. "That's where me and Ray had that run-in with a wild boar."

Elizabeth's daddy sat up straight in his seat, looking about with interest. When he'd struck it rich with his rent-to-own business several years back, he bought a patio home in a fashionable gated community in Augusta. But Elizabeth knew Dwayne was still a small-town Southern boy to his marrow, feeling most at home in tiny hamlets with dirt roads, smoky roadhouses, and family-owned meat-and-three cafes, the "three" standing for the slow-cooked vegetables that always accompanied the entrée on the plate.

Taffy yawned. "I hope the Presidential has

an in-room Jacuzzi. I want to soak some of this road dust off of me."

"It's supposed to be on the main thoroughfare," Dwayne said. "Must be a brand-new motel, because it wasn't here three years ago when I visited Ray."

They passed a Hardee's, a barbecue place called the Big Pig, and a Bumper-to-Bumper auto parts. Beyond the cluster of businesses was a light-studded arrow with the word "motel" on it. The arrow pointed to a row of dilapidated mint-green cinder-block units with an empty, cracked kidney-shaped pool set in concrete out front. Faded letters painted on the building identified the place as the "Heart of Dry Branch Motor Inn."

"Heck, if we're in the heart of Dry Branch, I hate to see its nether parts," Taffy said with a grimace. "I wonder who'd stay in such a dumpy—"

"Here it is, the Presidential." Dwayne swung the car into the lot of the motor court. He tugged on his chin. "Funny. This place don't look brand new." Then he pointed to a portable curbside sign with letters that spelled out, "Presidential Inn. Under new management."

"Oh, new *management*," Dwayne said, reading the sign. "And they changed the name."

"Dwayne, I wouldn't let my roaches stay here," Taffy said, glaring at the building with narrowed eyes. "Although I'm sure they'd find plenty of their friends around."

"They're advertising free color TV," Dwayne remarked. "Doesn't look so bad to me."

"Yes it does!" Taffy and Elizabeth said in unison.

"Well, let me go to the office." Dwayne opened the car door and swung his legs out. "I'll cancel my reservation and see if they can't suggest some other place to stay."

"I'll go with you." Taffy emerged from the car, tying a red scarf over her hair. "Clearly you're not capable of making our lodging decisions."

"Wait for me," Elizabeth said as she unbuckled her seat belt.

The only other car in the parking lot was a primer-paint-gray El Camino with a Hefty bag billowing from its passenger window.

"Classy clientele," Taffy remarked.

The three trudged to the office, only to see a note affixed to the flimsy wooden door that said "Motel guests, please check in at pawn shop across the street."

"This is just getting better and better," Taffy said as they crossed the two-lane road. The pawn shop, a square building with barred windows, was called "Quick Silver Pawn and Bail Bonds."

They pushed open the door and entered the dimly lit shop. A dark-haired woman was reading a John Grisham paperback behind a glass display counter filled with watches, jewelry, and an assortment of small electronics. A curly-haired toddler tugged at her sleeve, saying. "Mama, Mama?"

"I want to cancel my motel reservation," Dwayne said, holding his cap with both hands.

The woman reached for a battered book underneath the counter. "Was it an hourly, nightly, or weekly reservation?"

Dwyane chuckled deep from his chest. "You hear that, Taff?" He winked at her. "They take hourly reservations."

"That ain't funny, Dwayne Polk," Taffy said.

The woman looked up from her work for the first time and squinted at him. "Uncle Dwayne? Is that you?" She stood up and smoothed the front of her denim maternity dress. "I'm your niece, Dorrie. And, oh my lord, is that Elizabeth standing behind you?"

"Dorrie?" Elizabeth said, a puzzled look crossing her face. She had a hard time reconciling this very pregnant woman with the sharp-featured, gangly-legged tomboy of her childhood.

"I know. I'm a lot wider around, and I don't have that Prince Valiant haircut anymore, but it's me, Dorrie." She darted from behind the counter and drew Elizabeth into an embrace. "I haven't seen you since we were kids."

The toddler scampered after her and raised his chubby hands, saying, "Up! Up!" Dorrie mussed his curls and hefted him into her arms. "This is my boy, Toby."

"What are you doing here in Dry Branch?" Elizabeth said, after she'd introduced Taffy to Dorrie.

"I live here now," Dorrie said. "Moved from Atlanta three years ago."

"Oh," Elizabeth said.

"I think what Elizabeth meant is what are you doing in this here pawn shop?" Taffy said, looking around with distaste. "We heard you were a fancy-pants lawyer."

That was exactly what Elizabeth had meant. Leave it to Taffy to cut to the chase.

Dorrie laughed. "I don't work here. This is my husband Skip's business. His regular help didn't show, and he had to run out to make a bank deposit. I'm just looking after things until he gets back."

"Skip Mahoney? Baloney-breath Mahoney?" Elizabeth said.

"I don't call him that anymore," Dorrie said with a laugh. "Now I just call him honey."

"You and baloney-breath Mahoney are husband and wife?" Elizabeth asked with disbelief. "You used to throw pinecones at him. You put fire ants in his swim trunks."

"It was all just foreplay," her cousin said, a mischievous glint to her eyes, and Elizabeth finally recognized a glimpse of the old Dorrie from her girlhood. "But whatever you do, don't tell him about the fire ants. Skip never knew it was me. He thought it was Paulie Simmons, and to this day he still snubs Paulie when he sees him at the driving range."

"So this is Skip's place?" Elizabeth said.

"This place, the Presidential across the street, and the Party-Time Liquor store next door," Dorrie said, unpeeling Toby's hand from her cheek. "Skip's like the Donald Trump of Dry Branch."

"I'd figured you'd be out at the hospital with your mama," Dwayne said.

"I was up there this morning. Ray's still in a coma," Dorrie said. Ray was Dorrie's stepfather, and they weren't especially close. Her real father died when Dorrie was just two.

"We're going to head out to the hospital ourselves," Dwayne said. "About them motel reservations—"

"Considered them canceled. Our customers are mainly migrant and construction workers who stay by the week." Dorrie picked up a nearby phone book and leafed through it. "You'd probably be more comfortable in a chain. There's a Sleep Cheap Inn, about five miles away on Frontage Road. It's not the Waldorf-Astoria, but their rooms are clean, and they offer a free continental breakfast. I'll make a reservation for you.

"I'll see you later on, Elizabeth, and we'll catch up," Dorrie said after she'd made the reservation.

Dwayne followed Dorrie's directions to Marion County Medical Center, a hospital that serviced Dry Branch and several other small towns in the county. They were directed to the intensive-care waiting room, where they found Georgia, Ray's wife, snoozing on a molded plastic chair.

Georgia startled when she saw them standing over her.

"Dwayne!" she cried, clutching his shirt and pulling him toward her. She threw her arms around his knees and started sobbing. Dwayne, who wasn't used to such emotional displays, awkwardly patted her head as if she were a pet German shepherd.

She finally released Dwayne, leaving behind an orange pancake makeup stain on his jeans.

"I'm Dwayne's wife, Taffy." With a stiff arm, Taffy held out a two-foot-long pecan log. "Sorry to have to meet you at such a troubling time, Georgia."

Georgia dumped Taffy's gift into the chair beside her and said, "I don't know why you can't smoke in this darn place."

"Where's the doctor?" Dwayne asked.

"He was just in here," Georgia said. "Ray's the same. Just lying there like a lump. Doctor says he don't know when or if Ray will snap out of it."

She started crying again, and Elizabeth knelt to comfort her, offering her tissues from a cellophane package in her purse.

The Polks kept Georgia company in the waiting room for the rest of the day, occasionally slipping off to the hospital cafeteria for a cup of coffee or a slice of pie. Skip and Dorrie dropped by briefly, just as the streetlights outside the hospital window winked on. After they left, a stiff-legged Dwayne rose from his chair and said it was time to get checked into the motel.

The plan was to return to the hospital the next morning, and then head back to Cayboo Creek around noon.

"Ain't a thing I can do for old Ray," Dwayne said in a mournful voice as they stood in the brightly lit lobby of the Sleep Cheap Inn, waiting for room keys. "But I wanted to be here for Georgia at least."

The next morning, alert from hot showers and a hasty breakfast of coffee and apple Danishes, the Polk family returned to the intensive-care ward.

During the evening, a seventeen-year-old boy had been seriously injured in a car accident, and his large, boisterous family was sprawled around the waiting room, making it their own. A portable playpen had been set up in the middle of the room; coolers filled with sandwiches and soft drinks were strewn over the floor; and a set of false teeth floated in a cloudy glass of water. Everyone in the family, except for a child in diapers, had a cell phone.

Georgia was scrunched up against a wall, wrapped in a patchwork quilt, burrito-style, watching the scene around her with puffy-eyed dismay and jumping every time the theme from *Batman* or the latest 50-Cent song blasted from a cell phone.

Close to noon, after Dwayne had made several guilty references to shoving off, an unshaven doctor in a rumpled white coat strolled into the room. The waiting area, which had been as lively as a block party, went silent. Even the toddler, who'd been pushing his toy corn popper back and forth across the floor, stood motionless and looked up at the doctor with wary brown eyes.

"Good news, Mrs. Polk," said the doctor. "It looks like your husband Ray is coming out of his coma."

A middle-aged woman with mascara-streaked cheeks rushed to the doctor's side.

"What about our Steven? Is there any news about him?"

"I'm sorry. Your son's condition is unchanged," the doctor said.

Both Dwayne and Georgia followed the doctor into Ray's room, while Elizabeth and Taffy flipped through a stack of outdated magazines. After a few minutes, a smiling Dwayne returned, saying, "Ray blinked at me. I says 'Ray, if you recognize your baby brother, give me a sign.' Then he blinked twice, clear as day."

The Polks decided to stay in Dry Branch one more night to see if Ray's condition improved. Elizabeth called Timothy to see how he was managing.

"Everything's great here," Timothy said. "Take as many nights as you need. Ferrell's been handling things at work."

"Don't forget," Elizabeth said. "Great-grandma Tobias could always lend a hand with Glenda. And if you need a break, either Mavis or Chiffon would probably be willing to—"

"I'm her father," Timothy said abruptly. "I don't need any help."

The Polks stayed at the hospital another full day and finally left around seven to eat ribs and hash at the Big Pig barbecue restaurant. Then they returned to the hotel, and Elizabeth fell asleep watching a Monty Python movie on HBO. She was startled awake by a knock at her door. The digital clock on the lamp table said it was five o'clock in the morning.

"Elizabeth, it's your daddy," said a voice in the hall. She slipped into her robe and opened the door to her father, whose face was gray from shock.

"Ray's dead. Georgia just called. We need to go see her."

After dressing and running a comb through her hair, Elizabeth met Taffy and her daddy in the lobby of the hotel and they all drove to the hospital.

"The doctor says he didn't feel a thing," Georgia sniffed into a wadded tissue after they'd joined her in the hospital cafeteria. "I thought he was going to pull through."

Dwayne took solace in the fact that Ray had regained consciousness before he'd died. "Least he knew his little brother was there for him at his darkest hour," he kept repeating.

After arranging for a funeral home to pick up the body, the family went back to Georgia's house to discuss future plans. There'd be no coffin; Ray had asked to be cremated and have his ashes thrown in the Atlantic Ocean at the Grand Strand in Myrtle Beach.

Elizabeth called Timothy to tell him about this latest development.

"What's wrong?" Elizabeth asked when he picked up the phone. "You're all out of breath."

"Nothing!" he snapped. "Everything's fine. Don't you trust me?"

"Course I do," Elizabeth said. She heard a muffled wailing sound in the background. "Is that Glenda crying?"

"Glenda is as happy as a lark," Timothy said quickly.

"The reason I was calling is that I'll probably have to stay a couple more days. My uncle Ray died."

The line went dead silent for a moment.

"Timothy, are you there?"

"Yeah, I'm, uh, just in shock about your uncle. Are you all right?"

"Yes. It's very sad, particularly for Daddy and Aunt Georgia, but Uncle Ray and I weren't that close. Still, I think I should stay for the funeral. Are you sure you're going to be able to handle things?"

"I said I would, didn't I? There's nothing to this," he said, but his voice sounded tired and thin. "How many more nights did you say?"

"I'm not certain. No more than three at the very most. Are you sure you can manage? If you can't, I'll rent a car and—"

"Of course not," Timothy interrupted. "Glenda and I will wait for you to come home."

Too many freaks. Not enough circuses.
—Sign on the bulletin board of the Bottom Dollar
Emporium

CHAPTER TWENTY-SEVEN

Mrs. Tobias sat at a booth in a pool hall, sipping a glass of sweet iced tea, while Rusty shared a pitcher of beer with his friends, Sheila and Larry.

"Rusty, are you sure your old lady doesn't want a mug of beer? There's plenty to go around," Larry said, wiping a white line of foam from his upper lip. He was pale and fleshy, with a few strands of hair combed over an age-spotted pate.

"Gracie doesn't drink beer." Rusty slipped

a protective arm around Mrs. Tobias's shoulder. "She's more of a champagne kind of gal."

"Go ahead. Take yourself a swig. Miller's the champagne of beers," Sheila said with a hacking laugh, recklessly waving her cigarette about. She bared a set of yellow teeth, the color of margarine.

Mrs. Tobias smiled, but felt miserable. Why had she let Rusty drag her to this unpleasant place? When he told her he wanted to teach her how to shoot pool, she'd balked initially. Bowling was one thing, but pool? Weren't pool halls dangerous places teeming with unsavory characters? Rusty persisted, claiming that pool halls had changed for the better over the years. "It's a family activity now, wholesome as mother's milk," he'd said. "And they're not called pool halls anymore, they're billiard parlors."

He'd finally worn her down, and they'd driven to Chalky's on the Aiken-Augusta highway. A tournament was in full swing, and every pool table was taken.

Rusty turned to leave, and Mrs. Tobias was grateful. *Family activity, my foot,* she thought as glanced around at Chalky's patrons. Nobody in *her* family had tattoos or wore trousers so low they barely covered their bottoms. But just as Rusty pushed open the exit door, they were hailed into the lounge by his friend Larry, who insisted they sit down and share a pitcher of beer.

Everything's wrong tonight, Mrs. Tobias thought. The trouble began when Rusty arrived at her house, driving a flashy black pickup truck. He'd apologized, saying that his Honda was in the shop and that he'd borrowed his brother's vehicle. The back window of the truck featured a sticker of a nasty little cartoon boy urinating on the ground.

"My brother Bruss has a lot of backwoods Georgia in him," Rusty said with a hearty laugh, as if that excused his sibling from displaying such a distasteful image on his truck.

"I didn't know you had a brother," Mrs. Tobias said as Rusty helped her up into the passenger seat. "In fact I know next to nothing about your family."

As it turned out, his brother Bruss, who installed swimming pools for a living, was Rusty's only family. His father, who'd been a drinking man, had a succession of jobs, including peanut farmer and John Deere salesman. He'd taken off when Rusty was eight, and his mother raised her boys while working the night shift at a fabric mill. She'd died of pancreatic cancer four years ago. It sounded like a grim upbringing.

"That's my story," Rusty said. Rain splattered the front windshield, and he turned on the wipers. "What's yours?"

"There's very little to tell," Mrs. Tobias said. "My parents are deceased. My father was a local business owner, and my mother was a homemaker."

Never mind that the business her father owned was a prosperous printing company that made him a millionaire by the age of fifty. He'd sold the company before he died, and Mrs. Tobias had inherited the proceeds.

"No brothers or sisters," she continued. "I have a daughter named Daisy, who's a businesswoman." No sense in mentioning that her daughter was CEO of Hollingsworth Paper Cups, a company she'd acquired from her late husband.

"I know that our families are worlds apart," Rusty said, as if he knew she'd omitted some details about her background. "But when I'm with you, it feels like we come from the same little tribe."

Mrs. Tobias thawed somewhat at his remark. Rusty said such charming things, and it did feel extremely natural to be in his company. But there were several things about him that continued to rankle her. For instance, she wished he'd trade in his leather jacket for a suit coat every once in a while. And that strong accent of his! "Hire yew" was "How are you?" "Bares" were "beers." Sometimes she could scarcely understand him.

She kept recalling her recent meeting with her mother-in-law. Cecilia could be a terrible snob, but she'd also made some valid points. It *was* difficult for people from two such different worlds to mesh.

Mrs. Tobias became even more convinced of that as the evening wore on. The lounge in Chalky's seemed shabby and mean under the sickly light of a Molson Gold sign. The carpet was water-stained, and the yeasty smell of spilled beer soured the air.

And these friends of his! Sheila was picking her teeth with a long, red fingernail while Larry and Rusty discussed the revolting things they found under houses.

"A decomposing king snake about six feet long," said Larry, who was a termite inspector. "I thought it was a length of rope."

"Last week I cleaned the ducts in a house

out in Hephzibah and came nose-to-nose with a mama opossum. Three little baby opossums were hanging from her—" Rusty took a quick look at Mrs. Tobias's face. "Maybe we ought to change the subject."

"I don't know how you boys get the courage to crawl under houses all day long," Sheila said from behind a thick screen of smoke. "You're a pair of unsung heroes."

"Ready to go, babe?" Rusty asked.

"Let's do." Mrs. Tobias winced at the word "babe." The first time Rusty had used the endearment it had made her feel youthful, as if she were a young woman strutting about in a miniskirt instead of a sixty-four-year-old matron in a tailored linen suit. But now, in the presence of Larry and his flashy wife, the term seemed proprietary and vulgar.

They returned to the truck, and Rusty slid a Jefferson Airplane CD into the player.

"Didn't you tell me you liked Italian food?" he said over Grace Slick's wails.

Italian came out "Eye-talian." He was constantly mangling the English language. Why hadn't it bothered her before?

"Yes," Mrs. Tobias said, holding on to the

dash as the truck trundled out of the parking lot.

"Good, because I'm going to take you to one of my favorite restaurants tonight."

They ended up at Moretti's House of Cannelloni, a chain restaurant that featured heavy, sauce-laded Italian dishes like spaghetti and lasagna. When Mrs. Tobias had said she favored Italian food, she meant the lighter cuisine of Tuscany, dishes seasoned with fresh herbs, lemons, and capers. But Rusty probably wasn't aware of the distinction.

"Excuse me, I need to visit the little boy's room," Rusty said shortly after they'd been seated in the eatery.

After he left, Mrs. Tobias took stock of her surroundings. On a far wall there was a watercolor mural of a gondola drifting through Venice. "O Sole Mio" played in the background, and each red-checkered table blazed with candles stuck in Chianti bottles. *Moretti's certainly won't get any points for originality,* she thought as she unfolded a napkin on her lap.

"Anything striking your fancy?" Rusty asked as he returned to their table.

"I don't know." Mrs. Tobias put down the oversized menu. "Maybe Bruno's Caesar Salad."

"Is that all? I'm going to have Mama Moretti's Pasta Sampler. I could eat a horse."

Mrs. Tobias noticed a group of servers assembling around a nearby table. A kazoo sounded, and they launched into an Italian song, presumably "Happy Birthday." Mrs. Tobias pitied the poor red-faced birthday woman who was slowly sinking in her seat, thinking, *What an embarrassing display!*

A waitress in a white apron set a small loaf of bread on the table and took their orders. When the food came, Mrs. Tobias's Caesar salad was swimming in dressing, and there wasn't an anchovy in sight. Rusty dove into his towering plate of Chef Boyardee–like pasta with gusto, splattering tomato sauce on his shirt.

"Tonight's a very special night," Rusty said, after he'd devoured about half his food. "Do you know why?"

Before Mrs. Tobias could answer, a phalanx of grinning servers headed in their direction. She glanced behind her in a panic, praying her table wasn't their intended target. But there was no one seated behind her, and the staff people continued their determined march to her table. What did they want with her? It was at least six months before her birthday.

There were eight of them, and they closed in like lions around a Christian. A kazoo tooted, and their clear, young voices reverberated throughout the restaurant. Every patron's head swung in her direction, and hundreds of eyes were fixed on her face.

Why are you rubber-necking, she wanted to say. *Haven't you ever seen people sing in a restaurant before? Get back to your overcooked manicotti!*

After the torture ended, a baby-faced waiter set a covered silver platter in front of her. The birthday tiramisù, Mrs. Tobias presumed.

"What was that all about?" Mrs. Tobias said, trying to hide her mortification. "It's not my birthday."

"No," Rusty said with a self-satisfied grin. "They were wishing us a happy anniversary. Did you know we've been dating now for a whole month?" He lifted his glass of Merlot. "It's been the best month of my life."

"I need to visit the powder room." Mrs. Tobias tossed her napkin on the table.

"Aren't you going to take a peek?" Rusty asked. He indicated the silver dish the waiter had left behind.

Mrs. Tobias sighed and lifted the lid. There was a small piece of paper underneath.

"Lo sposerete," it read. Mrs. Tobias didn't know Italian, so she assumed it meant "Happy anniversary."

"How sweet," she said, crumpling the paper and putting it in the pocket of her jeans. "Now if you'll excuse me—"

"But—" Rusty stammered.

"I'll be back right back," she said.

But she wasn't coming back; she knew that the minute she rose from the table. There was no denying it. She and Rusty didn't belong together, and she couldn't bear to tell him and see the hurt in his dark brown eyes. She rushed past the restrooms and headed for the front door. There was a doughnut shop next to the restaurant, and she could call a cab from there.

Mrs. Tobias wiped a tear from her cheek. As much as she hated to admit it, Cecilia was right. Rusty was a dear man, but she simply couldn't handle the vast differences between them. Tonight's events had made that glaringly clear. She and Rusty might as well live in different solar systems.

Wal-Mart is not the only saving place.
—Sign outside Rock of Ages Baptist Church

CHAPTER TWENTY-EIGHT

"Chicken wings, barbecued ribs, and some of them little crock-pot meatballs that Dooley favors," Attalee recited from a handwritten list. "Sounds yummy, don't it? Trouble is, ribs are kind of messy. Remind me to tell the caterer to put Wet Ones on all the tables."

She glared at Mavis, who was at the checkout counter punching figures into an adding machine. "Are you listening to me?

I'm talking about the food at my wedding reception. This is important."

"I'm listening," Mavis said.

"No, you ain't," Attalee said. "You're still stewing." She took a pencil from behind her ear and added more items to her list. "Fried mozzarella sticks and nachos. I almost forgot about them. And what's your opinion on marinated shoe leather? Yea or nay?"

"Sounds delicious," Mavis said.

"A-ha!" Attalee pointed her pencil at her. "You *weren't* listening to me. Quit your moping. It wasn't that bad."

Mavis looked up from the adding machine. "A geyser burst from my bra. What could be worse?"

Attalee considered her question for a moment. "Janet Jackson at the Super Bowl. A geyser's better than a bare nipple, don'cha think?"

"You're not making me feel better," Mavis said.

"Then come here, and let me tell you about my honeymoon," Attalee said, motioning her over.

Mavis switched off the adding machine, walked to the break area, and dropped into a seat beside Attalee.

"Birdie just flew out of the banquet without saying a word," Mavis said in a small, strained voice. "She didn't even apologize to me."

Attalee ignored Mavis's comment and stuck the brochure under her nose. "Now it *was* a toss-up between Pigeon Forge and SOB. But since Dollywood don't open until late April, Little Pedro won by a sombrero."

"SOB?" Mavis glanced down at the glossy travel magazine. "South of the Border? That tacky tourist trap off I-95? You're not going there for your honeymoon?"

"You never 'sausage' a place," Attalee said, affecting a Mexican accent. "And what do you mean tacky? *Roadside America* called it 'one of the seven wonders of American kitsch.'"

"Kitsch means tacky," Mavis said.

"Well, I don't care. It says here they got three hundred and five acres of fun." Attalee pointed to a page in the brochure. "We'll be staying in the 'heir-conditioned' honeymoon suite. Free champagne and waterbeds."

"What's there to do?" Mavis asked.

"A whole mess of things. There's an indoor golf course called the Golf of Mexico, an arcade, fourteen gift stores including an adult-only outlet store," Attalee said, wagging her eyebrows in a suggestive manner. "Indoor swimming pool, fine dining in the Sombrero Room restaurant, and an elevator up to the two-hundred-foot sombrero tower. You walk around in the brim of the hat and gaze down at the Interstate and miles of loblolly pines."

"I see," Mavis said.

"As they say, there's 'sometheeng for every Juan,'" Attalee said. "So as long as me and Dooley can tear ourselves from our king-size waterbed—"

"Time to go back to work." Mavis stood.

"Wait!" Attalee said. "What's new with Brew? If you speed things along, maybe we can have us a double wedding."

"He called last night to see if anyone else had RSVP'd for the reunion. He also told me he was going to be pretty busy this week, finishing up his house. But he promised we'd see each other at the reunion Saturday night."

"Birdie will have a fit when she sees you paired up with Brew."

Mavis stuck out her lower lip. "He's not taking me to the reunion. Brew thought it was best if we went stag since we were the ones who put it all together. But I'm sure I'll get a dance or two."

"And Birdie?"

Mavis sighed. "Brew says Birdie keeps throwing herself at him. He'll probably dance with her out of politeness."

Attalee grunted. "No one at the reunion will even know he's your beau."

"I know he's my fellow," Mavis said, retying the apron of her uniform. "And that's what's important. And when this reunion is over, Brew and I will have the time to be a real couple."

Work is the curse of the drinking classes.

—Slogan on Dwayne Polk's T-shirt

CHAPTER TWENTY-NINE

Elizabeth and Dorrie sat on the back stoop of Uncle Ray's saltbox house, watching a warm breeze stir the damp clothes on an old-fashioned metal umbrella-shaped clothesline. Dorrie wore a pair of cork sandals and a dark cotton shift, while Elizabeth sweated in her long-sleeved black turtleneck, wool skirt, and tights. Dry Branch was over a hundred miles south of Cayboo Creek, and Elizabeth had forgotten how much warmer the weather could be. Spring hadn't officially begun, but the temperature was seventy-five degrees. The two cousins had been eager to escape the hordes of people who'd gathered in the tiny house after Ray's memorial service.

"Remember how we buried a time capsule in the backyard near the tire swing?" Dorrie asked.

"I do remember," Elizabeth said. Her eyes swept the overgrown grass. "You think it's still out there?"

"Nope," Dorrie said. "We buried a *Ferris Bueller* video, and I got bored about a week afterwards and dug it up."

Elizabeth laughed. "What else did we have in there? I don't remember."

"Let's see," Dorrie said, cocking her head in thought. "A Rainbow Bright doll, bald as a billiard ball; a Cyndi Lauper poster; a pack of those trashy trading cards we used to collect. What were they called?"

"Garbage Pail Kids." Elizabeth giggled into her hand. "I had all of them, and they were so disgusting. Meemaw always threatened to throw them away, so I'd hide them underneath my mattress."

"Those were the days." Her cousin tilted her head toward the sky. The day had started out overcast, with a backdrop of gray clouds. Now golden veins of sunlight seeped through the haze.

"I had big dreams back then." Dorrie poked a twig into the dirt, her face obscured by a sheet of dark hair. "First, I wanted to be a roadie for Duran Duran. Do you remember that?"

"Yes," Elizabeth said. "And I wanted to be a soap-opera star on *General Hospital.*"

Dorrie jabbed Elizabeth's arm with her stick. "Because you were all gooey over Jack Wagner."

"I admit it, but you had a thing for Corbin Bernsen on *LA Law.*"

"Guilty. I was hot for Corbin, but I wanted to *be* the Susan Dey character."

"That's one dream that came true."

Dorrie didn't respond. Instead she dusted the dirt off her hands and stared up at a string of crows on a telephone line. The silence between the cousins stretched for such a long time that Elizabeth feared she'd introduced a taboo subject.

"I was this close to making partner at the law firm," Dorrie finally said, pinching her index finger and thumb together.

"And?" Elizabeth gently probed.

"And I felt like an imposter." She whipped her head up and looked at Elizabeth with pained eyes. "Who did I think I was, wearing pinstripes and designer pumps? Sometimes I prepared contracts that involved millions of dollars. It scared me. I was terrified that eventually I was going to be found out."

"Found out how?"

Dorrie tossed her twig in the dried-out yard. "That I was just plain, old Dorrie Polk from Dry Branch." She slipped her hands between her knees and exhaled deeply. "Long story short, I came back here one weekend and hooked up with Skip. We had a long-distance relationship for a couple of months, and then I found out I was pregnant. I married Skip, had my kid, and a year later got knocked up again. Finally, I was doing what everyone here expected me to do in the first place. My family never did cozy up to me as a corporate lawyer."

She flipped her long hair over her shoulder. "I heard you had a high-powered marketing career a while back. Did you find it as hard to escape your small-town upbringing as I did?"

"I wasn't a marketing executive long enough to feel like an imposter," Elizabeth said in a drowsy voice. Her eyes were closed and the sun warmed the thin skin of her eyelids, making everything look rosy. "But it probably would have happened to me eventually."

"I left Atlanta 'cause I felt like I didn't belong." Dorrie rubbed a hand over her swelled belly. "And even though I love Skip and my son, I still feel out of synch in Dry Branch. I just wonder, is there ever going to be a place for me in this world?"

Elizabeth was about to respond when the screen door squeaked open and Skip, who was holding Toby, stuck his head out the door.

"Hon', where's Toby's diaper bag? He's walking around sopping wet."

Dorrie lifted herself up from the cement stoop with her elbows. "Luckily, I don't have the time to think too deeply about all this," she said to Elizabeth with a half-smile. "Real life is constantly interfering."

The door thwacked shut behind her as Dorrie joined her husband inside the house. Elizabeth continued to bask in the sunlight.

She, too, wondered if she'd ever find her place in this world, one where she would feel comfortable in her own skin. Chiffon had discovered her niche as a photographer. Mavis was happiest when she was running the Bottom Dollar Emporium, and Birdie loved being publisher of the *Cayboo Creek Crier.* Where was Elizabeth's place? Would she ever stop feeling so at odds with her lot in life?

The next morning Dwayne, Elizabeth, and Taffy headed for Myrtle Beach with Ray's ashes stored in a cardboard box in the trunk of the Trans Am. Georgia stayed behind in Dry Branch.

"Myrtle Beach just brings back too many memories of Ray," she'd said through her tears. "I can't face it just yet." The Polks promised her they'd take pictures of the moment when Dwayne tossed the ashes into the waves of the ocean.

Taffy couldn't wait to get to the beach. At the memorial service, she kept whistling the song "Myrtle Beach Days" under her breath until Dwayne elbowed her in the side, at which point she quickly switched to "Taps."

Elizabeth had called Timothy a couple of times in the last two days since Ray's death, but he'd seemed distracted and had kept their conversation brief. Elizabeth missed him, and her arms ached to hold her daughter. Thankfully, Dwayne was planning to scatter his brother's ashes at sunrise, per Ray's request, and then they could all head back to Cayboo Creek.

Taffy fidgeted in her seat as they passed the numerous billboards along Highway 501 advertising Myrtle Beach attractions.

"Dolly Parton's Dixie Stampede, Carolina Opry, Ripley's Haunted Adventure," Taffy recited as she passed each sign.

Dwayne, who'd been somber for the last few days, perked up a bit.

"Crazy Horse exotic dancers, Gentleman's Oasis, and A to I Cup Lingerie Shop." He let out a phlegmy laugh. "I want to see an 'I' cup for myself. Must be one of the seven wonders of the world."

"Watch the road, Dwayne," Taffy snapped. "You're weaving."

After traveling a few more miles, they entered Myrtle Beach proper with its mishmash of Wings T-shirt shops, themed miniature golf courses, and Calabash Seafood Buffets.

"My blood pressure is dropping ten points just being here in this tropical paradise," Taffy said with a contented sigh.

"I feel mine rising," Elizabeth said, after

they'd passed miles of highway lined with all-you-can-eat buffets, pancake restaurants, and tourists shops. "Where's the palm trees and the sand?"

"I think we'll have to turn off the main drag to see the shore." Taffy nibbled on an arm of her sunglasses. "There's a seagull, Dwayne. Follow that bird."

Unfortunately the seagull, instead of flapping its way to the beach, perched on the roof of a Dunkin' Donuts. Elizabeth spotted a sign across the street that said "Public beach. One mile."

"Turn here," she said, pointing to the sign.

They drove along Ocean Boulevard, which was bordered with hundreds of hotels in saltwater-taffy colors of pink, green, and yellow.

"I'll choose the hotels from now on," Taffy said, surveying the offerings as they cruised down the road.

She picked a white high rise called Buccaneer By the Sea, mainly because she saw a Jaguar parked in the registration area.

Dwayne read the sign on the marquee. "Welcome shaggers." He reached over the car console to squeeze Taffy's knee. "I guess that means us, sugar."

"Hmmph." Taffy slapped at his hand. "We ain't in England. If we shag here, it's going to be to 'Sixty-Minute Man' on the dance floor. I wouldn't mind going out on the town tonight."

But, as they soon discovered, their evening activities would be limited. The desk clerk said that Myrtle Beach rolled up the sidewalks during the winter, and many attractions, restaurants, and nightclubs were closed for the season.

As the three of them sat in the lobby bar, Taffy plunged a plastic swizzle stick into her piña colada. "Can you believe it?" she said. "We're smack in the middle of the fun capital of the Southeast, and there's nothing to do. Even the lazy river in the hotel isn't open."

"I have a novel idea," Elizabeth said. "Why don't we go to the beach?"

"The beach?" Taffy made a face. "So we can get all sandy and smell like a fish?"

"Do they sell beer on the beach?" Dwayne asked.

"Probably not this time of year," Elizabeth said.

He wrapped his hand around his Budweiser can. "Then I'm happy to stay put."

Elizabeth decided if she was going to get

a glimpse of the ocean this trip, she'd be forced to go alone.

She left Taffy and her daddy in the bar and rode the elevator to her hotel room, where she slipped into a windbreaker. It was shortly after five, and the temperature had dropped several degrees as the sun sank into the horizon.

Feathery pampas grass swayed in the breeze as Elizabeth crossed the gentle, sloping dunes to reach the sugary, white sand of the beach. She took a whiff of the briny air and felt completely lifted from the chaos of commercialism just yards away. The sun bled sherbet shades of orange and pink as it plunged into the sea.

She kicked a conch shell with the toe of her tennis shoe, spooking a covey of sandpipers, who hurried away on spindly legs. Looking up at the vast sky, she felt as small and insignificant as a speck.

Did it really matter where she fit on such a huge planet?

Elizabeth continued to walk the beach, even as the sky turned a shadowy purple and the lapping waves receded from the shore. The mantra "a place for me" repeated in her thoughts. Reaching the braced, sea-washed wood of the breakers, she turned to trudge back to the hotel. She thought about her cousin Dorrie, and how she'd been frightened into giving up her career dreams. She thought about the isolation and boredom she'd experienced as a stay-at-home parent, made even worse by the disbanding of her Mommy Time group. There just didn't seem to be any answers.

Then, there was an abrupt mental click, like a puzzle piece sliding into place. Suddenly, she knew exactly what she should do.

It's perfect, she thought, quickening her pace along the sand as her mind blossomed with a fully formed idea. Elizabeth couldn't wait to get home to Cayboo Creek and discuss her brainstorm with Timothy. Finally she'd found a solution to her dilemma that would satisfy them both.

Coffee, chocolate, men. Some things are just better rich.

—Overhead underneath the dryers at the Dazzling Do's

CHAPTER THIRTY

Some people toss back whiskey shots when they're upset, others find solace in boxes of Little Debbie swiss rolls or cartons of Mayfield Moose Tracks Ice Cream. Whenever Mrs. Tobias felt blue, she sought comfort in the plot of soil in her backyard garden. In the last few days she'd dug up three basketfuls of weeds, fertilized her pansies, and prepared the soil for spring bulbs.

At first, she refused to admit that anything was amiss. *I'm right as rain,* Mrs. Tobias had said to herself as she attacked the soil with her wooden-handled trowel. Forget the fact that she compulsively checked her answering machine whenever she went inside, even though the message light never blinked but blazed steadily, like a cruel red eye. Once she even drove to a convenience store and called herself from a phone booth to make sure her machine was functioning properly.

Mrs. Tobias didn't know why she expected a phone call from Rusty. After all, he was the one who'd been wronged. Still, it seemed as if he'd given her up too readily. Shouldn't he have put up more of a fight?

Clearly his feelings for her didn't run very deep. *Maybe he's even moved on,* she thought to herself as she tore big handfuls of clover from the dirt. Maybe he and that cigar-smoking Minnie from the flea market were, at this very minute, listening to The Mamas and the Papas on Rusty's car stereo en route to a game of cosmic bowling.

"She can have him," Mrs. Tobias whispered to herself, accidentally pulling up a few sprigs of rosemary along with a clump of weeds. A sour taste of indignation rose in her throat at the thought of Rusty and Minnie together. How dare he take up with someone else so soon after his relationship with her? She got so worked up, she had the urge to call Rusty and give him a piece of her mind. It was only after she'd bumped her knee against a flagstone that she came to her senses and remembered that the pairing of Rusty and Minnie had merely been an invention of her imagination.

She couldn't trust her thoughts anymore. They flew about pell-mell, like deflating toy balloons. Sometimes *she* felt like the betrayed party. Shouldn't Rusty have checked on her to make sure she hadn't been spirited away from the restaurant by a band of thugs? How did he know she hadn't hit her head and wasn't wandering around town with amnesia?

Sometimes, Mrs. Tobias just felt plain sad. *Pillow Talk* came on TV the other evening, and she immediately changed the channel. Rock Hudson reminded her too much of Rusty.

And then there were the times when she called him while he was at work, just to hear his voice on the answering machine. Those were the most confusing times of all.

Mrs. Tobias got up from her crouching position in the garden and shook the pins and needles out of her legs. Inside the house, she could hear the faint ring of the phone. Adrenaline surged through her blood as she sprinted inside, the back door banging behind her.

"Hello?" she said breathlessly.

"Hello, dear," said Cecilia. "You sound winded. Did I catch you in the middle of your morning calisthenics?"

"No, Cecilia," Mrs. Tobias said, trying to disguise the disappointment in her voice. "I just came in from the garden."

"Lovely day for it, although my hip tells me we might be in for an afternoon shower."

"I'm sorry it's bothering you." Mrs. Tobias opened the refrigerator and grabbed a bottle of spring water.

"Guess who I ran into at the club yesterday? Rutherford Spalding. You remember Rutherford? He's an oncologist at University Hospital."

"Oh yes, Rutherford," Mrs. Tobias said. "I remember him very well." Harrison used to call him "the anteater" because his nose was so long.

"Did you also know that he's been recently widowed?"

"No, I didn't," Mrs. Tobias said. She remembered his wife, a white-haired woman with an imposing shelf of a bosom.

"We were chitchatting in the grill, and your name came up. It seems Rutherford has fond memories of you."

"Really?" Mrs. Tobias said.

"Oh yes," Cecilia said in a girlish voice. "He got dewy-eyed at the mention of your name."

"I see where this is leading, Cecilia, and I don't—"

"Nonsense," Cecilia interrupted. "You obviously long for male companionship or you wouldn't have been at Jacque's kissing that leather-clad ruffian. And you couldn't ask for a more appropriate suitor than Rutherford. I urged him to call you. I certainly hope you'll agree to an outing with him."

Mrs. Tobias was about to protest further, when she stopped herself. After all, an evening on the town could provide her a much-needed diversion from her wild swings of emotion. And perhaps, if she went out with someone from her old social circle, it would further convince her of Rusty's unsuitability as a beau.

"Very well. If Rutherford calls and asks

me out, I'll go. Thank you, Cecilia, for thinking of me."

"We'll find the right man for you yet," clucked Cecilia, clearly enjoying her new role as a Yentl.

A few hours later, the phone rang while Mrs. Tobias was heating tea on the stove.

"May I speak with Mrs. Harrison Tobias, please?" a male voice said when she answered the phone.

Mrs. Tobias picked up the whistling kettle from the burner. "This is she."

"Gracie, this is Rutherford Spalding."

Rutherford's voice sounded deeper on the phone than what she remembered, and his speech was cultured and as crisp as Melba toast. There was no dropping of 'g's or muddying of vowel sounds, just lovely, well-formed enunciations.

Rutherford engaged in the requisite small talk and then launched headlong into the true purpose of his call.

"Would you care to join me for dinner Saturday night?" he asked. "I know it's short notice, but—"

"That would be wonderful, Rutherford," Mrs. Tobias said.

And that was that. After a few moments

he ended their conversation, and she stood by the phone, contemplating what she might wear for their date.

It's for the best, Mrs. Tobias thought. For the first time since her dreadful evening at Moretti's House of Cannelloni, she didn't feel the need to take refuge in her garden. Perhaps her every waking moment would no longer be plagued by thoughts of Rusty. The last few days had been more trying than she could ever have imagined.

A closed mouth gathers no foot.
—Message in fortune cookie at Dun Woo's House
of Noodles

CHAPTER THIRTY-ONE

Mavis stood in the aisle of the Bottom Dollar Emporium, modeling her reunion dress for Attalee. It was a pink duster with a mandarin collar and gold embroidering down the sides.

Attalee stuck two fingers in her mouth and whistled.

"Thank you," Mavis said. She liked the way the dress emphasized her soft curves. "Do you think it's too flashy?" she asked. She touched the slight fuzz of mustache above her upper lip. The area stung from a recent application of Jolene bleach.

"You look pretty as a speckled puppy, and you know it," Attalee said as she swiped at the counter with a damp rag.

Mavis fingered the silky fabric of her dress. "It doesn't seem right, though. There's no one else here beside you to admire it."

"Well, Elizabeth is out of town. Mrs. Tobias is . . . I don't know where she is; she's been lying low for a couple days." Attalee stopped to think for a moment. "That's everyone."

"No it isn't." Mavis sank into a vinyl stool at the soda fountain.

Attalee snapped her dishtowel. "Purge that bra-busting broad from your mind. She ain't fit to roll with a pig."

"Birdie always had such good fashion sense," Mavis said with a wan smile. "She'd suggest just the right accessories for this dress."

The phone rang, and Mavis hurried to the front of the store to answer it.

"No, Brew," she said. "The mail's come, but I didn't get any more RSVPs. Yes. I'm looking forward to tonight as well." Mavis hung up the phone and returned to her perch at the soda fountain.

"So is everyone from your high school class coming to the reunion?" Attalee asked.

"A good many, considering the short notice," Mavis said. "Prissy Stevens, Brew's old girlfriend, didn't respond, and I'm grateful for that."

"Are you afraid Brewster's going to warm up a pot of old soup?" Attalee asked.

"I don't think so," Mavis said. "But it's a relief not to have to worry about her."

"What about old Hank Bryson? Wasn't he in your high school class?"

Mavis smiled at the mention of her friend. She hadn't seen Hank since he sold his hardware store over a year ago and moved to California to be closer to his daughter.

Attalee leaned across the counter. "Hank always had a sweet spot for you."

"Oh pooh," Mavis said, waving her off. "Elizabeth used to say the same thing, but I never saw it. It's not like he ever asked me out on a date. We were just buddies."

"I think he would like to have been bosom buddies, but he just didn't have the nerve to ask you out."

"You TiVo too many soap operas." Mavis stood up. "I better change out of this dress before I muss it."

"Old Hank," Attalee muttered as she mashed the button on the Oster milkshake machine. "He was the right man for you, I tell you," she shouted over the roar of the Oster.

"Who's the right man?" Mrs. Tobias said, peering around the corner.

"Hey, Mrs. Tobias." Mavis motioned to Attalee to cut off the machine. "I didn't hear you come in. How are you?"

"I'm curious," Mrs. Tobias said with a smile. "What man are you talking about? That Brew fellow?"

"No," Mavis said. "We were actually talking about Hank Bryson. You remember him. Big fellow that used to come into the store? Always wore overalls?"

"He and Mavis are star-crossed lovers." Attalee squirted a dollop of whipped cream on her milkshake.

"We are not," Mavis said. "Attalee's imagination works overtime. Besides, my heart belongs to Brew now."

"You'll forget all about Brew once you lock eyeballs with Hank across the dance floor," Attalee insisted. She took noisy slurps from her straw. "He's your destiny. I have a psychic knack for knowing these kinds of things."

"Well, Miss Cleo, I've got a news flash for you," Mavis said to Attalee. "I didn't hear a word from Hank about the reunion. I don't even know if he got his invitation."

"Tonight's the night, isn't it?" Mrs. Tobias said. "Your dress, by the way, is very flattering. I assume you're wearing it to this evening's festivities?"

"I am." Mavis made an awkward 360-degree turn so Mrs. Tobias could see how nicely her dress hung.

"Your dance card will fill up in a hurry," Mrs. Tobias said, fingering her earrings. "I, too, have a big evening planned for tonight. I'm going out on a date."

"Where are you and Rusty off to? Maybe we could double-date," Attalee asked. She clapped a hand over her mouth. "I forgot. Rusty's supposed to be a secret."

"Never mind," Mrs. Tobias said. "Rusty's out, and Rutherford is in."

"What happened to Rusty? Y'all were perfect for each other," Attalee said with a scowl.

"Rutherford is even more perfect." Mrs. Tobias turned to Mavis. "He's a respected physician in Augusta, and—"

"So?" Attalee said, with a burp. "Rusty's a doctor."

"A duct doctor, Attalee," Mrs. Tobias said in a firm tone. "Rutherford is an oncologist. He treats cancer patients."

"Does he fill out the seat of his Levi's as nicely as Rusty does?" Attalee asked.

"Rutherford doesn't wear Levi's." Mrs. Tobias's fingers tensed on the handle of her pocketbook. "I do recall him cutting a dashing figure in his Armani suits."

"Does he have Rusty's sexy, lopsided smile?" Attalee said, circling Mrs. Tobias. "Is he easygoing and funny? Does he look at you the way Rusty does, like you were the most beautiful gal he's ever put his sights on?"

"Stop!" Mrs. Tobias said with a bang of her heel. "Rutherford has other qualities that I admire in a man. Rusty's too small-town, too backwoods, too . . . common!"

As soon as the words flew from her mouth, she paled as if she wished she could snatch them back.

Attalee slowly set down her milkshake. "What about Mavis and me? Are we common, too?"

"No," Mrs. Tobias said, on the verge of tears. "You're my dearest friends. You must know that."

"Course we do." Mavis patted Mrs. Tobias's back. "Quit picking on her, Attalee. Mrs. Tobias knows if a fellow is right for her or not. You need to stay out of people's love lives."

"You never saw Rusty and Mrs. Tobias together," Attalee insisted. "They were like Loretta Lynn and Mooney. A match made in heaven."

"I need to go." Mrs. Tobias dabbed at the corner of her eye with a gloved finger. "I've got a million things to do today."

"Don't let Attalee chase you off, Mrs. Tobias," Mavis said.

"It's not that." Mrs. Tobias picked up her purse. "I'm just in a rush."

After she left, Mavis swiveled her stool to face Attalee. "Sometimes you go too far."

"Don't care what nobody says: Rusty was right for her," Attalee said, clanging soda glasses as she reshelved them. "See how she went back to wearing them proper little suits and those silly white gloves? She needs loosening up, and Rusty's the one to do it. Heck, we've known Mrs. Tobias a couple of years, and we still don't call her by her given name."

"It's just Mrs. Tobias's way," Mavis said. "But you shouldn't have run her off like that. She's our friend, and you insulted her."

"Nope, that wasn't it," Attalee said, her black eyes glittering under the fluorescent light above the soda fountain. "She wasn't insulted. She left because she knew I was speaking the truth about Rusty, and she ain't ready to face it."

"Attalee—"

She held up a wrinkled finger. "You heard it here first. Mrs. Tobias is in love with Rusty Williams. And a date with some rich doctor ain't going to change that."

All men are animals, some just make better pets.
—Cross-stitch pillow in Taffy Polk's bedroom

CHAPTER THIRTY-TWO

The first thing Elizabeth saw when she opened the front door to her house was Maybelline's snout buried deep in a Domino's pizza box.

"What are you doing, girl?" she asked. The dog had the box pinned down with her paw as if it were prey. When Elizabeth knelt down to pick it up, Maybelline emitted a low growl.

"You'll make yourself sick, Missy," Elizabeth said, snatching the box away. "Timothy?" she called out as she walked into the living room.

The house had a sour, dirty-sock smell about it. Elizabeth threaded through an obstacle course of Glenda's toys to find her husband, garbed in a bathrobe and sprawled out on the couch. His mouth was wide open, and he was snoring over the sounds of a Clifford the Big Red Dog video playing on the TV. A copy of *Dr. Spock's Baby and Child Care* lay open on his chest.

Elizabeth shook his shoulder. "Timothy, are you okay?"

"What's that?" he said with a start, blinking through bleary, bloodshot eyes. His face flooded with grateful relief as he recognized her. "Elizabeth, you're home."

He immediately sprung from the couch and buried his face in her sweater. "Thank God, you're back." His hair was matted with dried baby cereal.

"Where's Glenda?" she said, gently extracting herself from Timothy's embrace.

"In her room," Timothy said. "She was up all night, so she's probably exhausted. Please don't wake her up."

Elizabeth hurried down the hall to the nursery, and Timothy followed close at her heels, as if he feared letting her out of his sight. As she passed the kitchen she noticed several empty pizza boxes on the counter.

"Timothy, why was Maybelline eating pizza from the box?"

Timothy shrugged. "We ran out of dog food. I kept meaning to get to the grocery store, but . . ."

"Never mind." Elizabeth entered the nursery and stood over Glenda's crib. Her daughter was dozing on her back, her long, dark lashes fluttering in slumber.

"I missed my baby so much," Elizabeth tucked the blanket around Glenda and discreetly checked her diaper. "What a little angel!"

"Ha!" Timothy snorted. "She may look angelic now, but you should have seen her last night. Red-faced and screaming. Kept spitting out her strained peaches. On purpose."

Elizabeth tossed her husband a surprised look. Until today, Glenda could do no wrong in his eyes. He often bragged she was the perfect child.

"And yesterday morning, she refused to let me change her diaper," he continued, scratching his bare chest. "Wriggled like a worm on the changing table. Took me twenty minutes to put on one Huggie, and then guess what she did?"

"Went tee-tee in it?" Elizabeth planted a light kiss on her daughter's smooth forehead.

"How did you know?" Timothy asked.

"Been there, done that," Elizabeth said lightly. She put a finger to her lips and tiptoed out of the nursery.

"I'd planned to take her out yesterday for a short stroll in the park," Timothy said. "But a simple diaper-changing took an hour, and then she needed a nap and so did I. Time kept slipping away from me. The next thing I knew it was six o'clock, and I hadn't even gotten dressed."

"You're preaching to the choir, honey." Elizabeth knelt down to pick up a collection of plush toys from the carpet.

"And just try to fit in a shower. It's impossible, because—"

"Because you can't hear the baby monitor over the shower, and if you put Glenda in the bathroom in her walker, she cries when you pull back the shower curtain," Elizabeth said.

"Yeah." Timothy snapped his fingers. "Exactly."

Elizabeth went into the kitchen and peeked into the refrigerator. "I guess I'll need to go to the market soon, and . . . Ugh!" She held her nose as she slammed the door shut. "Something's hurting in there, but I'll figure out what it is later."

Timothy hung his head in shame and stared at his bare feet.

"I'm sorry, honey, I didn't mean to pick on you," Elizabeth said, touching his wrist. "Besides a few pizza boxes and some clutter, this place is in pretty good shape. And I know Glenda loves spending time with her daddy."

Timothy still didn't look up, so she wrapped an arm around his shoulder. "Why not take a long, hot shower? You'll feel much better."

"No I won't. I don't deserve to feel better." He glanced up at her with eyes ringed by dark circles. "Not after the way I treated you."

"What do you mean?"

"I acted so high and mighty, insisting you stay home with Glenda, when I had no idea what it was like," he said, sagging against the kitchen counter. "While you were gone, I thought I was going crazy. Every day was the same as the next. The tedium, the exhaustion. My brain was turning to mush."

"You never let on," Elizabeth said. "When I

spoke with you on the phone you seemed fine."

"Most of the time I was lucky to *find* the phone." Timothy rubbed his hand over the stubble on his chin. "I had to stop myself from begging you to come home. I kept thinking it would get better."

"I'm sorry you had such a rough time."

"It wasn't all terrible." A faint smile played at Timothy's lips. "Glenda tried to pull herself up on the coffee table yesterday."

"No!"

"And when the *Big Blue House* was over on TV, she waved bye-bye to the bear."

"Wow," Elizabeth said. "I wished I'd been here."

Timothy slapped the kitchen counter with the flat of his hand. "I can't believe I screwed up that arrangement with Mrs. Pirkle. She was a terrific sitter. Even I could see that."

"That's water under the bridge, honey," Elizabeth said. "And the marketing job was probably going to take more hours a week than I expected. It would have been too much for me to handle."

Timothy reached out to brush a strand of her hair out of her eyes. "I just want you to know, Elizabeth, that whatever you decide to do with your life, I'm behind you one hundred percent." He swallowed. "And I'm sorry for the bullheaded way I behaved. I had no idea what you've been going through."

"It's getting better. Really it is. Some days I'm even dressed before noon," she said with a laugh. "But going back to my high-powered career isn't the solution. I want to be the kind of mother Glenda deserves, and that, unfortunately, limits my options."

"But being a good mother doesn't mean you have to sacrifice everything you love about your life," Timothy said.

"You're right," Elizabeth said as she sat at the kitchen table. "And I'm not going to. I did a lot of thinking while I was gone, and I think I've discovered the perfect solution to everything. I believe I've finally found my place in the world."

"Your place? What do you mean?"

"Come here," Elizabeth said patting the chair next to her. "I'll tell you all about it."

"You Done the Wrong Women Wrong"
—Selection F-7 on the jukebox at the Tuff Luck
Tavern

CHAPTER THIRTY-THREE

Mavis heard the lyrics to the song "Yakety Yak" drifting down the halls of the high school long before she reached the gymnasium. The tune transported her back to the late 'fifties when she'd spent countless afternoons at the Capri Theater on Main Street, scaring herself silly with the Fright Fests. The theater screened movies like "The She Creature," "The Mole People," and "I Was a Teenage Werewolf." After the show she'd gaze into the large windows of Vickery's department store, admiring the wool-blend twin-set cardigans. Or she'd wander into the record store, to buy a chart single like "To Know Him Is to Love Him" by The Teddy Bears.

In each one of these memories, Birdie was by her side, grabbing Mavis's shoulder in a tense part of the movie or gabbing a mile a minute as they walked down the streets of Cayboo Creek, arm in arm. The sudden rush of memories saddened her, and Mavis wiped a stray tear from her cheek and willed herself to stop. She'd just have to put Birdie out of her mind for tonight.

As she entered the gym, the blue and white streamers hanging from the ceiling brought her alma mater to mind: "Here's to our dear blue and white, Flying Squirrels we will unite . . ."

She couldn't remember the rest of the words, probably because whenever the band played the school song, her attention had been focused on Arnold, her future hus-band, as he cavorted around the gym in his squirrel suit.

Arnold's costume had been retired in 1975. The seniors that year thought the fly-ing squirrel was too tame a mascot for a sports team. The current mascot at Cayboo Creek High School was a fierce, sharp-toothed wildcat, which never failed to startle Mavis at the occasional games she attended, making her nostalgic for the more innocent days of the class of 1959.

"Hi, Flump. You in a slump?" asked a wiry man in porkpie hat.

"Morty? Is that you?" Mavis said.

Morty Ames, former class comedian, had always called her by her last name in high school, usually along with a rhyme. Unfortunately, Flump rhymed with all kinds of unpleasant words: chump, frump, grump, and plump.

"One in the same," Morty said, answering her question. "Jeepers, look at this place. It's like stepping into a time machine."

Mavis nodded. Brew had done an admirable job of creating a vintage mood in the gymnasium. The walls were plastered with posters of 'fifties icons like Davy Crockett, Chubby Checker, and Pat Boone. A disc jockey, his slick black hair styled into what they used to call a duck butt, spun Jerry Lee Lewis and Bobby Darin tunes on an old-fashioned hi-fi. And in the far corner of the gym, a hula-hoop contest was underway.

"Feels like old times." Mavis took a good look at Morty. It was hard to reconcile the washed-out, gray little man standing beside her with the vigorous, freckle-faced Morty Ames of her youth. "What have you been doing all these years?" she asked.

"Car salesman. I work at a lot down in Camden." He pointed a finger at her. "You know, Flump, you'd look great behind the wheel of a sporty little Daihatsu."

Suddenly Mavis spotted Brew across the gymnasium. "Excuse me, Morty. There's someone I need to speak with."

"Sure thing," Morty said, tipping his hat. He eyed her backside with appreciation as she brushed past him. "Hey, Flump, I see you still have a nice—"

She whirled around, a prim look on her face. "Morty Ames. Watch your tongue."

He held up a hand. "I'll keep it decent. See you around, Flump."

Mavis was about to approach Brew when Dolores Lewis sidled up to him. Dolores had been a cheerleader in high school and, like many of Mavis's female classmates, had once had a big crush on Brew.

Dolores, who was now fifty pounds heavier than she was in 1959, seized Brew's arm and was whispering in his ear. Mavis felt awkward speaking to Brew while he was with Dolores, so she decided she'd visit the powder room first, hoping to catch him alone afterward. She was anxious for him to admire her pretty new dress.

Mavis entered the ladies' room and checked her lipstick in the mirror. Then she went into a stall to pull up her pantyhose. Over the last few minutes they'd worked their way down her thighs, giving her a bow-legged, John Wayne gait.

As she tugged at her stockings, the outside restroom door opened and the strong scent of gardenia perfume floated in.

"Did you see Brewster Clark?" Mavis recognized Dolores's high-pitched, babyish voice. "He's still a cutie pie. If I wasn't happily married to Harry, I'd be barking up his tree."

"Yes, I saw Brewster," replied a low-pitched female voice. "And I think he's a terrible cad."

"Why do you say to that, Trixie?" Dolores asked. Mavis remembered Trixie Scarsdale, head of the pep squad. When Brew played quarterback for the Flying Squirrel football team, the bouncy, red-headed Trixie had been one of his greatest fans. Mavis was surprised to hear her badmouth him.

"Do you know he talked me into writing all his term papers during our senior year?" Trixie said.

"Really?" Dolores said.

"All the while leading me to believe I was his girlfriend. Then when prom time came along he asked Prissy Stevens instead of me."

"He was always crazy about Prissy," Dolores said. "But, Trixie, you shouldn't hold a forty-five-year-old grudge. I'm sure Brew's changed over the years."

"Don't bet on it. He's still a user," Trixie said. "Earlier I complimented Brew on all the hard work he'd put into the reunion. I asked him where he'd gotten the 'fifties posters on the gymnasium wall, and how he managed to find all of our classmates. He hemmed and hawed, and finally had to admit he hadn't done a speck of the work himself. He told me that Mavis Flump and Birdie Purdy planned the entire event. Mavis contacted the classmates, and Birdie handled the food and decorations."

Mavis gasped aloud. She heard an even louder gasp come from the stall next door.

"Mavis Flump and Birdie Purdy?" Dolores said. " I remember those girls. They were like

two peas in a pod. You never saw one without the other." There was a sound of a compact snapping shut. "Let's get back out there.
I heard that Merle Jones is here, and he still
has all his hair."

Mavis stood motionless in the stall after
the women left, her mind swirling with shock.
She couldn't believe her ears. Birdie had
decorated the gym, not Brewster! He'd lied
to her. What other things had he been lying
about? She had to find Birdie. She needed
to talk with her right away.

As she fled from the stall she nearly
knocked heads with her best friend.

"Birdie!"

"Oh, Mavis!"

"Were you in the stall next door? Did you
hear what Trixie said?"

"Every word."

"Can you believe it?"

"That scamp!"

"He's gotten the best of both of us."

Birdie took a hesitant step toward Mavis.
"Mavis, I don't know what to say. I fear we've
made a terrible mistake. I've missed you so,
and . . ."

"Me, too," Mavis said quickly.

"I'm so sorry," Birdie said. "Do you think we might . . . that is . . . is it possible that you and I . . ."

"Say no more," Mavis said holding out her arms.

Falling into a tearful embrace, the two women tried to talk at once and through their conversation, they quickly discovered that Brew had been a two-timing scoundrel ever since he'd moved to Cayboo Creek. He had dinner at Birdie's house on Monday, Wednesday, and Friday and at Mavis's on Tuesday, Thursday, and Saturday. Sunday was his day of rest.

"It sounds like we were his personal chefs," Birdie said, bitterly. "He never once took me out to a restaurant or even to a movie. And he always left right after dinner."

"It was the same with me," Mavis said. "I can't believe I was so foolish. One day Elizabeth told me she saw his car parked outside your house. When I asked Brew about it he told me you'd lured him over there, saying you needed his help with home repairs."

Birdie stomped the heel of her gold party shoe against the bathroom tiles. "He told me *you* were the one coaxing him over to your place with squeaky doors and leaky faucets.

That's why I was so angry with you. I didn't understand why you were trying to steal my boyfriend away from me."

"He was supposed to be my date at the Business Person of the Year banquet," Mavis continued. "I guess he was worried he'd see you there, so he made up a story about having a flat tire."

"I feel so foolish."

"Same here," Mavis said, twisting a button on her new dress. "We were snookered."

Birdie took a lace hankie from her clutch purse and swiped at her eyes. "I felt terrible about your bra. I kept wanting to call you afterwards to apologize."

"Things haven't been the same at the Bottom Dollar Emporium without you," Mavis said in a soft voice.

Birdie linked arms with Mavis. "Let's never, *ever* let anything separate us again."

Mavis smiled. It felt glorious to have her dear friend beside her again, just like in high school.

"I promise if you do."

If you're going to walk on thin ice, you might as well dance.
—From the Methodist Church bulletin

CHAPTER THIRTY-FOUR

As Mrs. Tobias sat in Rutherford Spalding's silver Lincoln Town Car, the leather seat beneath her got warmer by the minute.

"Oh my goodness," she said with alarm. "I think I'm in the hot seat."

"If your seat's getting too warm, you can turn down the heat with the climate control center on your armrest," Rutherford said.

"How clever!" She surveyed the buttons

and made a small adjustment to the temperature.

Rutherford's Lincoln was like a plush parlor on wheels. And Mrs. Tobias felt at home beside her date, who looked especially debonair in a cashmere topcoat and an English ascot hat. Both items had obviously been purchased at Gents, where all the distinguished men of Augusta bought their clothes. Harrison had refused to shop anywhere else, even purchasing his boxer shorts and wool socks from the clothier.

How lovely to have a well-dressed, predictable man at the wheel! With Rutherford there'd be no impromptu excursions on the evening's agenda. No sudden dashes into a drive-thru restaurant for chili dogs, no impulsive suggestions of Putt-Putt games or midnight canoe rides. And no rock music blaring from the car stereo. Rutherford kept his radio tuned to an investment station, whose motto was "all about stocks, all day long."

"I thought we'd go to the club," Rutherford said. "It's prime-rib night."

Mrs. Tobias gave a nod of approval. For years, she and Harrison had gone to the Summerville Country Club on Saturday nights for their fabled prime-rib night, and when Rutherford's car passed through the stone-columned entrance of the club, Mrs. Tobias felt a strong sense of déjà vu. Glancing at the driver's seat, she almost expected to see Harrison at the wheel.

Rutherford parked, and helped her out of the vehicle. As the liveried valet took the car keys, Rutherford warned him to be mindful of the Lincoln's touchy accelerator.

The pebbled path to the club's entrance was lined with lights, and Rutherford took her arm to guide her inside, just as her husband used to. The coat checker was the same one who had been there for years, a chatty black woman named Yolanda.

"Nice to see you, Mrs. Tobias," Yolanda said, putting her coat on a hanger. "I'll take good care of this pretty fur of yours."

Yolanda addressed Mrs. Tobias as if she'd seen her only three days ago instead of three years. Maybe she hadn't even noticed her absence.

The sound of jazz floated from the spacious, formal dining room, and Mrs. Tobias recognized the song, "The Girl from Ipanema."

"Are the Two Tones still playing here?" she asked as they strolled in the direction of the music.

"It wouldn't be Saturday night without the Two Tones," Rutherford said.

They stood at the threshold of the dining room as the three white-coated musicians who made up the Two Tones played on the same tiny stage near a seldom-used dance floor. For some reason, it irritated Mrs. Tobias that the group still had a regular gig at the club. Didn't they have any aspirations beyond playing "Take the A Train" to a bunch of overprivileged socialites who didn't know Chicago-style jazz from fusion?

Where did that unkind thought come from? After all, Mrs. Tobias hadn't been able to distinguish between the different types of jazz until Rusty had explained it to her when they'd visited a smoky underground club in downtown Augusta.

The maitre d', a short, compact fellow named Godfrey, greeted Rutherford. "What a pleasure, Mr. Spalding, to have you and your lovely companion as our dinner guests tonight," Godfrey said.

Godfrey had also called her the "lovely companion" when she dined here with Harrison. Mrs. Tobias wondered if he even noticed that she wasn't Rutherford's wife, and if all aging white matrons looked alike to him.

Godfrey reserved most of his fawning for male members, as they were the rulers of the Summerville Country Club. Men had a private grill and smoking room. Women could be members in their own right, but they were not allowed to serve on the board of directors or to play golf on Saturdays, unless accompanied by a male member.

They followed Godfrey to a white-clothed table near the window. The maitre d' pulled out her chair, while Rutherford adjusted the silverware to his liking. After she'd been seated, he said, "I'm delighted you agreed to accompany me tonight."

"My pleasure." Mrs. Tobias unfolded her napkin and spread it over her lap.

Rutherford had taken off his cap in the lobby. He was bald, save for a bit of grayish fuzz bordering each large ear. His nose was long and thin like a toucan's. Candlelight shone in the lenses of his square, heavy-framed glasses, but the flattering lighting did nothing to enhance his rather plain appearance.

"I wonder if they have oxtail soup?" Mrs. Tobias said as she glanced at the menu. *Where had that comment come from?*

"Soul food at the Summerville Country

Club?" Rutherford let out a laugh. "That would be the day."

After they ordered (prime rib, naturally, and a cup of French onion soup, an appetizer the club was famous for), Rutherford began to complain about the rising costs of malpractice insurance. By the time he'd switched the topic to his latest golf game—he'd scored an eagle on the club's tricky sixteenth hole—the bread server had stopped by their table.

Mrs. Tobias was familiar with the country club's bread ritual. She was supposed to choose one piece of bread from the basket, and the server, using a pair of silver tongs, would place her selection on a small plate.

She peered into the basket, but couldn't decide what kind of bread she felt like eating.

"Why not just leave the basket on the table?" Mrs. Tobias said to the bread server, a lanky, blank-faced boy who looked to be fresh out of high school. "That way if I want more bread you don't have to come back over here."

The young man gave her a startled look and then glanced at Rutherford for guidance.

"Gracie, if you want more bread"—Rutherford glanced at the server's name tag—"William, here, will be glad to bring it to you. Isn't that right?"

"Yes, sir," William said.

"Furthermore, I think there's something common about having a breadbasket on a table," he continued. "This isn't Shoney's, after all."

"I'll pass on bread," Mrs. Tobias said to William, losing interest in the whole discussion.

As soon as William moved on to the next table and the waiter had brought out their soups, Rutherford began a fresh diatribe about the plummeting stock market.

As she listened to the drone of his voice, Mrs. Tobias felt like the Bill Murray character in the movie *Groundhog Day,* living the same day over and over again. She'd heard this conversation before—or one very like it—only it had been Harrison sitting across the table from her instead of Rutherford. She'd tasted this soup hundreds of times before (too salty and mushy with bread; for the club's signature soup it was actually quite awful). And she'd heard the Two Tones play "Sweet Georgia Brown" so many times she knew when the saxophone player would take a breath.

Suddenly it was clear. Her former life of quiet predictability didn't suit her anymore. She'd changed since Harrison's death. She was no longer a "lovely companion" who listened with great attention to the men in her life. Instead, she had her own views and opinions, and sometimes, even though it scared her, she relished doing crazy, out-of-character things, like eating ice cream for breakfast or hopping on the back of a motorcycle, or even kissing her date in a restaurant.

"I read in the paper that the astronomy club is having a star party tonight on the grounds of Augusta State University," Mrs. Tobias said abruptly, when their prime-rib dinners arrived at the table. "Let's go, shall we?"

"Gracie," Rutherford chortled. "What a madcap notion! A star party. Besides, if we were to leave now, we'd miss the Two Tones' next set."

Later, after dessert and coffee, Mrs. Tobias complained of a terrible headache, and Rutherford agreed to take her home.

"Perhaps we can have dinner at Jacque's sometime next week," Rutherford said as he escorted her to her door.

"Rutherford, you're a lovely man, but—" Mrs. Tobias began.

"Do you have someone else on your mind?" he asked.

"What?" Mrs. Tobias said, in a surprised voice. How could he possibly have guessed?

"I felt it, too," he continued. "The ghost of our late spouses, hovering over our table. Your mind was on Harrison and mine was on Victoria. When you ordered cheesecake for dessert, I almost protested. You see, Victoria always chose the bread pudding."

"Yes, Rutherford," Mrs. Tobias said, grateful that he'd provided her with an excuse not to see him anymore. "You're correct. There were painful ghosts haunting our table tonight. I'm so sorry."

"I understand perfectly." He planted a dry-lipped kiss on her cheek. "Good night, Gracie, and good luck."

As soon as she shut the door behind her, Mrs. Tobias dashed into her bedroom to change into the pair of jeans she'd tossed in the back of her closet. Then she prepared a thermos full of hot cocoa and took a blanket from the linen closet.

She drove to the college campus and saw

a crowd of people congregated on the crest of a hill. Several telescopes were set up at various points in the grass, and the night was noisy with the mating songs of crickets.

Mrs. Tobias made her way to the party, her eyes gradually adjusting to the gloom. She spread her blanket on a flat area beside a monstrous oak tree. Leaning against the rough bark of the trunk, she gazed at the light of the stars searing through the gauzy darkness.

She'd been there for only ten minutes when she felt someone drop beside her on the blanket. The familiar scent of leather reached her nostrils.

"It's a little bit cloudy for a star party," Rusty said.

Mrs. Tobias's heartbeat quickened. She pinched the tufts of yarn that had come unraveled from her blanket.

"What are we supposed to be looking for?" she asked softly. "Meteor showers?"

"March is a bad month for meteor showers. Leonids-Ursids are in the sky, but they're hard to see. The big attraction tonight is Saturn's rings. They're at maximum tilt toward the earth."

"Is there anything you don't know?" Mrs. Tobias asked.

"Yup. There's certain things that stump me." Rusty nibbled on a blade of grass. "Like why my best girl ran off from me the other night."

"That is a puzzler," Mrs. Tobias said. "I didn't know the answer myself . . . until tonight."

"Care to clue me in?"

Mrs. Tobias looked up at Rusty, who was staring at her with dark, wounded eyes.

"When I left the restaurant that night, I wasn't running from you; I was running from myself," she began in a faint voice. "I was turning into someone I didn't recognize. It frightened me, and I wanted to return to the familiar. Yet when I revisited my old world, the one my late husband cherished, I found I didn't fit there anymore . . . Maybe I never did."

Rusty turned to her, searching her face. "So who are you now, Gracie Tobias?"

"I'm still working on that. Every single day," she said. "For instance, I know I like star parties—even if I don't know what to look for—though maybe I'm not crazy about pool halls." She laughed. "Who would have thought that a sixty-four-year-old woman would be reinventing herself in this way?"

"I wonder." He paused for a beat. "Is there a part for me in your reinvention?"

"Yes," she said, finally meeting his eyes. "I think you're the biggest part of all. I missed you terribly, Rusty. I came tonight hoping you'd be here."

"I missed you, too," he said, capturing her hand and giving it a squeeze.

They sat in companionable silence, staring up at the shifting bank of clouds.

"I don't see Saturn," Mrs. Tobias said finally. "And I certainly don't see its rings."

"You can't see Saturn's rings with the naked eye," Rusty said. "We'd have to look through a telescope. But I think it's too overcast to see them tonight anyway."

"What a pity!"

"Saturn's rings are overrated," Rusty said. He fingered his collar and spoke in a halting voice. "I was afraid the question I asked you that night at Moretti's scared you away. You haven't mentioned it."

"Question? What question?"

"I wrote it on a piece of paper." Rusty's face was cloaked in shadows and she couldn't see his expression. "The waiter brought it to our table."

Mrs. Tobias suddenly remembered the slip of paper underneath the covered platter at the restaurant.

"I put it in my pocket," she began. "There was something written in Italian—" She reached inside the front pocket of her jeans. They were the same ones she'd worn to Moretti's. "I still have it."

"There's writing on both sides," Rusty said.

She retrieved the slip of paper and unfolded it. Rusty took a lighter from his pocket and illuminated the note.

"Lo sposerete." She glanced at Rusty. "I thought that meant 'happy anniversary.'"

"Turn it over for the translation," he said in a thick voice.

With a flick of her wrist, she turned the paper to the other side.

"Will you marry me?" Mrs. Tobias read. She scarcely recognized the shaky, high-pitched tone that left her lips.

Rusty reached into the pocket of his jacket and extracted a small jewelry box. "I've carried this since the night you ran away. It was supposed to go with the question."

Slowly, with fumbling hands, she opened the box and nearly dropped it when she saw the diamond ring inside.

"Rusty," she whispered. "It's beautiful."

"It can't compare with Saturn's."

"Will you put it on my finger?"

Rusty let out a long exhale of breath. "You mean . . . ?"

"Yes." She vigorously nodded. "I will marry you."

"Oh Gracie, I can't believe it. I had so much hope, but . . . Dang." He wiped at the tears coursing down his face. "There I go again. Bawling like a baby."

Mrs. Tobias took a handkerchief from her purse and blotted his tears. "Don't worry, my dear Rusty. It's one of the things I love most about you."

He smiled and plucked the ring from the box and slid it along her finger.

She held the diamond close to her face, and Rusty reignited his butane lighter so she could see it.

"You're right," Mrs. Tobias said. "Compared to this, Saturn's rings *are* overrated."

Church Parking Only. Violators will be baptized.
> —Sign in the parking lot of the Rock of Ages
> Baptist Church

CHAPTER THIRTY-FIVE

Arm in arm, Mavis and Birdie left the ladies' room and walked down the locker-lined hall that led to the gymnasium. As they got closer, they heard the plaintive voice of Connie Francis singing, "Who's Sorry Now?"

"Sounds like they're playing Brew's song," Birdie said with a huff. "I can't wait to see the look on his face when he sees the two of us heading in his direction."

Mavis giggled. "Remember what we used

to say to people like him in high school? DDT!"

"Drop Dead Twice!" Birdie hooted. She playfully grabbed her friend's arm. "You tell him, Mavis."

As they shared a private laugh, Dolores tore out of the gym, her two chins jiggling as she ran. "You won't believe who's here," she announced to no one in particular. "Prissy Stevens! She just pulled up in a white stretch limousine, and she's inside."

"I'll bet she's tubby, just like Dolores," Birdie whispered to Mavis. "The pretty ones always go to seed."

"I admit I'm curious," Mavis said as they hurried inside.

When they entered the gym they couldn't even get a glimpse of Prissy. She was sur-rounded by a crowd of her classmates, all vying for her attention. Finally there was an opening in the crowd, and Birdie and Mavis were able to get a peek.

In high school, Prissy's most envied fea-ture had been her head of long, wavy hair that had shimmered on her shoulders like a golden veil. The fair hair of her youth was now gone, replaced by a more mature, but still gleaming, silver mane. She looked every bit as stunning as when she'd been voted homecoming queen in 1959. Her ears and slender neck dripped with diamonds that could scarcely compete with the sparkle of her bright, blue eyes. Dressed in a silk claret-colored cape, she was like a beautiful, plumaged bird.

"Hmmph," Birdie said. "Can you say 'plastic surgery'? And what's with the Little Red Riding Hood getup?"

Mavis could scarcely breathe, she was so taken aback by Prissy's loveliness. Apparently some people's stars never dimmed.

The deejay played "It's All in the Game," and time seemed to stop. Prissy cocked her head as if listening to a private melody, and Brew, who'd emerged from the shadows of the gym, tugged at his black bow tie and headed in her direction.

He reached the spot where Prissy was standing and, for a moment, the pair stood motionless staring into each other's eyes. Then, he held out his hand, and Prissy shyly accepted it. Brew encircled her waist with his arm and the couple began a slow dance across the freshly waxed gym floor. Prissy's cape twirled around her feet, making her look as if she were floating on air.

"How beautiful!" Mavis rummaged through her purse for a Kleenex.

"How can you say that?" Birdie demanded. "Brew's such a jerk."

"He *is* a jerk," Mavis agreed. "But a very dashing jerk. I never thought I'd say this, but I think he and Prissy belong together."

Birdie folded her arms across her chest. "You know what I think? I think he planned this whole reunion on the off-chance she would come."

"I bet you're right." Mavis sighed. "It's actually very romantic when you think about it."

"How can you still believe in romance? He used *us* to get to her," Birdie said. "I, for one, am done with men."

"Birdie, you sure look purty," crooned a male voice directly behind them.

"Morty? Morty Ames," Birdie said, turning to greet their classmate. "Look at you!"

"I 'Ames' to please," said Morty, appearing at her elbow. "Any chance I can get a dance, Purty Birdie?"

The deejay had replaced the slow number with "Splish, Splash I Was Taking a Bath."

"I guess so." Birdie gave him her arm. "If you promise not to step on my feet."

"I'll try, Purty, but it's going to be a trick to

avoid those big, old planks of yours," Morty said, pointing to Birdie's shoes.

"Morty Ames, you haven't changed one bit," Birdie said. Her tone was cross, but she was smiling.

Mavis watched the pair head toward the dance floor. Birdie was right; she *was* a romantic at heart. Brew's awful behavior couldn't change that. Mavis fervently longed for male companionship, but she was also a realist. Maybe she'd never meet the right man. Maybe Arnold would be the one and only love of her life.

She thought about her first date with her late husband and how sweaty his palms had been when he'd held her hand during a showing of *Gigi* at the Capri. He'd spilled popcorn on her lap and got a terrible case of the hiccups during the love scene when Gaston, the suave French hero, asked Gigi to marry him. Despite Arnold's awkwardness, Mavis knew after their first date that he was the man for her.

Deep down she'd always known that Brew wasn't a suitable beau. He was too good-looking, too polished. Mavis had always been attracted to diamonds in the rough, like her dear departed Arnold, perhaps because she was one herself. Her sparkle wasn't as obvious at Prissy's, but it was there all the same.

Mavis decided to get herself a cup of punch, and maybe, after her thirst had been quenched, to take a little stroll around the gym. No telling who she might run into.

She headed toward the refreshment table and saw a fellow standing in line for punch, tapping his loafer to the music. He was deeply tanned and dressed in a trendy suit, but there was something familiar—

"Hank?" Mavis asked. "That can't be you!"

"Mavis!" Hank said. "Did I drop something?" He glanced at the ground for a minute and then looked up with a sly grin. "It must have been my jaw."

"Hank?" Mavis said in a puzzled voice.

"I hope you know mouth-to-mouth, Mavis Loomis, because you're taking my breath away," Hank said with a guffaw.

Who was this tanned, fast-talking fellow? Certainly not the shy, bumbling Hank she used to know.

"I didn't think you were coming," Mavis said. "I sent you an invitation, but I didn't hear a word."

"I know." Hank shoved his hands in his

pockets with studied casualness. "You know how bachelors are. They have to keep their options open."

"It's good to see you. And look at you! You're so put together. Everything matches." Mavis indicated his monochrome forest-green tie, shirt, and jacket.

"It's from the Regis Philbin collection." He fingered his tie. "Everyone dresses like this in California."

"The land of milk and honey obviously agrees with you," Mavis said. "Your color's good. And you've lost a few pounds." Hank also seemed taller than she remembered.

He patted his abdomen. "I play a little squash. Toss around a few weights."

Mavis wasn't sure what to make of this new, flashy version of Hank. Conversation petered out between them, and they both stared out at the couples swaying on the dance floor.

Dolores waddled by. "There you are, Hank. You suave thing, you. Don't you forget to save a dance for me."

"You can count on it, doll-face," Hank said with a wink.

Mavis took a step away from him. "It's been great to see you, Hank." This Hugh

Hefner version of her old friend was not altogether appealing. "If you don't mind, I think I'll go and mingle a bit."

"You're not getting away without a dance," Hank said, grasping her hand and leading her to the floor—this from a man who could barely look her in the eye when he used to ask her out for coffee.

Hank gyrated around the dance floor with an assortment of slick and vigorous moves. Mavis got out of breath just watching him. Dolores was bopping nearby, and she kept glancing over at Hank and waving. Mavis guessed that Hank's spiffy dance routine was for Dolores's benefit, and she didn't care to be used in that way. Hank might as well have been another Brew.

The song ended and was replaced by the Everly Brothers singing "All I Have to Do Is Dream."

"Thank you for the dance, Hank," Mavis said as she headed back to the refreshment table.

"Hey, gorgeous. Where's the fire?" Hank said, following her.

"I thought maybe you'd like to dance with Dolores. She's free now."

"Wait a minute, Mavis."

She turned and caught sight of his face, which looked like it was melting. Dark droplets coursed down his cheeks and gathered in rivulets in his collar.

"What's happening to your face?"

"What do you mean?" Hank said with a shrug. Mavis withdrew a handkerchief from her purse and pressed it to his cheek.

"This," she said, pointing to the brown streaks on the cloth.

"For Pete's sake!" Hank touched his face in panic. "That's my bronzer. I must be sweating it off."

"Bronzer?" Mavis said. "Your tan is a fake?"

Hank nodded and shuffled his feet. "I have a confession to make. My tan's not the only thing that's not real," he said in a sheepish voice. "I'm also wearing elevator shoes and a waist cincher."

Mavis lowered her voice. "You mean a girdle?"

He cast his eyes to his shoes. "I prefer the term 'waist cincher,' but, uh, yeah."

"Oh."

"And all that sweet talk you've been hearing from me. I got it out of a book called *How to Wow Women.* And I stole my dance moves from John Travolta in *Saturday Night Fever.* Must have watched that darn video a hundred times."

"I thought some of your steps looked familiar," Mavis said.

"I suppose this ruins everything," he said, wearing such a hangdog look that she felt sorry for him. Apparently all of his bravado had been washed away with the bronzer.

"Your secret's safe with me," she said. "It's nothing to be ashamed of. Everyone wants to look nice for their high school reunion. If you go in the bathroom and splash water on your face I'll bet Dolores won't even notice."

"Dolores? Who said anything about Dolores?" Hank took a deep breath and nervously cleared his throat. "You're the woman I wanted to wow."

"Me?" Mavis said, completely surprised.

"Yes," he said. "You've been on my mind for a long while."

"I . . . I never knew."

Hank took a quick intake of breath. "When I lived here I was just too darn shy to court you. I could never get up the nerve to ask you out. So I decided to come back to Cayboo Creek as a new, improved Hank. Didn't work so good, I guess."

"Gosh," Mavis said, studying his bronzer-striped face. "I kind of liked the old Hank."

A deep, red blush seeped up from Hank's neck. "Care to dance?" he asked softly.

"Love to," Mavis said.

He escorted her to the floor and rested one hand on her waist and guided her with the other. His palm was clammy with sweat, just like Arnold's used to be, and his dance steps were now slightly out of sync with the music.

That's more like it, Mavis thought as she rested her cheek against his chest, feeling as if she belonged in his arms. Let Prissy have the perfect Prince Charmings of the world. Mavis preferred real men, waist-cinchers and all.

If you smoke after sex, you're doing it too fast.
—Graffiti in the ladies' room of the Tuff Luck Tavern

CHAPTER THIRTY-SIX

Mavis hummed "I Could Have Danced All Night" as she waltzed with a broom down the housewares aisle of the Bottom Dollar Emporium. She was so lost in her reverie, she didn't notice when Birdie pushed through the front door.

Birdie watched Mavis glide around the floor for a moment, than interrupted her solo dance by saying, "The party's over, but the memories linger on."

"Oh!" The broom clattered to the floor. "You startled me."

"I'm sorry." Birdie shook out her wet umbrella. "I smell coffee. Just what I need. It's practically a monsoon out there."

She patted the damp bag she was holding. "I brought some doughnuts."

The women retired to the break area, and Mavis waited as Birdie poured cups of coffee for both of them.

"Just like old times, huh?" Mavis touched her mug to Birdie's.

"It's so good to be back," Birdie said as she selected a chocolate-covered doughnut from the open bag. She smiled at Mavis. "I bet your dogs are barking today. You and Hank wore a groove in that dance floor."

"You and Morty didn't sit out too many numbers," Mavis teased.

"Guess where we went after the dance?" Birdie whispered.

"Where?" Mavis leaned closer to her friend.

"Thrill Hill!" Birdie said, suppressing a giggle.

"You didn't?" Mavis gasped. "People used to gossip about Thrill Hill in high school. But I never went."

"Neither did I," Birdie said. "Nice girls didn't go to Thrill Hill. They worried they'd ruin their reputations."

"How was it?" Mavis asked eagerly.

"Exciting." Birdie took a swallow of her coffee. "I half-expected a policeman to shine a flashlight in the window."

"Oh my," Mavis said with an involuntary shiver.

"There we were, parked under a magnolia tree, admiring the full moon. Then, just as Morty's arm was inching towards my shoulder, we heard an unearthly moan. I was terrified. All those scary lovers'-lane stories ran through my head. I thought, what if some maniac was lying in wait in the dark?"

Mavis's eyes grew rounder. "What happened then?"

"Morty got his flashlight from the glove compartment and went to investigate, with me creeping behind him," Birdie continued. "Turns out there'd been a car parked nearby. We didn't see it because it was hidden behind a row of bushes. The moaning just kept getting louder and louder. It sounded like a dying coyote, and then, when Morty shone his flashlight in the window of the car, I saw the most disturbing sight of my life."

Birdie's story was interrupted by the rumble of thunder and the jingle of the bell above the door as Attalee stormed in.

"There she is!" A soaking wet Attalee leveled an accusing finger at Birdie. "The peeping Tom. Is there no place a gal can go to get some privacy with her fellow in this town?"

Mavis burst out laughing. "So Attalee was the one who was moaning. What on earth were you doing?" She held up her hand. "Never mind. I don't want to know."

"Get your mind out of the gutter," Attalee said, wringing water from her long, gray hair. "We were just necking. I told you me and Dooley had trouble finding places to be alone. Thrill Hill was our love nest, until Birdie and her beau came around and broke up the party. That hill's not big enough for the both of us."

"Not to worry, Attalee," Birdie said. "I'm done with Thrill Hill." A secretive smile crossed her face. "But I'm not necessarily done with Morty."

"So you like him?" Mavis said.

"Maybe. He's no Brew," Birdie sighed. "But that's probably a good thing. Morty's invited me to come to Camden and test-drive a new Daihatsu. Who knows what that might lead to?"

"A sales contract and 2.5 percent financing?" Attalee said.

"You *know* what I mean," Birdie said. "Enough about Morty; I want to hear about last night."

"Well, Dooley was hot as a pistol," Attalee said, rubbing her hands together. "But I guess you gathered that from my howls of pleasure. I'm telling you, it's getting harder and harder to save myself for the wedding night, 'specially when he starts lolling his tongue in my ear."

"Attalee, I saw what happened between you and Dooley last night, and I'm desperately trying to forget it," Birdie said. "I want to hear about Mavis and Hank."

"So do I," Elizabeth said, having caught the tail end of Birdie's comment as she came through the front door. She slipped out of her rain slicker and sat down with the others. "What's the dish?"

"The romance of the decade," Birdie said, her eyes cast heavenward. "Hank and Mavis were dancing in each other's arms all night long."

"What happened to Brew?" Attalee demanded. "I thought he was the man of your dreams."

"It's a long story," Birdie said. "But, in a nutshell, Brew threw us both over for his old high school sweetheart, Prissy Stevens. But that doesn't matter. The most important thing is Mavis and I have resolved our differences. We've vowed never to let anything or anyone get in the way of our friendship again."

"Here, here," Elizabeth said clapping her hands.

"So Hank came to the reunion and the two of you finally made a love connection," Attalee said. "Didn't I tell you he was the man for you?"

"It was a magical evening, and I'll never forget it," Mavis said. "Too bad Hank's on his way back to California. He took an early flight this morning."

"So." Birdie tugged on Mavis's sleeve. "When's he coming back?"

Mavis shrugged. "Who said anything about his coming back? He lives in California now."

"Yes, but what about last night?" Birdie demanded. "The air in that gym just crackled with chemistry. You two were meant for one another."

"So we're supposed to drop everything and run off together?" Mavis got up to refill her coffee mug. "We're not teenagers, you know."

Birdie's face dropped. "I realize that, but you'd think the two of you would have discussed a future of some sort."

"And you call *me* overly romantic," Mavis said. "We exchanged e-mail addresses, and I'm sure we'll keep in touch. But California and South Carolina are thousands of miles away from each other."

The front door opened, bringing in a pair of customers. Mavis smoothed the apron of her uniform. "Let me go wait on these folks."

As Mavis crossed to the cash register, Birdie spoke in a low voice to Attalee and Elizabeth. "You should have seen the two of them together. It was like Romeo and Juliet, Cleopatra and Marc Anthony—"

"Mittens and Lulu," Attalee said, taking off her glasses and wiping them with the corner of her soda-jerk jacket.

Birdie rolled her eyes. "Dare I ask?"

"They're the names of the two cats that live behind me at the Shady Oak," Attalee said. "They get passionate every Saturday night in the alley."

"I might have known," Birdie said with a frown. "I think Mavis is being awfully casual about this. Last night, she and Hank were like two kids in love."

"Speaking of kids." Attalee turned to Elizabeth. "Where's your crumb-snatcher?"

"She's with a sitter," Elizabeth said. "I have lots of errands to run today."

"I thought I saw your car parked in front of the courthouse earlier when I went to pick up my wedding license," Attalee said. "What were you doing there? Paying a speeding ticket?"

"Nope." Elizabeth smiled. "It's kind of a secret. I'm having a special party for Glenda's first birthday, and I'll make the announcement then."

"A secret? I can't wait to hear," Birdie said. "It's been such a whirlwind of social activity lately. The Business Person of the Year Banquet, the high school reunion, Attalee's wedding—"

"My bachelorette party," Attalee said, slurping the cream out of a donut.

"Your *what*?" Birdie said.

"The night before the wedding, after the

rehearsal dinner. Gotta have one last fling." Attalee licked the sugar from her fingers.

"What, pray tell, are we going to do?" Birdie asked.

"I'll give you a hint," Attalee said. "It'll be a night you'll never forget."

The overhead bell jingled once again, and Mrs. Tobias walked in shaking the rain from her umbrella. Mavis, who was checking out her customers at the cash register, greeted her and said, "Help yourself to some hot tea in the break area."

"Thank you, Mavis," Mrs. Tobias said. "I'll do that."

She sauntered over to the back of the store. "Hello everyone! What a gorgeous day!"

Attalee gazed out the window and saw the trees thrashing in the high winds of the thunderstorm. "It is, if you like to dodge lightning bolts."

"I enjoy a little pyrotechnics now and then. Livens things up a bit," Mrs. Tobias said as she untied her rain bonnet.

"I'm glad you're here, Mrs. Tobias," Birdie said. "Attalee insists on having a bachelorette party after her rehearsal dinner. Now you can imagine what that might entail—"

"Some sowing of wild oats, I assume." Mrs. Tobias sat next to Attalee. "Sounds like great fun. I can't wait."

"You heard what the lady said," Attalee said to Birdie.

"But—" Birdie said.

"Give me five, girlfriend." Attalee held up a hand for Mrs. Tobias.

"You're not yourself today," Birdie said, as she watched Mrs. Tobias slap palms with Attalee.

"No, I'm not, Birdie." Mrs. Tobias pulled off her glove and extended her right hand. "I've been transformed by love."

"Would you look at that?" Elizabeth gulped. "Mavis, get over here."

Mavis shut the cash-register drawer and darted over. "What is it?"

"Look who's engaged!" Elizabeth picked up Mrs. Tobias's hand to examine the ring more closely.

Attalee squinted at it and grunted. "I hope you and that fancy-pants doctor will be very happy."

"No, Attalee." Mrs. Tobias shook her head. "I followed my heart. You were right. Rusty's the one for me."

"I knew it!" Attalee said, throwing her

scrawny arms around Mrs. Tobias's neck. "You done good."

Mavis beamed at her friend. "And I'm so happy for you, Mrs. Tobias. We can't wait to meet this fiancé of yours."

"He'll be attending Attalee's rehearsal dinner," Mrs. Tobias said. "You'll all get a chance to meet him then."

"You're next." Attalee pointed at Mavis. "Wait and see. You'll be jumping the broomstick before the year's out."

"What's this?" Mrs. Tobias asked.

"Nothing," Mavis said. "Hank came to the reunion, and we had a few dances. Now he's back in California, and I'm still here in Cayboo Creek. That's all there is to tell."

"That's wonderful, Mavis," Mrs. Tobias said. "I want to hear all the details."

Mavis vigorously shook her head. "No more talk about me. This is your moment."

"But, Mavis," Mrs. Tobias protested.

"End of story," Mavis said. "Tell us how your fiancé proposed. We're dying to know."

Mrs. Tobias smiled and began to speak. As she talked about Rusty's proposal, it was clear she was so excited she could barely contain herself. Mavis wondered if she would ever find that kind of joy with a beau of her own. For the umpteenth time that day, she relived the moments she danced in Hank's arms. Maybe last night wasn't the end of their story. Did she dare hope that it was only the beginning?

Friends don't let friends take home ugly men.

—Bumper sticker seen in the parking lot of
Highballs

CHAPTER THIRTY-SEVEN

Attalee's rehearsal dinner was held at the Pick of the Chick restaurant, chosen because it was the site of her first date with Dooley. The wedding party plowed through overflowing baskets of fried chicken and vinegar fries. Guests raised their Mason jars filled with iced tea and toasted the bride and groom.

Attalee, who wore a red velvet dress with a lacy white collar, blushed like a maiden during the proceedings, and Dooley couldn't keep his eyes off her.

"I'm the luckiest son-of-a-gun alive," he said over and over, as he fingered the string of his bolero tie.

Rusty, who was Dooley's best man, had been introduced to everyone present by a shy but obviously proud Mrs. Tobias. The Bottom Dollar Girls adored him from his first lopsided grin and firm handshake.

At eight-thirty on the dot, after everyone had finished eating, a black limousine slid into the parking lot of the Pick of the Chick, and the driver leaned on the horn. Attalee leapt up from the booth and said, "Here's our ride, gals."

"I feel a pounding headache coming on," Birdie said, rubbing her temples.

Attalee jerked Birdie up from her seat by her elbow. "There's champagne in the limo to take care of that."

Timothy whispered into Elizabeth's ear. "Don't do anything I wouldn't do."

"You'll probably be home long before me," Elizabeth said, scooting out of the booth. "Call the baby-sitter if you're going to be any later than midnight."

Timothy and Rusty were taking Dooley to the Tuff Luck Tavern for his bachelor party.

"Don't get too wild, Attalee," Dooley warned with a wag of his finger. "You've got a wedding to attend tomorrow."

"Don't you fret, sugar booger. I'll be just fine," Attalee assured him after pecking his cheek. Then she raised her arms and danced an impromptu jig in the aisle of the restaurant. "Come on, ladies, let's boogie!"

As Elizabeth, Birdie, Mavis, and Attalee approached the limo, they were greeted by the driver, whose muscles strained against his snug tuxedo.

"Ladies," he said, removing his driving cap to reveal a tumble of shiny black hair. "I'm Hugh, your driver for this evening. Where's our blushing bride?"

"Right here, handsome." Attalee stepped forward. Hugh grinned and removed a white veil from a bag he was holding and placed it on Attalee's head. Then he pinned a button to the front of her dress.

"Buy me a shot; I'm tying the knot," Attalee said, reading the button's message. "Ya-hoo! Time to par-tee!"

Hugh proceeded to hang plastic leis

around the necks of the other women and place cardboard crowns on their heads. "Your chariot awaits," he said, opening the door.

Birdie climbed in first, screamed, and immediately backed out of the limo. "There's a naked man in there!"

"No, madam," Hugh said calmly. "That's just Paul the Pleasure Doll. He's made of latex and won't hurt a fly."

Birdie held a trembling hand to her chest. "What is he doing back there?"

"You gotta have a blow-up doll at a bachelorette party. Everyone knows that," Attalee said, climbing inside the car.

"I don't know if I'll survive this evening," Birdie said as she warily entered the limo behind Attalee.

"Girls Just Want to Have Fun" was playing on the limo's stereo as they got settled inside, and Mrs. Tobias popped open a bottle of champagne and poured everyone a portion. Birdie downed hers quickly and held her glass out for a refill.

"What are those things on the crown of your veil?" Elizabeth asked Attalee, who was cuddled up in the corner of the car with Paul the Pleasure Doll.

Birdie, her paper crown askew, reached out to touch Attalee's veil. "Hmmm," she said, a puzzled look on her face. "They feel like rubber balloons, only thinner . . ." She snatched back her hand as if she'd touched hot coals. "Are they what I think they are?"

"You were real close when you said 'rubber,'" Attalee cackled.

"Another glass of champagne, please," Birdie said to Mrs. Tobias, who was holding the bottle.

Mavis, who was generally a teetotaler, nursed her drink. "Bachelorette party or not," she said, "I'm glad we're all together. Attalee's getting married tomorrow, and now Mrs. Tobias is engaged. Things won't be the same."

"Why?" Elizabeth said, taking Mavis's hand. "Nothing has to change between us. I want us to be close always."

"Nothing's changing with me," Attalee said, wiping champagne from her lip with the back of her hand. "Marriage just means I'll be finally getting a little liver for my pup." She elbowed Birdie, who was sitting next to her. "If you know what I mean."

"I fear that I do," Birdie said.

"And I might be around *more* often," Mrs.

Tobias said, as she poured another round of champagne. "After we're married, Rusty wants me to move from Augusta to Cayboo Creek. He's always dreamed of building his own house there."

"That would be wonderful." Mavis grinned and lifted her glass. "To the Bottom Dollar Girls. Long may we live!"

"Here! Here!" Elizabeth said as they all clinked their champagne glasses together.

"Oh look." Birdie handed her cell phone to Mavis. "How sweet! I got a text message from Morty. Morty's the fellow I danced with at the reunion last night," she explained to the others. "Read it. It's so cute."

"'Hi, Bird. What's the word?'" Mavis read the message in the window of the phone. "Sounds like Morty, all right."

"I've got to send him something back." Birdie stroked her chin in thought. "What's rhymes with 'Morty'?"

Mavis sighed. It seemed everyone was attached to a man except for her. Just before she'd left for Attalee's rehearsal dinner, she'd checked her AOL mail, but the little cartoon mailbox was closed up as tight as a drum. Hank had been home for several days, and he still hadn't bothered to e-mail her. Clearly, their shared evening had meant more to Mavis than it had to him.

After a forty-minute drive in the limo to Columbia, South Carolina, and several glasses of champagne, Hugh parked in front of a nightclub called Highballs. The marquee read "One Nite Only! Hunk-O-Rama."

"I knew it," Birdie said, staring out the window. "This is one of those male strip joints with scantily dressed chipmunks."

"You mean, Chippendales," Elizabeth said with a hiccup and a giggle. "I've never done this before, but I've always wanted to."

"Wait a minute, ladies." Mrs. Tobias rummaged in her purse and withdrew an envelope filled with dollar bills. "We'll all need some mad money. To tip the dancers."

Birdie shook her head in disapproval, but still grabbed a handful of bills before she exited the limo. Elizabeth and Attalee also took some money and joined Birdie in the parking lot. Only Mavis and Mrs. Tobias remained inside the car.

"I'm curious," Mavis said. "How do you know what goes on in strip clubs?"

"Keep this to yourself, but I planned this whole evening," Mrs. Tobias said in a low voice. "Don't misunderstand. I tried to coax

Attalee into having a sweet little tea or a shower, but she insisted she wanted a wild bachelorette party."

"You're the one responsible for her condom veil and Paul the Pleasure Doll?" Mavis asked in disbelief.

"Guilty," Mrs. Tobias said with a blush. "Everything's included in one package and, believe me, this was the tamest one available."

Attalee poked her head in the car. "Come on, slowpokes. You're missing the party."

Music thumped in their eardrums as they approached a warehouse-sized building, glowing with tubes of purple and pink neon. Packs of giddy young women jostled to get inside, several wearing veils just like Attalee's. The night air was filled with a mingling of perfumes and excited, high-pitched voices. Clearly, this was a favored venue for bachelorette parties.

The Bottom Dollar Girls inched their way toward the entrance, paid the cover charge to a bouncer, and were ushered into the nightclub. The interior of Highballs was decorated in the same colors as the garish neon lights outside. Thick carpeting and wall coverings served to mute the loud music blasting from the club's sound system. Attalee's party took a seat at a table near the stage. A bare-chested waiter, wearing only a glow-in-the-dark necklace and a loincloth, delivered a bottle of champagne to their table.

Within moments after the waiter popped the cork, the curtains of the stage slowly parted and an unseen master of ceremonies was heard over the microphone.

"Gals, it's time to give a big Highball welcome to Hunk-O-Rama!"

Shrieks and whistles pierced the air, accompanied by bawdy calls of "take it off" and "show some skin."

The music boomed, and yellow and pink spotlights whirled across the nightclub. Then, a siren wailed, and a group of uniformed men marched onstage: a firefighter, a policeman, an EMT, a highway patrolman, and a doctor.

"Gals, here they come! Hunk-O-Rama! Attention all damsels in distress, who wants to be rescued?" shouted the emcee.

The crowd of women roared and screamed their answer. The emcee introduced each dancer by name: Sarge, Dante, Buck, Rod, Maximus, and Hot Chocolate.

To the pulsating beat of the 'sixties song

"Rescue Me," the members of Hunk-O-Rama shimmied out of the confines of their uniforms until they were stripped down to satin G-strings.

"My goodness." Birdie peeked at the stage through parted fingers. "They're wearing dental floss."

The dancers' slick, overinflated muscles reminded Mavis of He-man action toys. The stripper named Maximus had left the stage and was gyrating only a few feet from their table.

"Here's your chance, Attalee!" Mrs. Tobias shouted over the din. "You can spend some of that tip money." She pointed at a group of women who were eagerly tucking bills into Maximus's G-string.

With a trembling lower lip, Attalee turned to face her. "Can we go home now?" she asked.

"What?" Mrs. Tobias said. "We just got here."

"Please?" Attalee pleaded. She looked on the verge of tears.

Mrs. Tobias patted her shoulder in sympathy. "Of course, dear. It's your night. We'll do whatever you want." She picked up her pocketbook from the table. "Ladies, I think At-talee's had enough," she announced to the women.

"Thank goodness," Mavis said, hopping up from her seat. Elizabeth nudged Birdie's side. "Are you ready?"

Birdie was so transfixed by the spectacle onstage that it took Elizabeth a few tugs on her arm to bring her out of her spell.

"So soon?" she asked.

"Come on," Elizabeth said, helping her up.

The women gathered their coats and made their way out of the club. Attalee, Birdie, and Elizabeth walked several steps ahead of Mavis and Mrs. Tobias.

"Poor dear," Mrs. Tobias said to Mavis as they reached the limo. "I think Attalee got overwhelmed. Sometimes we forget how old she is."

"It's not like Attalee to cut an evening short," Mavis said.

The women settled into the sumptuous seats of the limousine, and the driver aimed the nose of the car in the direction of Cayboo Creek. On the ride home, Attalee was un-characteristically sullen and kept her face pressed against the window.

"Are you all right, dear?" Mrs. Tobias asked Attalee.

"She's probably just in shock," Birdie said. "I've never seen so many wiggling backsides in my entire life."

"Or maybe she's sleepy from all the champagne," Mavis said with a yawn. "I know I'm ready to hit the hay."

Attalee turned to face the others. Tears trailed down her careworn face.

"It's Burl," she said in a quavering voice. "That dancer, Dante, with the skimpy red-and-white-and-blue drawers, reminded me of him."

Burl was Attalee's late husband, who'd been hit by a bread truck over ten years ago. Mavis found it hard to imagine what the hard-bodied, raven-haired Dante would have in common with the bald, slack-bellied Burl.

"They both have that sexy little gap be-tween their front teeth," Attalee explained. "Remember how Burl used to whistle every time he talked?"

"Yes, dear," Mavis said.

"Burl was my husband for almost fifty years," Attalee said, scanning the faces of her friends. "And I'm replacing him with an-other man. It don't seem fitting."

"I see." Mrs. Tobias handed Attalee a tissue. "Sounds like last-minute nerves to me."

"What if me and Dooley aren't right for each other? What if we end up fussing all the time?" Attalee honked into the tissue. "And what will he think when he finds out I wear a chin strap to bed every night?"

"You do?" Birdie said, leaning forward with interest. Mavis poked her in the ribs.

"Fiddle-faddle," Mrs. Tobias said. "We girls all have our little beauty secrets. Men know it's mostly an illusion. The important thing is, do you love Dooley?"

Attalee blinked away her tears. "I reckon I do."

"Then don't fret," Mrs. Tobias said. "I read a saying in the latest issue of *Reader's Digest*: 'Leap and the net will appear.' Life demands that we take risks, and if we somehow stumble, there will always be someone at the bottom to catch us."

"Like me," Elizabeth said. "I'll be there to catch you anytime you need me, Attalee."

"Me, too," Mavis concurred.

"As will I," Birdie chimed in.

"You see, Attalee," Mrs. Tobias said. "You can't make serious mistakes when you have friends who love you."

* * *

The trip back to Cayboo Creek was mostly silent. The driver softly whistled "Good Night, Ladies" over the sounds of Birdie's snores. Everyone was on the verge of slumber except Mavis. She was alert as a sentry as she kept replaying Mrs. Tobias's last comments in her mind.

When the limo driver dropped her off at her home and the other women bade her drowsy good-byes, Mavis unlocked her front door and made a hasty beeline to her office. There she sat down at her computer and signed on to AOL. As she stared at the empty mailbox on the screen, she wondered if she'd made a mistake in not e-mailing Hank first. Was it possible that Hank was constantly checking his computer waiting to hear from her? At the reunion he had admitted being shy about approaching her in a romantic way. Perhaps his bashfulness had returned when he'd gotten back to California.

Leap and the net will appear. Mavis closed her eyes and pictured the smiling faces of the Bottom Dollar Girls. Even if Hank, for whatever reason, never responded to her e-mail, her friends would be there to listen and to help ease her disappointment. Quickly, before she lost her nerve, she typed him a message:

Dear Hank,
Had a wonderful time at the reunion. Hope you had a smooth plane ride back to California.
Respectfully,
Mavis Loomis

P.S. I can't stop thinking about you.

Her hand shook as the cursor hovered over the send button. *Leap,* she urged herself, and she pressed down on the computer mouse. The message sailed out of her in-box through the pixels of cyberspace, headed for its gentle landing in Hank's mailbox.

Mavis's heart beat like a snare drum as she shut down her computer. Risk-taking was exhilarating! She couldn't remember the last time she felt so alive. Now she'd just have to wait and see if her act of courage would pay off.

Being over the hill is much better than being under it.
                    —Sign outside the Senior Center

CHAPTER THIRTY-EIGHT

The next morning, Mavis assisted a hung-over Birdie with the zipper of her bridesmaid dress in the small choir room just off the sanctuary of the Methodist Church.

"Shouldn't Attalee be here by now?" said a bleary-eyed Birdie.

Elizabeth, who'd already donned her bright purple dress, had a look of dread in her eye as she studied her reflection in the mirror. "Am I retaining water, or is it this dress?"

"It's all those bows and puckers," said Mrs. Tobias, who was standing behind her. "They aren't very flattering."

"This dress reminds me of something Cher would wear if she'd guest-starred on *Little House on the Prairie*," Elizabeth said, frowning into the mirror. "Oh well, anything for our little bride. She *is* late, isn't she?"

"Maybe her case of cold feet returned," Birdie said, slipping into her dyed shoes.

"I'll give her a call," Mavis said. She headed for the door and almost bumped into Attalee.

"No need to call," said a weak voice. "I'm here."

They all turned toward the door to see her. Attalee appeared to sway on her feet in the entryway; her gray hair was a tangled nest, and her eyes were nearly swollen shut behind her glasses.

"You *look* how I *feel!*" Birdie said, rushing to her side. "But I didn't think you drank nearly as much champagne as I did. Come along, and we'll help you with your hair and makeup."

"Ladies?" Rusty's voice came from the hall. "Is everyone decent? I wanted to know if—"

"Come on in. You need to hear this, too," Attalee said as she feebly gestured him inside.

"There you are," said Rusty, wearing a powder-blue tux. "I have a question about the procession: Do I stand to the right or the—"

"Ain't going to be no procession. Not for me," Attalee said in a barely audible voice. "No wedding neither."

"Attalee," Birdie tutted. "What's this nonsense? I thought you were over your jitters. We'll get some coffee into you, and you'll feel like a new woman."

Attalee violently shook her head. "This ain't about jitters. And I'm not hung over. I'm not getting married today, because . . ." A strangled sound escaped her mouth. "Dooley's dead. And it's all my fault."

"What?" Mrs. Tobias led a shaking Attalee to a folding chair in the corner of the room as the others looked on in shock. "Tell us what happened."

It took several moments before Attalee could gather her composure to speak, and when she did, her words were continually stalled by sobs.

"I took your words to heart, Mrs. Tobias," Attalee said in a pained whisper. "Last night when I got home, I had a powerful yen to see Dooley. I realized how much he meant to me, and I just wanted to hold him close. My room-mate Myrtle had moved out of the apart-ment, so we could finally have our privacy."

She wiped her eyes with a corner of her blouse and continued. "He came over in two shakes, and I greeted him wearing one of my brand-new nighties. We'd waited so long to be alone. One thing led to another and . . . I guess it was just too much for his heart. When I woke up this morning and leaned over to give him a good-morning kiss, his lips were cold as stone. I called an ambu-lance, and the paramedics screeched over. But it was too late. He'd been dead for hours."

A hush fell over the room. One by one, the women gathered at Attalee's side.

"You didn't kill him, you know," Mrs. Tobias said, stroking back Attalee's disheveled hair. "It was just his time."

"He was my man," Attalee said, covering her face with her hands. "And I loved him."

"What a terrible shame!" Rusty's eyes welled up with tears. "Dooley was a real good egg." He paused, as if trying to gain control of his emotions. "I'll speak with the minister, and tell her there won't be a wedding today."

"Yes," Birdie said with a nod. "I'll stand outside and inform the guests as they arrive."

Attalee lifted her head and cried. "All my beautiful plans. A wedding was meant to take place today." As Mrs. Tobias handed her some fresh tissues, some of the misery drained from Attalee's expression; her face grew curiously thoughtful.

"Wait a minute," she said choking back a sob. "My plans don't have to go to waste." She grasped Mrs. Tobias's wrist. "You and Rusty are engaged. You could get married today. Everything's been arranged."

"Dearie, you're just distraught," Mrs. Tobias crooned. "You're not thinking clearly."

"Yes, I am," Attalee insisted. "That way there'd still be a wedding. Please, Mrs. Tobias. It would mean the world to me, and I know it's what Dooley would want."

"Sweetie," Mrs. Tobias said, "you're talking out of your head. Rusty and I can't get married today."

"Why not?" Attalee looked at her through smudged eyeglasses.

"We can't get married without a license," Mrs. Tobias said with nervous, darting eyes. "We'd have to apply first, and that takes a couple of days."

"I'm friends with Fred over at the courthouse," Birdie offered. "He'll pull some strings for me. I could be back with a marriage license in a blink."

"Yes, but—" Mrs. Tobias tugged at the pearls around her throat. "I don't think—"

"All the people you love are here." Mavis put a hand on Mrs. Tobias's shoulder. "It could be so romantic."

Rusty stepped forward. "I'm willing if you are, Gracie."

Mrs. Tobias paused. "I don't know. I think—"

"I'll call your daughter. She'll want to be here," Elizabeth offered.

"You claim to love this fellow, don't you?" Attalee said. "Or are those just words."

"Not at all. I just—" Mrs. Tobias stammered, and then she looked over at Rusty, whose whole body was tensed as he waited for her reply. Everyone in the room looked as if they were holding their breath.

"Yes," she finally said, looking into his Rusty's dark, hopeful eyes. His shoulders relaxed and his face broke into a heartbreaking grin. "I do, Rusty. I really do."

Mrs. Tobias decided she could say those words one more time that day.

"Jump," said Attalee in a ragged whisper after Mrs. Tobias agreed to be a bride, "and the trampoline will appear."

Mrs. Tobias stood in front of the mirror adjusting her veil. The only person left in the choir room was Mavis. Elizabeth and Birdie had gone home with Attalee to help her freshen up for the wedding.

Mrs. Tobias frowned at her reflection. "I look ridiculous in Attalee's dress, don't I? I've never see a gown so garishly white. I feel like a big, fluffy snowflake."

Mavis circled Mrs. Tobias, appraising the dress. "It *is* a bright white. But I guess with Attalee you're lucky it isn't purple or hot pink. It's a perfect fit though. You and Attalee must be the same size."

Mrs. Tobias whirled to face Mavis. "I don't know if I can do this, Mavis. I feel ridiculous. This is the last dress I would choose for my wedding. I love Attalee, and it's one thing to take over her wedding day, but to also wear her dress?" Mrs. Tobias looked down at her

gown in dismay. "A wedding day is a very serious, dignified occasion after all, and this
frock is—"

The door opened and Birdie strode in. "Attalee's coming this way with Elizabeth. Y'all
be sure and make a big fuss over how she
looks."

Elizabeth entered the choir room first,
urging Attalee inside. Attalee shuffled into
the room, powdered and lipsticked, her hair
braided and piled up on top of her head.

"Attalee, you're a picture of loveliness,"
Mavis said, clasping her hands together.

Her comment didn't elicit even a microme-
ter of response from Attalee. Her eyes remained empty-looking and her expression
haggard—that is, until Mrs. Tobias turned
around to face her.

"Oh my Lord," Attalee said, looking at Mrs.
Tobias with wide, unbelieving eyes. "Oh my
God in heaven."

"See?" Mrs. Tobias said, tugging on her
veil and turning to Mavis. "I've just upset her
further. I'm sorry, Attalee. I found I just can't
do this dress justice. I'll take it off and—"

"You look just like Glinda the Good Witch
of the North," Attalee interrupted, blinking
back tears and beaming at Mrs. Tobias.

She slowly walked to the center of the room where Mrs. Tobias was standing and reached out to make a small adjustment to the veil. She then bent down to smooth the train. When she stood, she planted a light kiss on Mrs. Tobias's cheek.

"I can't tell you how much this means to me," she said in a whisper. "You're a beautiful bride."

Mrs. Tobias touched her cheek and turned to face the mirror. No longer did she see the yards of blinding white satin, or the puffed-up sleeves. She just saw the reflection of a woman who was willing to do what it took to help Attalee through her sorrowful time.

"I do look beautiful," Mrs. Tobias said. "And I'm ready to walk down the aisle to my groom."

Later, as Mrs. Tobias stood outside the sanctuary waiting for her signal to go in, the front door to the church opened, and Daisy Hollingsworth stepped inside.

"Mother?" Daisy said as she spotted Mrs. Tobias standing outside the door. In her tailored, dark sheath and matching pumps, Mrs. Tobias's daughter was the picture of elegance.

Mrs. Tobias parted her veil and glided over to her daughter.

"Mother?" Daisy repeated, a bewildered look on her face. "Is that you under all that satin and lace?"

"I'm afraid so." Mrs. Tobias adjusted her train. "Thank you for coming. I'm sorry it's so last-minute. I didn't expect to get married to-day."

"I didn't even know you were *engaged*. What's the rush?"

"It's a long, involved story," Mrs. Tobias said. "You see, Attalee was supposed to get married today, but—"

The pianist in the sanctuary started play-ing the first few bars of "The Gambler."

"Sorry, dear. I must go," Mrs. Tobias said. "That's my cue."

"You're walking down the aisle to a Kenny Rogers song?" Daisy asked.

"Yes," Mrs. Tobias pulled the veil over her face. "It was Dooley's favorite. Wish me luck, darling."

"Who's Dooley?" Daisy said, but Mrs. To-bias didn't have time to answer; she was on her way to the altar.

Mrs. Tobias took measured steps as she walked down the aisle toward a beaming

Rusty. Her friends, including Attalee, were all crying into their bouquets.

Matilda Long, the Methodist pastor, recited a short prayer, and then smiled at Mrs. Tobias and Rusty, saying, "I understand the couple has written their own vows for the wedding ceremony. You may begin."

Mrs. Tobias startled. She hadn't written any vows, and neither had Rusty. Attalee and Dooley had, but the minister had forgotten to make the adjustment in the service.

An awkward pause followed and the minister, who by this time had realized her mistake, whispered, "Shall we skip the vows and get right to the ceremony?"

"No." Mrs. Tobias surprised herself by speaking aloud. "There's something I would like to say to my betrothed."

The minister nodded. "Please proceed."

She swallowed hard and locked eyes with Rusty. Her words came slowly at first, then tumbled out as if she'd been holding them back for far too long.

"Sometimes you meet a person, and no matter how hard you try to resist him, you find yourself spiraling into love. Almost as if there were other forces at work, much bigger than yourself, guiding you along." Mrs. Tobias's voice caught in her throat and she had to pause before she could continue. "It's what happened to me when I met you. I couldn't help but fall in love with you, Rusty Williams."

The church was so still, you could have heard the exhale of a moth.

"Gracie," Rusty said, putting a steadying hand around her waist to still her shaking. "My dearest. I love you so."

They clasped hands and faced the minister. "I think we're ready to become man and wife," Rusty said. As the minister began the wedding ceremony, a wave of muffled sniffs and joyful murmurings spread throughout the congregation.

The reception dinner, which was held in the church's small fellowship hall, was jolly, despite the sadness over Dooley's untimely death.

"I'll be spilling my tears over Dooley later," Attalee said, raising her glass of sparkling cider from her spot at the head of the table. "But today belongs to Rusty and Mrs. Tobias."

"She's not Mrs. Tobias anymore," Mavis pointed out as she passed a platter of fried mozzarella sticks to Elizabeth. "She's Mrs. Williams,"

"I'm Mrs. Williams, now, that's true," Mrs. Tobias said. "But isn't it about time all of you just called me Gracie?"

Everyone at the table was momentarily at a loss for a response. Then Attalee clapped her hands together and all of the guests joined in on her applause as the new couple exchanged a chaste kiss. Then the deejay started the music for the evening with the selection "May I Have This Dance for the Rest of My Life?"

"Mrs. Williams, can I have the honor?" Rusty whispered into her ear.

"Absolutely," Mrs. Tobias said, giving him her hand.

The two took to the floor, swaying to the music and beaming at one another. After a few measures, Timothy and Elizabeth joined them. Attalee watched them for a moment and then, as if in a trance, rose from her seat and began a slow, dreamy dance with an invisible partner. Her eyes were closed and her lips were parted as she swayed to the music. As the melody sighed from the stereo, and her feet shuffled from side to side, she could swear she felt Dooley's wiry arm wrapped around her waist and his warm breath in her ear as he whispered, "I love you, dumpling."

"The Last Word in Lonesome Is Me"
—Selection H-4 in the jukebox of the Chat 'N' Chew

CHAPTER THIRTY-NINE

It had been several days since Dooley's funeral and a pall hung over the Bottom Dollar Emporium. Mavis never saw Attalee cry, but each morning her friend came to work pink-eyed and subdued. During the day, she would stand behind the soda fountain with a dishtowel, drying the same petal-lipped glass over and over. Mavis had to call her name more than once before she'd snap out of her daydream.

Mavis was also feeling morose lately, but for a different reason. She checked the inbox in her computer several times each day, but there was never a return e-mail from Hank. Her cheeks burned with shame every time she thought of the brazen e-mail she'd sent him the night of Attalee's bachelorette party. How could she have been so free with her emotions? Either Hank didn't return her ardor or she'd scared him off for good.

Mavis's evenings were as lonely as ever. A grief-stricken Attalee always went home immediately after work, and Birdie had been stepping out most nights with Morty Ames. Then, to make matters worse, Mavis had run into Courtney Cooper, the real-estate agent, who'd given her some disturbing news about Brewster.

"He eloped with that woman, Prissy Stevens, right after the reunion, and they're living together in New York City," Courtney had said. "Brewster's hired me to handle everything with the sale of his aunt's house, because he's not coming back to Cayboo Creek. When I went to inspect the property, I found some obituary notices he'd left behind in his bedroom about Prissy's husband, who died a year ago. Guess he's had his sights set on Prissy for a while."

Mavis had always suspected that Brew had used her to plan the reunion so he could hook up with Prissy, but it didn't help her sour mood any to have it confirmed.

One evening, just as Mavis was turning out all the lights in preparation to close the store, Mrs. Tobias came in.

"Hey, Mrs. Tobias. I mean Mrs. Williams. I mean Gracie," Mavis said, tapping her temple as if to jar loose the correct information. "How was your honeymoon?"

"Delightful. I got back late yesterday afternoon." Mrs. Tobias glanced around the store. "Where's Attalee? I want to tell her all about South of the Border. We took rolls and rolls of photographs."

"It was real decent of you and Rusty to go there. I know you did it for Attalee," Mavis said in a low voice. "I'm sure South of the Border wouldn't have been your choice as a honeymoon spot."

"It was more fun than I'd expected. Rusty and I kept imagining it through Attalee's eyes," Mrs. Tobias said. "And it would have been a pity to waste all those arrangements." She looked in the direction of the soda fountain. "Where is Attalee? Are the two of you ready to go?"

"She's in the back hanging up her uniform." Mavis frowned. "And where are we supposed to be going?"

"Don't tell me you've forgotten Glenda's first birthday party?" Mrs. Tobias said.

Mavis pressed her hand against her cheek in distress. "Heavens to Betsy. I surely did. It's just been so crazy around here, what with the funeral and—thank heavens I bought a present for Glenda ages ago. I've got it in the back."

She strode to the stockroom and called out to her friend. "Attalee! We almost forgot. Glenda is having her first birthday party tonight."

Attalee stepped out of the back room, her thin shoulders sagging as she hobbled toward them. For the first time ever, she carried herself like the octogenarian she was.

"Y'all go on without me." Her fingers fumbled to fasten the top button of her thin cotton coat.

"Elizabeth will be so disappointed," Mavis said.

"She'll understand," Attalee said, refusing to meet her eyes.

"Oh dear," Mrs. Tobias said, dramatically wringing her hands. "I guess those presents Rusty and I brought back for you will just have to wait."

"Presents?" Attalee said, a flicker of interest registering in her eye.

"Yes. Lots of them!" Mrs. Tobias said. "A whole bag full. Rusty and I got you a souvenir everywhere we stopped, and we took so many pictures. We wanted you to feel like you'd been right there with us the entire trip."

"Did you get a shot of the Great White fiberglass shark?" Attalee asked softly. "The biggest one in the world? They mentioned it in the brochure."

"Of course!" Mrs. Tobias said. "And a panoramic shot of the sun setting on the sombrero tower."

"I bet that was just breathtaking." Attalee fidgeted with the sleeve of her coat, and she cleared her throat. "Well, maybe I could go for a little while. I'd hate to seem ungrateful."

"Lovely!" Mrs. Tobias said. "Let's all pile into my Caddie. Rusty will be meeting us there."

Mavis retrieved her present from the

stockroom and locked the front door. Then the three women climbed into the car, and Mrs. Tobias took a right turn out of the parking lot of the Bottom Dollar Emporium.

"Where are you going, Gracie? Elizabeth's house is to the left," Mavis said as she adjusted her seat belt.

"We're not going to Elizabeth's house, remember?" Mrs. Tobias said. "The invitation instructed us to go to her grandmother's old house in Dogwood Village."

"That's right," Mavis said. "I guess this all has to do with Elizabeth's big surprise."

After a few minutes, they arrived at their destination. Several cars were already parked in the yard, and a large, colorful sign was erected near the door.

"A Place for Us," Mrs. Tobias said, reading it aloud. There was a painting of a mother and a small child walking hand-in-hand. "That Elizabeth. I wonder what she's up to now?"

The trio emerged from the car, arms loaded with presents for Glenda. A smiling Chiffon met them at the door and snapped their pictures as they walked inside.

"I'm the official photographer for this

event," Chiffon said. "Wait until you see what Elizabeth's done in such a short time."

They entered the front room, painted in bright primary colors. A long table was set up for a birthday party, and helium balloons in all colors of the rainbow were tied to each cane-backed chair. Laid out on the table was a pink-and-white frosted sheet cake with icing script that said "Happy Birthday, Glenda!" Elizabeth stood in the middle of the room surrounded by a group of well-wishers. When she spotted her friends, she bounded toward them.

"I'm so glad you're here," she said, her cheeks flushed with excitement. "Put your packages down. I can't wait to show you around."

The women stacked their gifts on a chair and glanced about the room with wonder.

"How charming!" Mrs. Tobias noticed a watercolor mural on one wall depicting a group of youngsters playing in a park. "What's this all about, Elizabeth?"

"It's a place for children and their parents," Elizabeth explained. "This is the birthday room. Parents can rent it out for parties, and I'll help them with all the decorations and games. It's an alternative to those over-priced, noisy parties at pizza restaurants and arcades."

"I've already reserved this room for Gabby's birthday party in two months," Chiffon said as she snapped pictures of the group. "No more Mozzarella Monkey for me."

"I'm going to offer packages with themes like dress-up tea parties for girls or space blast-off parties for boys. It will be an old-fashioned kind of fun," Elizabeth explained.

"Did you tell them about the meeting room?" Chiffon asked.

"I'm getting to that. Follow me." Elizabeth led them through the hall and stood by an open bedroom door.

"Meemaw's old bedroom will be used for Mommy Time meetings or informal gatherings of mothers so they won't feel so isolated during the day," Elizabeth explained. "For a small membership fee, moms can drop in for coffee and cookies or a little chat and bring their children along."

The room had been painted a restful light blue, and sunlight poured in through the large window looking out to a backyard with a tire swing. There was a mishmash of comfortable seating places: two big-bottomed wicker chairs with daisy-patterned cushions, a low-slung Victorian love seat, and several overstuffed armchairs. A stack of magazines and a squat, red vase filled with fresh white tulips graced a long, wooden coffee table.

"If a mother is really feeling stir-crazy she can drop off her child for up to three hours for a few dollars extra," Elizabeth said.

She led them to a bedroom across the hall that had been set up for children. Framed nursery-rhyme characters of Little Bo Beep and Jack and Jill hung from the walls and an assortment of clear bins stored toys and books. Several sleeping mats were stacked in a corner, and a small portable crib was set up by the window.

"In the kitchen I've got coffee, of course, and snacks, but Meemaw's old table can be used for crafts like scrapbooking," Elizabeth explained. "Later, I might hire some people to give art lessons or teach baby massage classes. There's so many possibilities."

Timothy had joined the group of women by this time and was holding Glenda, who was decked out in a pink taffeta party dress. "Isn't this a great idea? My wife's a genius," Timothy said.

"I don't know about that." Elizabeth took

Glenda from his arms. "But it's been the perfect compromise career-wise. I'm able to take my daughter to work with me to a place I'll know she'll enjoy. And I've found a job that excites me. I'm just bursting over with ideas."

"You can take the girl out of the business, but you can't take the business out of the girl." Mavis hugged Elizabeth. "You've done it again."

"Yes, indeed, you have," Mrs. Tobias said, joining her in the embrace.

"Good going, gal." Attalee eyed the presents on the chair. "You think we can get this party on the road?"

Taffy and Dwayne came in carrying a giant stuffed panda, and Daisy Hollingsworth arrived with a small wrapped box from Tiffany's. Birdie scooted in late—the city council meeting she'd been covering ran over—but she'd brought Glenda a wooden rocking horse with a yarn mane.

After everyone at the party had arrived, including Rusty, and they'd been given a personal tour of "A Place for Us," cake and soda were served in the birthday room.

Glenda was treated to a miniature cake of

her own, which she promptly dived into headfirst, much to the delight of her parents, as well as Chiffon, who was capturing every sticky moment with her camera.

Attalee, who was finally allowed to open her gifts, couldn't get over the loot she'd received from South of the Border. Among her presents were three different kinds of back scratchers, a snow globe, a shot glass filled with seashells, and a T-shirt that said "My friends went to South of the Border, and all I got was this stupid T-shirt."

Additionally, Mrs. Tobias had prepared a photo album for Attalee of all the attractions she and Rusty had visited. In every photo, either Rusty or Mrs. Tobias held up a hand-lettered sign saying "Wish you were here, Attalee."

"I ain't never in my life seen nothing as nice as this." Attalee hugged the album to her chest. "I'm much obliged."

The party broke up shortly afterward, since the guest of honor was getting cranky and needed a diaper change. Mrs. Tobias dropped Mavis and Attalee off at the Bottom Dollar Emporium.

"Where have you decided to live?" Mavis

asked Mrs. Tobias as she helped Attalee gather up her gifts from the backseat of the car.

"I'm living like a gypsy," Mrs. Tobias said. "Currently we're staying at Rusty's house. I'm putting my house in Augusta up for sale, and hopefully we'll find a suitable lot here in Cayboo Creek to build our new home."

"It'll be such a treat to have you so close by," Mavis said as she climbed out of the car.

Mrs. Tobias's smile was visible in the weak green light of the dash. "My life is here in Cayboo Creek now."

Mavis and Attalee waved good-bye as Mrs. Tobias put her Caddie into reverse, and then Mavis helped Attalee to her car.

"Endings are hard, and they don't get any easier no matter how old you are," Attalee said as she loaded her trunk with her gifts. "I felt like my world ended when Dooley died. It does my heart good to see all the beginnings going on in other folks' lives."

"Like Elizabeth and her business. Or Rusty and Mrs. Tobias," Mavis said.

"And that little young'un turning one year old," Attalee said. "She's got a heap of beginnings to look forward to."

Mavis kissed Attalee's cheek. "So do you, dearie. You just wait and see."

She waited until her friend had gotten safely into her car. As Mavis headed for her own vehicle, she noticed a light left on over the soda fountain.

I thought I'd turned them all off, she thought as she unlocked the front door of the Bottom Dollar Emporium. Striding to the back, she passed her office door and her eye caught the blue glow of her computer monitor.

It's been over a week since the reunion, she chided herself. *There's not going to be any mail from Hank. Not today, not tomorrow, maybe not ever.*

Still, she couldn't stop herself from checking. She wondered when she'd finally give up on him. Mavis signed on to the computer and heard the familiar AOL voice say, "You've got mail."

Right, Mavis thought. Probably just some of that silly spam she occasionally received. She'd likely open her in-box and find an e-mail from a mortgage refinancing company or a firm peddling Viagra. It couldn't be Hank. Not after all this time.

Mavis held her breath as she clicked on

the box, preparing to feel disappointment. Instead, her heart jumped when she saw an e-mail from HardwareMan38.

Hi Mavis. When I got home from Cayboo Creek my computer had crashed, and I just retrieved your e-mail today. I, too, had a fine time at the reunion.
Best,
Hank

P.S. I can't stop thinking about you either. What do you think we should do about it?

Mavis read the e-mail several times just for the sheer pleasure of it. *He can't stop thinking about me,* she thought over and over. His ending sentence, "What do you think we should do about it?" was the most exciting one of all. His words held the promise of some sort of future between the two of them. Maybe he was thinking of moving back to Cayboo Creek, or maybe he was willing to pursue a long-distance relationship for a while.

Mavis sat at her desk and eagerly typed a reply:

Dear Hank,

So good to hear from you again. I don't know what we should do, but whatever it is, I hope I will see you again very soon.

Fondly,

Mavis

She hit the send button and sighed, knowing for certain that this time, her response would be warmly welcomed. She didn't know what was going to happen between her and Hank, but through the courtesy of their computers, they were planting the seeds for their future.

How wonderful, Mavis thought, as she printed out Hank's e-mail so she could continue to marvel over it when she got home. It looked like she was getting her own beginning.

ACKNOWLEDGMENTS

I'm lucky to have so many fabulous people in my life. My husband is a mensch. He cooks for me, doesn't complain when I work into the wee hours, and keeps an eye on my teenager when I'm on tour. He's the best-est! Thanks also to my son Brandon who has grown into a fine young man. I'm very proud of him.

Thanks to my mom, Magda Newland. I'd be living in a poorly decorated cardboard box if it weren't for her. She brings beauty into my life every day.

I don't know where I'd be without my dad. He's my web master, cheerleader, photographer, and weekly lunch partner. His wife Judy is also a dear. I must have some good karma to have such great parents.

If it weren't for my beautiful and stylish sister-in-law Susan Gillespie, I'd still be wearing acid jeans. I love her and my brother Ken dearly. Also thanks to my brother Tim and his wife Debbie.

I am deeply grateful to my editor Denise Roy, who has taught me more about polishing a manuscript than anyone. I simply cannot express how much her guidance and wisdom has meant to me and how blessed I am to have her as an editor.

Thanks to Jenny Bent, my agent. She has alays beeen my greatest champion and took a chance on me when nobody else would. I owe her my career, and she continually re-routes me when I go off track.

Also great waves of gratitude go to Rebecca Davis, my publicist, and her assistant Alexis Saarela, who make sure my tours go without a hitch. Thanks also to Marie Florio for all her wonderful work with sub rights.

Thanks also to Annie Orr and Jessica Mae Pavlas, who make the wheels of publishing turn smoothly.

Thanks to the Dixie Divas (Jackie Miles, Julie Cannon, and Patty Sprinkle) who are like sisters, and the Red Room Writers (Kyle Steele, Rhonda Jones, Renee Mackenzie, Nancy Clements, and Steve Fox), who are family. Thanks also goes to all the great members of the Girlfriends Cyber Circuit.

I'd be nowhere without friends, so thanks to my favorite traveling companion Michele Childs. Other dear friends include Harriet Spear, Collin White, Laurie Adams, and Sandra Vantrease.

Thanks to the Morris Museum of Art for always throwing me a marvelous party and to Erica Cline and *The Augusta Chronicle* for letting me write columns for them. Finally thanks to all my readers, and your appreciative letters of support.